TRULY
TERRIBLE
PEOPLE

LIARS, LOVERS & LOSERS

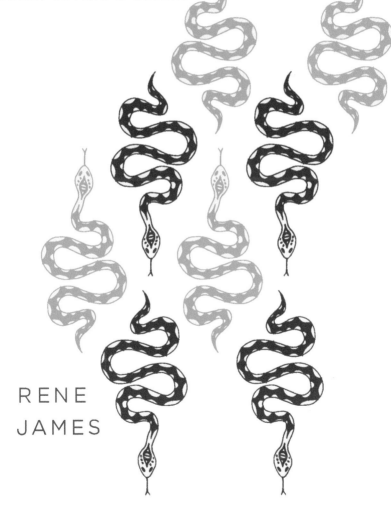

RENE
JAMES

Truly Terrible People

Author: René James

Copyright © René James (2021)

The right of René James to be identified as author of this work has been asserted by the author in accordance with section 77 and 78 of the Copyright, Designs and Patents Act 1988.

First Published in 2021

ISBN 978-1-914366-48-2 (Paperback)

Book layout by:

      White Magic Studios
      www.whitemagicstudios.co.uk

Cover Design by:

      Katarina Nskvsky

Published by:

      Maple Publishers
      1 Brunel Way,
      Slough,
      SL1 1FQ, UK
      www.maplepublishers.com

For my sisters, Naomi & Rylee.
I'll tell you when you're older.

CONTENTS

ACKNOWLEDGEMENTS

This book has been a long time coming, and there are a lot of people in my life I owe thanks to.

My grandparents, to start. If they had never turned my teenage bedroom into a guest room; for that one friend that visits every 2 years; and moved me out into a caravan in the driveway, I would have never been bored enough to write the first line.

I need to thank my parents, for allowing me to move out of the caravan and back into the house when that spider crawled across my pillow 3 weeks later.

But really, my parents never stopped supporting me. Wincing through my atrocious grammar and spelling errors, they never failed to make me feel like I was onto something special.

I need to thank my oldest brother, who despite witnessing my many, many, hobbies and career paths over the years, believed in me enough to invest in my future.

And thank you to my wonderful publishing team at White Magic Studios, and all the talented illustrators that worked on this project with me.

Riomaretha, mr_hand.art, and Oksana Fedorova, I know I can be a bit of a nightmare. For a writer, I am not the best at expressing the vision I have in mind. I know. And it takes an extraordinary artist to understand me anyway.

Acknowledgements to the 8.

You know who you are, and I couldn't have done this without you.

TRULY TERRIBLE PEOPLE

This is a story about 8 friends, and yes, from a distance, you could call them friends. But perhaps I ought to start off a little more honestly. So, this is a story about 7 students, 1 unemployed narcissist, endless dysfunction, fleeting friendships, fleeting romances, and if you don't think about it too much, something worth writing about.

I'd like to begin this exposé by telling you a little about where this horrible lot lived; putting aside their extravagant origins, which as you read on, will realise is a huge part of everyone's identity.

The group lived in an unmarked building around the corner of Rugby Avenue, right bang in the middle of the notorious Holy Land borders in South Belfast. Being just a 5-minute walk to the Queen's University, these students, and as mentioned, an unfortunate tag-along, resided in 2 flats on the second floor, splitting the group in half.

In the first flat, as addressed, Flat 5, lived Reece, Zasha, River, and Damian. An odd choice of flatmates, on paper, seeming to mesh perfectly with Zasha and River's love for the finer arts, Reece and Damian's bubbly and adjustable nature, and to be frank, the dual love for excessive drinking. Beneath the surface however, the group got on like a house on fire; continuously sparking and spreading.

We'll get to that later though.

The flat next door was undisputedly more orderly than Flat 5. Flat 6 had four rooms shared between Will, Nora, Amy, and Jackson; a collectively sound group of people that seemed to fit the brief for a flat in the Holy Lands. Meaning, at least 3 of them started off with enough income to pay off the household's following damages from frequent house parties and unwanted visits. But once again, we'll get to that.

Each flat's downstairs was generally the same, both having a questionable lounge suite and kitchen with at least 2 appliances out of order on each side. Flat 6 however, was lucky enough for Amy's mother to drop off a working microwave, kettle, and toaster. Whereas Flat 5 was restricted to cold meats and cereal for the first two weeks without an oven.

Let's skip to moving day.

AMY

IT JUST HURTS WORSE Y'KNOW, COMING FROM HIM...

JACKSON

NEED A WINGMAN?

REECE

DRESS LIKE A DETECTIVE
THINK LIKE A DETECTIVE

DAMIAN

IM NOT A DOCTOR!
I STUDY BIOLOGICAL SCIENCE!

ZASHA

I HAVE A BETTER IDEA...

RIVER

MEN ARE THE WORST

WILL

A FILM-MAKER'S GREATEST WEAPON...
SUSPENSE!

DETACHED

The 4th of September 2018, it was a Tuesday if I remember correctly. Amy, Jackson, and Reece moved in early. As the only three that lived in Northern Ireland all year round, they thought it convenient for them to pick up the keys. Amy and Jackson went into the property services building first.

Just around the corner from the flat, M&M was a tired two-story building right on the corner of University Avenue, opposite the Spar. Practically abandoned all year round with one heavy redhead behind the desk uselessly agreeing to repairs he knows they will never get to.

But this was moving day. So, on this Tuesday, the outside patio was swarming with unknowing delinquents excited to pick up their keys. Including Amy and Jackson.

As the only one who knew Jackson before the lease was signed, Amy was not surprised at his predatory comments on the girls waiting beside them. Rolling her eyes and brushing him off every time he referred to them as 'birds' and commenting on how their asses looked in their tight ripped jeans or how many buttons he wished were undone on a particular blonde sitting on the broken wall.

Amy's and Jackson's friendship were strange yet solid. Bonding over their mutual love for the Libertines and how they both liked to keep the teaspoon in their cup after stirring, yet every second interaction went something like this.

Jackson - "I would drink that girl's bathwater."

Amy - "Fuck up, Jackson."

Amy was quite a stern-looking girl, with a sullen face and pursed lips. She had a weighted nose, full cheeks, and brown almond eyes framed by almond brown hair; it was thin and only past her shoulder. She was tall, with enviously long legs and a slender torso. Attractive of course, and perhaps the reason why Jackson was so besotted with her on their first meet.

Jackson, very physically alike, was an even taller young man, starting with extremely thin legs, like twigs, and branching out at his waist to broad angular shoulders. His jaw could grate cheese, yet if you asked him, he would say "Metal," and his face was once again long, with large features. His smile was wide, and in constant action. He had slanted eyes; that if you looked close enough, you could tell were green; and his large forehead was covered with a large wave of brown hair. You could see in his face that he was a little older than Amy, with harsher skin and contoured lines in his cheekbones. He was in fact, 3 years older.

Within the next hour or so, Reece had picked up her own set of keys and had made her way down to the flat to meet Amy at the front door. "Amy!" she yelled, running down the side street over broken glass and takeaway boxes to give Amy a tightly squeezed hug. It had been a couple months since Reece had seen her and was perhaps a bit too excited for Amy's liking.

"Oh hey,"

"Where are you going?" Reece asked, noticing the car keys in Amy's hand.

"Just back to Lisburn. I moved in my stuff, but the flat is still wrecked, so I'm gonna stay at home tonight."

It was true, in her few moments at the flat, Amy had decorated her walls with dozens of Beatles posters she had ripped from an old calendar and had stuck kitten tarot cards above her bed, next to a shrine on her dresser with lit candles and cat ornaments. And to make the point, that she was indeed a cat person, she also had a cat lamp, Russian cat dolls, and would occasionally respond with "Meow" instead of perhaps, yes or no.

Seeming a little disheartened, Amy pulled the car door open and sat in the driver's seat.

"What do you mean *wrecked*?"

"Jackson will show you," Amy said, turning the key in the ignition.

"Jackson's here?" Reece asked, a little worried as she remembered back to the last time she had spoken to Jackson.

It was around 5 months before, the day the 8 of them signed the lease, and they all decided to go for drinks afterwards at a bar called Weatherspoon's. Jackson had sat next to Reece in a crammed booth that night and told her all about his Chinese, Italian and Irish heritage. Intrigued at first, Reece shared that her family came from South Africa, though she lived in England for most of her life. The two seemed to be getting on quite well until Jackson thought it was a good idea to tell the girl he's just met he's happy to share his sexual experiences with her.

Now Reece had had a couple months to think his offer over and surprisingly decided she would not need his services, which left a somewhat awkward lull in their relationship.

"Ha!" Amy laughed. "You'll be fine, text me how it goes, and I'll see you later."

"See you." Reece watched as Amy drove off, completely dismissing the one-way system, and headed for her parent's house in Lisburn.

With that, Reece made her way upstairs and into the first flat to her room, the ground-floor bedroom. The air smelled wet and stale, and light puffs of dust escaped the carpets upon touch.

"Lovely."

Being the biggest of the bedrooms, you would have expected a fight over Room 1's: pentagonal shape, the excessive cupboard space, and the dirty *but* unstained carpeted floors. However, the others were under the impression that if they were to get robbed—and they were—the ground floor bedroom would be the first target; wise choice when you live in the Holy Lands, and break-ins are more frequent than post. But this didn't bother Reece, and just days later, the flat would come to regret letting her have such a nice room when given her unapologetically messy and uncontained living style.

Placing her duvet and pillows on her bed and wheeling her suitcase underneath; thinking that was a sufficient amount of unpacking; she decided to knock on Flat 6's door.

It wasn't long before the door opened, and Jackson found Reece awkwardly grinning outside. "Hey," she said, opening her arms for an awkward hug.

Laughing at her attempt to act natural, Jackson opened his arms, and pulled her in.

Reece was a petite little thing, fitting snuggly under his chest, her wild long black hair within seconds shedding over his white jumper.

"Yo!" he said, finally pulling away and looking down at her.

Reece had a striking face, with a defined nose and large dark eyes; a small scar cutting through her left eyebrow. Her full cheeks and lips were coral against her olive skin, and her jaw was sharp. Unlike Amy, Reece had more rounded shoulders, chest, and hips, with a short narrow waist and was usually seen wearing tracksuit bottoms and vest tops.

"So...Amy said your flat is trashed?" Reece asked, looking quizzical.

"Yeah! Come look." Jackson turned, Reece following him into the lounge.

The smell of bleach was immediate from where Amy had tried to clean the stained wooden flooring, yet the smell of mould and damp was equally as bad. A broken wooden table was sitting in the corner, and ripped curtains hung over the windows.

"Upstairs is worse," Jackson exclaimed as he ran upstairs to show Reece the hole the size of a small person that went from his room into the bathroom.

"Well, that's just *lovely*... The Landlords are going to fix this, right?" she asked, looking up at Jackson's face, which seemed unaffected by the chaos around him.

"Yeah, they're sending over a maintenance man later today. They'll probably start with the broken lights and fire alarm though."

"Well, you can stay in our flat until it's fixed if you want. The others don't get here for a couple weeks, so there's spare rooms upstairs."

Although Jackson didn't take her up on the offer, the two did spend a lot of time together, falling into somewhat of a routine over the next two weeks. Reece would head off to work at a recruitment company during the day, tending the bar and serving tables, and Jackson would play football, search for jobs, and work on his CV. When Reece returned, she would *edit* his CV, and Jackson would teach her a sports fact she would forget almost instantly.

Did you know Juventus was founded in 1897?

And they would fall asleep watching movies on the black leather couch in the lounge. This became the norm for a while; there wasn't much else to do before the term started.

Amy would also visit the flat, littering her room with feline propaganda. Leaving her jealous boyfriend with Jackson, so she could tell Reece all about how their friend Matthew has gotten a lot creepier since he broke up with his girlfriend.

Next to arrive at the flat was River. Putting theatrics aside, he thought it best to pitch up unannounced at the dead of night, knocking loudly on the thick wooden door that separated himself and a 'scared shitless Reece' on the other side.

"H-hello?" Reece called out, running to switch on all the nearby lights, because murders only happen in the dark, and then braced herself behind the door and waited for a reply. "Jackson?" she called again, a little more dubiously as she knew Jackson was spending the night at his mothers'. Again, no response, Reece stood shell-white behind the door and watched as she heard a metal key grate inside the lock and jaggedly turn, grinding against the mechanics inside. With wide eyes, she watched as the door heavily swung forward, and a tall thin baby-faced boy stood outside.

"Hey, Kid!" River beamed, taking out his earphones and wrapping the wires around his phone.

"River! You scared the shit out of me! How did you even get your keys?"

"Eh, I've been here a while," he smirked, tilting his head to the side and resting his hand on his hip.

River was a complex-looking boy. Tall in frame, with slim rounded shoulders, a long thin midsection leading to broad 'feminine hips' as River described. His face was small and round, lacking a defined chin and his hair was soft and fair and waved over his ears and one eye. The eye that you could see was an orb of blue above a delicate nose. His eyebrows were dark and defined, like his eyelashes, which took Reece by surprise as she stared, wondering whether they were real or not.

It had been over 4 months since River had seen Reece but took no shock when she flung herself into his arms, squeezing his lower ribs a little too tightly. "Nice to see you too, Kid," he said, laughing to himself and looking down at the little girl wrapped around his waist. "You like red wine?" he asked as she pulled away and gestured to a bag slung over his green suitcase holding two obvious bottles.

"Nope, but I'll drink it anyway," Reece gleamed, and for the next couple hours, both River and Reece got rapidly drunk from delicate booze they had sloshed into coffee mugs, ending the night by falling asleep on the same black leather couch Reece hadn't moved from in weeks, prolonging the unpacking.

There were 4 rooms upstairs, River, being of sound mind and after the year in the flat, unsound body, took the room with the highest mould count. The mould started at the windows, sledging gently from the frames to the sill and spreading into the neat cavities of River's dresser. Granted, the mould took him for surprise days after he moved in and hung a perfectly pressed suit in the wardrobe to find it covered in frothy fungus a couple weeks later. The room *did* however, have an old-fashioned desk, perfect for storing aptitudes of poetry books and literature along the top shelf, and reasonable space for an old typewriter coiled with red and purple ribbon, not just for decoration I might add, River would use it to write notes to his flatmates, daily poems and the occasional list, only to be extra.

Following River's lead, Damian had also taken it upon himself to tell no one of his arrival, casually strolling in the following day, keys in hand and bumping into River at the door.

"Oh hey, Buckaroo!" River exclaimed, gleefully shocked as he looked Damian up and down, noticing his summer transformation from buff to ripped.

Damian, like Reece, was a lot smaller than River, barely reaching his shoulder. He had short fluffy brown hair and an untamed beard. Standing posed and upright, his muscular chest throbbed through his white t-shirt, leaving his bare white arms laced with purple veins. Putting aside his masculine features, Damian had a soft kind face, with kind eyes and a beaming smile.

"Oh, hey!" Damian exclaimed back, equalling River's enthusiasm with a posh British accent and opening one arm for a brotherly hug, which River replied by grabbing him and swallowing him for a tight embrace.

Unlike the others in the flat, River and Damian had spent most of the previous year together, living across the halls from each other in their first-year accommodation. The two had grown exceptionally close, bonding over their love for old films and their London heritage.

Finally pulling away, Damian looked around the dark bare hallway in search. "Where's Reece?" he asked.

Seeing his wandering eye, River laughed and pointed through to the lounge where Reece was sleeping under an oversized duvet on the black leather couch, keeping in mind that it was well into the afternoon, and this wasn't abnormal behaviour for the girl.

Smiling to himself, Damian walked in and stood next to the couch, looking down at the black-haired mess he called, "Reece?" he practically sang the words, and a pair of dark eyes slowly fluttered open.

Dazed at first, Reece looked around, noticing the bright light seeping through the blinds, and then to the boy who stood in front of her. Searching him up and down and slowly concluding that this was not River or Jackson. In an instant, her half-open eyes expanded, and she threw herself upright and grabbed Damian around his arms, screaming, "Damian! Hi!" burying her head in his chest.

Damian leaned over and tightly held her, his eyes brightening at the enthusiasm in her voice. River, still standing in the doorway watching over the two, smiled, and thought to himself how much he wishes this would be a good year for them all.

Not too long after, Will was at the foot of the stairwell shouting up to the flat, his faint Scottish accent bouncing off the bare white walls and echoing throughout.

Filled with excitement and nervous energy, both River and Damian raced down the cold concrete stairs to help Will with his luggage, leaving Reece to fall back asleep on the couch. Damian reached Will first, lunging off the last step, forcefully shaking his hand with one and wrapping the other around his back.

"There he is!" Will announced, with the flare and charm of a talk-show host.

Will was a relatively tall fellow with a healthy rounded frame and muscular legs from all his cycling up the Aberdeen mountains. Much like River, Will's face was soft and round, with two large dimples in the middle of his blushed cheeks. Looking like the poster child for Scottish youth, his auburn hair curled effortlessly over his pale white skin and complimented his bright blue eyes viciously.

"How have you been, my man?" Will asked, eyes widening as he too noticed Damian's serious development over the summer.

"Yeah, not too bad, not too bad," Damian replied, noting Will's concentration on his arms and subtly reaching over to the metal rail so he could tense his bicep.

Turning his gaze now to River, who had been patiently waiting a couple steps up to say hello, Will smiled and opened his arms, to which River fell into and squeezed. Like the others, it had been several months since River had seen Will, and it was only now River realised how much he had missed him.

"Hey Bud," River cooed, pulling away and grabbing one of the many suitcases Will had brought with him. "How was your summer?"

Will took a second to think about it, and River could see the alternate answers dance across his eyes, but instead, Will nonchalantly shrugged and said, "Aw man, couldn't tell you if I wanted to" and then proceeded to lift the heavy luggage up the flights of stairs to the flats, with River and Damian picking up the slack behind.

Walking through Flat 6's door, River and Damian still following, Will braced himself for the rumoured mess. Sure enough, stepping into the lounge, Will set his eyes on the dust clouds hovering above his head, the fridge door slowly wavering open, and a large boy polishing the wooden floor with a packet of wet wipes.

Jackson, who was on his hands and knees at this point, lifted his head and studied the newcomers, noticing the large Pulp fiction tee Will wore and thinking to himself whether he could pull off something that mainstream.

On the other hand, Will was looking down at Jackson, looking at the contoured lines in his angular face, and trying to work out whether Jackson was good-looking or not.

The space between the two contracted as if someone had tightened the leash on the tense air around them. And after what seemed like minutes, Jackson finally stood up, dropping the wipes onto the now clean floor, and looked down at Will. The height difference was apparent to both, making Will inertly squirm.

"How's it going, big lad, you alright?" Will exhaled, after a noticeable silence, extending one hand for a firm handshake.

"Not gonna lie, I've been better. We live in a bit of a shithole," Jackson laughed, strongly shaking Will's hand.

Damian, who had been waiting patiently behind Will at this point, was less obviously affected. Casually walking past Will to give Jackson a handshake of his own. "Don't know if you remember, I'm Damian," he said smiling, taking no hits from the boy who loomed a foot above him.

"Yeah, man, I remember. What you think of the place then?"

"I've seen worse, yeah," his voice lingered on the 'yeah,' not managing to convince anyone in the room that Damian Ormerod Campbell, of Bristol, had seen worse than a manhole in the bathroom and a bird's nest in the sink.

"Have you *though*?" Jackson joked.

"No. Nowhere."

Jackson's laugh screeched in a single "Ha!" that shot directly upwards and pierced through the thin walls. Although loud and obnoxious, Jackson had the kind of laugh that had no less than the effect to bring a smile to those around him. Like a magnet, reeling in laughter from those who heard.

Even Reece, who was not only in a different flat altogether, but was unconscious, woke to the loud sound of Jackson's laugh, her lips curving in her sleepily haze.

HOSTILE

Like a canon, the last 2 of 82 Rugby followed in shortly after.

Zasha, with much more flair and extravagance, announced her own arrival at the top of the stairs and awaited her welcome party. Reece was the first out the door, swinging it open and throwing her arms around Zasha's shoulders, both laughing, screaming, and jumping up and down, awaking the rest of the flat, who not long after were huddled around Zasha at the top of the stairs and cradling her in a group hug.

Zasha's arrivals, much like her disappearance, were always unplanned, uncoordinated, and uncertain. Let me help you understand.

Zasha had spent her summer travelling from one European country to the next, visiting her best friend in France, concerting in Amsterdam and Berlin, going back and forth to London where her mother and younger brother lived, and finally going back home to Russia to visit her inattentive father, and asking for money to pay for the next adventure.

The thing is, when you travel as much as Zasha, you end up acquiring a lot of luggage. Vintage rugs, coats, and scarves from her charity shopping down Mayfair. Hats, skirts, and shoes she had haggled German market sellers for, and trinkets she had brought from home for those days she missed the soft snow-laden streets of Moscow.

This, in turn, ended up being quite a predicament when she came to move into the small flat space of Belfast. Having to make back and forth trips from the Europa train station in a taxi to unload her luggage in shifts, and trusting in the good of mankind not to steal bags and bags of shopping from a quiet Café Nero hidden in the corner of the station.

Zasha also loved a physical change; it was quite known from all her stories of back home that Russian hairdressers were quite behind on the ideal styles and colours of the 21st century. Yet, every time Zasha travelled, she thought it patriotic to give them one more chance. 4 hours later, regretting her decision when she ended up with a mousey brown bowl cut that had the ends of her hair-splitting off at her cheek.

Lucky for her, she was quite an attractive girl, blessed with an angular frame and sharp cheekbones. Her small face was pleasantly round, and her button nose was surrounded by blurred freckles. Usually, Zasha had broken dry skin revealing a history of acne, but the sun had hidden this under a layer of a beautiful golden tan. Her eyes were small and ocean blue, and if you looked closely, you could see her left eye was minutely smaller than her right eye, which was at the top of her list of complexes.

Enjoying the warmth of Reece, River, Damian, and Will around her. Zasha took this moment in. It had been a long summer, much of it she spent alone, and so she missed this feeling. The feeling of being surrounded by people who want her there, and it took her a moment before she remembered that a taxi had been waiting outside for her next trip to the Europa.

"Oh fuck!" she exclaimed, worming her way out of the huddle and running down the cold stairs. "I have to uh—I'll be back!" she shouted as she ran out of the door, leaving the rest of them dazzled.

Maybe it was the ecstasy of the moment, perhaps it was the feeling of completeness, of having yet another one of the flat arrive, the feeling of seeing a family member after months apart, but the realisation that a hitch was just around the corner was a slow burn.

It was Reece who caught on first, as she and Will were dragging Zasha's abandoned suitcases up the unvacuumed stairs in Flat 5, reaching the top and thinking to herself where they would put her things. And it was in this instance Reece's eyes doubled in size, her pupils, which were already abnormally large, like a kitten, filled her iris, as she looked at Will with a wave of fear.

"What?" Will asked, now feeling a little uneasy.

"Zasha's room," she said, her eyes searching back and forth the line of closed wooden doors. It was like a game, to pick a door, the room behind would be Zasha's room for that year, and you see, since Zasha was one of the last to arrive, the pickings were slim.

"What about it?" Will asked again.

"You're in it!"

Now Will looked worried, and the two stood at the top of the stairs in shock and silence.

Now, this might not seem like a massive issue, but at this point in time, Will was on the lease for Flat 5, not wanting to part from Damian and River, and since no one else wanted the bottom floor room, the real fight over the rooms was over the large, long room over-looking the streets below. Quite a view, I might add. The issue, however, came about when Zasha had asked Reece to move her boxes into the room as a way of claiming it from overseas, but being the forgetful girl Reece was, this went over her head. So, when Will arrived and saw Zasha's bagsied room unclaimed, it was fair game.

In a bit of a panic, Reece nervously asked, "Do you think she's going to kick off?"

"No, she can't. There's no point. I got here first. What she gonna do?" Will's attitude did a 180, and he decided to take a less dramatic approach.

Reece, on the other hand; doubting Zasha's ability to remain calm; gingerly pulled Zasha's suitcase into the remaining room. The spare room.

It was tiny and could barely fit the luggage Will and she held, let alone the 10 filled carboard boxes currently sitting stacked at the bottom of the stairs.

"She's going to kill me. She said she wanted that room the day we viewed the flat."

"Fuck that, it is what it is. I got here first. It's only fair." Will tried to sound authoritative, psyching himself for his mature talk with Zasha.

Reece however, still panicked, felt guilty and quietly waited downstairs for Zasha's return.

Like the end of class, as if waiting to be dismissed, River, Reece, and Damian sat perfectly still on the small black leather couch in the lounge facing Will on the opposite sofa. Will was sat in the middle, leg over the other in a perfect right angle, arms sprawled outwards over the back of the seat, and grinning cheekily.

River, finding the silence uncomfortable, twirled his soft blonde hair between his fingers and tried to whistle, though the dryness of his throat just made him cough.

Reece, finding it hard to form words, sat in silence, her eyes constantly bouncing back and forth from the front door, to Will, to the window, and back to the door, with every small noise sending a jolt of panic through her body.

And Damian, sitting neatly, also with his legs crossed, as patient as ever, was taking in the quietness of the room, acutely studying the expressions on his friend's faces. He saw Will smirking across from him, the hollows in his cheek's constant, his eyes set on the painting on the wall. It was an odd painting, mainly just an array of bright colours, an expressionist style, it was there before they moved in, and Damian, now also looking at the painting, tried to like it, but the random display of blurred colour made no sense, and so he looked away, and at Reece instead. He noticed how her face twitched and how her large eyes moved across the room, her child-like hands were entwined, and her toes, which barely touched the floor, wrinkling and curling in stress. He then made eye contact with River, who was thinking the same thing as him, *what the hell is going on?* but both too timid to break the silence.

It wasn't long before the opening of the ground floor door could be heard from the lounge, and in unison, both Will and Reece took a deep breath in and held it.

The seconds which it took Zasha to drag herself and her luggage up the stairs were endless, the echoes of sharp breaths shooting through the walls. The ascent of the second set of stairs was much more painful to listen to, the thud of each heavy footing on the old carpeted steps followed by the thumping of the bags Zasha was holding that hit off the wall as she went higher. It seemed as if time had slowed. Like there was a never-ending number of steps. Will and Reece took one last second to exchange a look of fear before the—

"What the fuck? Will!" Zasha's yell could be heard from anywhere in the flat; the loud ear-ringing screech that made standing by glass a dire concern.

Like a dog responding to a whistle, Will threw himself off the couch and ran to the bottom of the stairs.

From the top, Zasha stood looking down at him, her eyebrows pushed so tightly together, creases developed elsewhere on her crinkled face. Thin red marks from where the bags had bound around her arms were prominent, and from a distance, looked like a pattern of cuts lashing across her skin. Her arms were crossed, like an upset child, and before Will could speak, she again shouted, "What the fuck is your stuff doing in my room? Is this a fucking joke?"

Attempting to laugh it off, Will chuckled and moved a step closer.

"No, Will, seriously fuck off, and get your fucking stuff out of my room."

Her words were knife-like, but still Will stepped closer, arms out and open-handed, as if approaching a wild animal. "Zasha, listen to me, you moved in last. There's still rooms in Flat 6."

"What? With Amy and Jackson? Fuck off." Zasha turned and stomped back into the room, leaving Will to call up after her.

"Zasha, stop being so immature. We can talk about this!"

"Immature?" she screamed, still out of sight, but her voice carried without fault.

"Urgh," Will sighed, leaning against the wall with his hand holding up his head. Just then, Will could hear Jackson and Amy pleasantly chatting as they came up the stairwell. They were with Nora, the last to arrive at the flat.

"So, is everyone here?" Nora asked Amy as they strode side by side, Jackson enjoying the view a couple steps behind.

"Uhh, I think so," Amy cooed, reaching the top and taking a second to look at Nora properly.

Nora was not as tall as Amy, though she would not be considered short. She had an athletic build with scrawny legs, and a defined collar bone. Her face, while still full, encompassed a thin, elegant nose and plump lips. Her hair was dark and sleek and effortlessly curled around her face, with a few odd layers that were burnt off with the misuse of a straightener. Her eyes, once again dark, were deep and hidden under thick healthy lashes. She wore a tight tank top and fitted jeans, sucked to her skin, revealing the lack of curves, yet standing with her hand on her hip, and that hip extended as far outwards as possible, humoured the illusion.

The not so faint sound of crashing and ruckus led Amy, Jackson, and Nora to the bottom of the stairs in Flat 5, where Will stood. The noise had also drawn-out River, Reece, and Damian to the same place.

"Hey, Torres!" Will exclaimed, excited to see Nora after the long summer, "how's it going, my dude?"

Nora dropped her bags in place and swung her arms over Will's shoulders, both rocking from side to side in a tight embrace. "Is that Zasha up there?" she asked dubiously as she pulled away, slightly chuckling.

"Yeah," Will sighed, "you see, we had a little disagreement about the rooms."

Nora, Amy, and Jackson looked mildly concerned, but before questions could be asked, a large bin bag filled with Will's clothing was thrown over the banister and down the stairs, startling Amy as it hit her mid-section,

"Fucking hell!" she yelled, and before the others could explain, a second bag followed in its path, hitting the same place. "Right, what the fuck?"

"Why does this make me want to have sex?" Jackson asked softly, an alarming sincerity in his voice, his gaze met with 6 pitiful stares. "Oh!" he gasped, his eyes widening, the back of one hand smacking against his palm. "That reminds me! One time this catholic girl from—"

But before he could finish, another screaming grunt could be heard from upstairs as the third bag, much heavier this time, holding Will's shoes, hit the wall and cascaded down the steps like an aging tumbleweed.

"So... I heard you guys have some spare rooms?" Will laughed.

Nora jumping on the bandwagon, nodded her head repetitively. "For me too."

"Yeah, we got you, man," Jackson said, picking up 2 of the 3 bin bags around their feet and leading Will and Nora through to the neighbouring flat, Amy following behind, leaving Reece, River, and Damian to deal with Zasha.

"Is this what this year is going to be like?" Damian whimpered, looking at them both, his eyes full of regret.

River took a moment to respond before saying, "Welcome to hell."

SHALLOW

I t had been several weeks since what would only be referred to as the 'Will and Zasha thing' and it was well into October. Reece was sitting in the lounge of Flat 6 on the floor, her short legs pinned together in front of her like a school child, and River, sitting idly by her, curled into her, his head resting on her shoulder, and Damian, sitting on the leather couch above them, playing with Reece's hair, running his fingers through it, but not making it to the end.

The smell of vanilla was faintly burning from the tealights Amy had sprinkled over the lounge, and the low rumble of the old kettle in the corner seemed to last forever, as it would be boiled, forgotten about for some time, and boiled again—on repeat.

The three of them spent hours discussing animated films, their costumes for Halloween, and the 'Will and Zasha thing' with River trying his best to sympathise, and Reece being adamant that yes, Damian should allow her to dye his hair black for 'Robin' from Teen Titans.

"Black hair is just hotter, think any Anime chare—"

"*Anime*?" River laughed, "you're talking about Damian, think basic white boy, gym shark, and putting himself to bed before 10pm!"

"Hold on, hold on. Are you saying I won't be able to pull off black hair?" Damian now intervening.

"Yes."

"He would! I've dyed hair before, piece of cake" Reece boasted, turning to Damian.

"You know what, I'll do it. If it looks bad my hair will just grow out."

"Oof, you sucker," River teased, giving Damian a weighted side glance from the floor.

"What? I genuinely think it will look good."

"Uh huh, she's basically turning you into McManus."

Reece choked. Throwing her hand over her mouth to cough into, and looking back at River, stunned.

It was completely dark outside, approaching the early hours of the morning when River brought up Alex McManus, a subject Reece had been dreading for a while now, and after a moment of silence, River reiterated, "Hey, Reece..."

"Yeah?"

"What happened with Alex?" River had been meaning to ask since they moved in, in fact, a lot of the flat had wondered what ever happened to Alex McManus. His name, over the course of a month turning into more of a conspiracy with no substance than anything else.

Reece's eyes grew with fear as she looked up at Damian in hopes of a way out, but he too was curious, and so without saying a word, Damian got up from the couch, put the kettle on boil, and stood by it, listening intently.

Reece laughed a little before trying to speak, but it was if the words were caught in her throat. "It uhh—was at the start of summer. I—"

Just then, as if written for dramatic effect, Jackson stumbled through the lounge door, wavering ever so slightly, dressed in skinny black jeans, a white t-shirt, and the only beige corduroy jacket he was ever seen in. His hair was distressed and slightly wet, and a tinge of orange makeup coated his collar.

Standing in the doorway behind him was a shorter girl, perhaps 5"5 or 5"6, she had a rounded pear shape frame, and fake tanned skin. She wore a red laced bodysuit, and a pair of skin-tight white jeans. Her face was rounded with a pointed nose and her eyes were red from rubbing. With matted brown hair, and smudged black shadow on her cheeks, she was quite the vision.

Feeling quite pleased with himself, Jackson stood in the middle of the room by Reece's feet, hands on hips and dramatically twisted around the room, grin as big as ever. "Well!" he laughed, "what—is—the—craic?"

After a moment of silent judging, River responded, "Just, chilling I guess." His tone dry. "Are you going to introduce your, uhh... friend?"

"Oh shit, yeah!" Jackson spun around and grabbed the strange girl's arm, drawing attention to the ink wrapped around it. She didn't seem phased as she was manoeuvred to the middle of the room and seated on the couch. "This is Dearbhla, we used to work together at Vodafone—"

"You worked at Vodafone? What!" Reece teased, meeting Jackson's gaze with playful eyes.

It was well known that Jackson had a previous career at Vodafone, before he was denied his monthly target bonus and left in a rage soon after, leaving him jobless and somewhat depressed. The flat, naturally, liked to look past his misery and remind him it was not nearly as dramatic as he makes it out to be. Like I said before, hearts of gold.

"Ha-ha-ha!" he laughed, sarcastically of course, as he grabbed Reece from the floor, tickling her sides and throwing her onto the couch beside him, making her cry with laughter and equally making everyone else in the room uncomfortable, especially Damian who had finished making coffee at this point and had quietly nipped out the room to bed, it was past his curfew after all, and sexual tension makes him sleepy.

Rolling his eyes at the juvenile antics, River turned to face Dearbhla, studying the tattoos on her right arm. At a closer look, River cringed at the poor artisanship and choice of design, noting the foreign word lashed across her forearm which undoubtedly meant 'courage' or 'stir-fry', the bold chain around her wrist, and the highly sought-after butterfly on her shoulder.

Unimpressed, yet unsurprised, River asked her coyly, "So, which is your favourite one?"

Dearbhla's drowsy eyes lit up, as she too looked at her arm as if she remembered she had one, before turning her wrist over to reveal an Indian elephant on her hand. "I like this one! It's an ele-eleph..."

"Elephant?" River answered, purely bewildered by this poor drunk girl.

"No! An Elephant!" she corrected, putting the back of her palm close to River's face so he could see it.

Just then Zasha entered the room, wearing blue bohemian trousers and a large multicoloured poncho, her thin hair tied back into an empty bun. Completely dismissive of the strange girl in the flat, Zasha looked around the room, saying, "Oh hey,

Reggie!" to Reece (a nickname that was developed in first year, origins unknown) and turned abruptly to River, asking, "River, do you wanna watch a film or—"

"Dear god, yes!" River exclaimed, pulling away from Dearbhla's tobacco powdered fingers and turning to Reece for a final "goodnight, Kid," before hastily following Zasha out the room, leaving Jackson and Reece exchanging a look of confusion, and Dearbhla finding crumbs on her jeans from a pizza she had eaten earlier, and dusting them off.

"So..." Jackson leant over to Reece's ear to whisper; one arm stretched on the couch behind her, his breath warm on the side of her face; "What do you think of her? Hot as fuck, right?" Jackson was smiling more than ever as he watched Reece's eyes scan Dearbhla up and down, the corner of her top lip raised as if being held by string.

"Uhh, yeah, she's really something. One to bring home to the family."

"Really?"

"No. She's a mess."

Jackson looked shocked as he pulled away to look Reece in the eye, trying to figure out if she was joking or not. "You're joking right?"

"No."

"You're mad—" Jackson smirked in disbelief before leaning over to whisper again, "Do you have any idea how much clout I'm going to get for this?"

"*Clout*?" Reece asked, tilting her head to the side, and hoping it wasn't a euphemism.

"Yeah, like, from the boys."

"Gross—"

Jackson laughed, "Ha! No. Every guy at work wanted to fuck her, she was like…The only good-looking girl at Vodafone, and I—"

"What!" Reece let out a gasp of laughter, causing Jackson to react by throwing his hand over her mouth.

"Let me finish. So, when the guys find out I'm the one who finally banged her, I'll y'know, get *clout*." He nodded as if to say, "So…yeah" at the end of a presentation, and slowly removed his hand from Reece's mouth.

"Firstly," she began, "you worked at Vodafone? Secondly, damn, slim pickings, and thirdly, you are all disgusting, and should be ashamed of yourselves."

"Yeah." Jackson continued to nod his head, filled with pride before realising that if he was to get *anywhere* with this girl, he should probably stop ignoring her.

Reece watched as Jackson stood up and walked to the door, calling for Dearbhla to follow him, and seeing her exhaust herself trying to get up from her slouch and run to Jackson's side.

"Well, yeah—" he said, giving Reece a last boyish smirk before leading Dearbhla upstairs, the sexual anticipation overpowering the vanilla.

Reece sat alone for a moment, thinking about Alex, thinking about how much she was hurting, and how much she would never admit she was hurting, before walking to the kitchen corner to put the kettle on boil for the final time that night.

Coffee was Reece's ice-cream.

Despite the pounding headache, Jackson woke up early the next day. The Sunday Morning light poured through his curtain-less windows in a blinding flood, and the faint chirping of small birds on the telephone lines could be heard. The smell of sweat and sex was prominent with a hint of black cherry from a Yankee Candle Jackson has been burning next to his bed.

His room, despite all, was quite inviting. The floor was clear with one storage box in the corner holding dirty clothes, and all jackets, jumpers and 'nice' t-shirts were hung in his cupboard, and the rest of his clothes were flat packed into a single neat drawer. To be honest, the only unseemly thing about Jackson's room was the view of the neighbouring flat's crusty walls, which he tried his best to cover up with a Juventus football shirt, and an Italian flag on the curtain rail. (This also acted as a reminder in case anyone forgot he was part Italian.)

In fact, if you didn't know the guy, you would have thought this was the room of a respectable workingman, with time to peruse the notable collection of books Jackson kept on his dresser, but not enough time to make a mess. That, or, this was the room of a minor neat freak, which; as I remember the way he would meticulously scrub dishes; is more accurate.

Jackson sighed as he lifted his head off his fluffy grey pillow and stretched his arms outwards, knocking Dearbhla's head with his hand. "Shit," he growled, running his other hand along the floor in search for his boxers, and quietly slipping them on under the covers. She didn't move, and for a second Jackson considered leaving her there as he changed for football, but the patches of foundation staining his sheets swiftly changed his mind.

Jackson loved football, he loved the thrill of the game, the atmosphere of the crowds, the way girls looked in the kit, but more importantly he loved that he wasn't half bad at it. Playing since he was 11, Jackson fell in love with the sport when he saw an Everton game with his father—up 'The Toffees.' They had just won a match against West Ham which spirited a growing hatred for 'The Hammers', and any opposition of 'The Blues' for that matter. Granted, Everton finished 5th in the Premiere League that year, but the admiration was already set in motion, and this was something Jackson could share with his dad. Who knew 11 years later, that same young boy would be playing twice a week with the 'Asian Community FC' with boots that had the words 'Send Nudes' embroidered down the vamp.

It wasn't long before Jackson was sat on the end of the bed fully dressed, dialling the number for a taxi to the door, and reaching over to Dearbhla to gently shake her awake.

"Hmm?" she cooed, nuzzling the side of her head into his hand. She was lying on her stomach, face smothered by the fluffy pillow, one arm tucked comfortably underneath and the other holding onto the bridge of Jackson's arm.

Now that the pillow had licked the paint from her face, you could see she was quite a pretty girl, with snow white skin and spotted freckles, however the missing fake eyelash was another thing all together.

"Yeah, urrm…" Jackson whispered, slowly drawing his hand from her face and grabbing his keys from the bedside table. "I've got to go. But I've called you a taxi. It'll be here, like, soon."

He paused for a second, looking at Dearbhla's confused scrunched face before turning and heading out the door and shutting it behind him.

Needless to say, the poor girl did not stick around.

In the neighbouring flat, things were a lot less exciting. River was the first to wake after falling asleep in Zasha's room, the cold draft from her broken window coaxing him out of his slumber. Stretching each long limb in either direction in a rather obnoxious pandiculation, River looked around the room.

As if stripped from a 90's catalogue, Zasha's room mirrored the 'pimped out' tour bus aura with mandala tapestries on her wall and hanging from her ceiling with looped green vines around the hem. A shaggy purple rug also ran adjacent to her bed; clumps of her hair wound in the fur, and small black bobby pins nestling between the tuffs.

Zasha's room was also quite large, big enough for anyone's knick-knacks, except maybe Zasha's, who, remember, had over 10 filled boxes worth of clothes, books and shoes she intended to sell online. Which over the course of the year spread like mould to the most gruesome areas, like behind the furniture and into the wet and dusty shoe cupboard by the front door. And as if space didn't matter, there again were no bare walls in Zasha's room; each corner having a string of fairy lights clipping abstract polaroids from her travels, and framed photos of familiar faces making it impossible to feel lonely in a room like hers.

River felt this as he slipped out from under the covers and tiptoed out the room and back into his own, making sure not to wake her.

In the room next door, Damian was lying perfectly still and straight under his own covers, the duvet neither creased nor ruffled, the kind of undisturbed arrangement that if a Corporal were to flick a penny onto the bed, it would bounce. This was the way Damian slept, like a vampire in a catacomb, and trust me, it's as distressing as it sounds.

Reece on the other hand, was the complete opposite. By this time, Reece had made the conscience decision to sleep in her own bed; as she realised, she can't keep getting mad at her flatmates from waking her up whenever they needed cereal. And her sleeping patterns reflected somewhat of an earth quake each night; pillows scattered around her floor, her thick duvet clinging to the end of the bed, and her sheets, undoubtedly ripped from their place while Reece slept the wrong way around, face first into the madness. And she would have stayed like that if Jackson didn't pop by for an early morning pep talk.

"Arise!" Jackson yelled, swinging Reece's door open and looking around the room, he was used to the mess and didn't seem phased when Reece didn't move. She slept like the dead. "Come on, get up!" he shouted again, going to her bed side and roughly shaking her awake.

"Huh? Jackson what are you doing?" Reece whispered, staring through the heap of tangled hair on her face.

She was wearing an oversized cotton blue work shirt River had given her; after she spilled red wine on it; and it took her a second to realise that's all she was wearing, bar underwear, before lurching upright and pulling her dismantled covers over her legs. "Jackson! It's like 6! What are you doing?"

Jackson laughed, noticing her scramble for the duvet. "It's 9 Reece, and you should lock your door if you didn't want me in here."

"Urgh, you're the worst," Reece growled. "...How was your night with Derbles?"

"Ha, her name's Dearbhla." (Pronounced Derv-la for anyone that didn't know).

"Sure thing, how's Derb-la?" she said, smiling mockingly.

"Well, I called her a taxi. I'm actually hiding out here until she leaves."

Jackson watched as Reece's jaw dropped, following her hand as it swept a pillow from the floor and was swung into his face, sending him a few feet back.

"What is wrong with you!"

"What?" he laughed, hugging the pillow and sitting down on the bed in front of Reece.

"You're just gonna leave? You have sex and then just, take off? Like, you don't even see her out?"

Jackson reached for her small hands and held them, smirking as he did so. "It was a one-time thing, she knew that."

Reece tried to rip her hands from his in an attempt to hit him, but he just squeezed tighter. "You know what?"

"What?"

"Someday. Some girl is going to come along and break your heart—"

"Ha!"

"Let me finish! And it is going to rip you to pieces—"

"Thanks—"

"And it'll change you."

"Oh yeah? How so?"

"Because you're finally going to know what it feels like, and you're not going to wish that on anyone." Her eyes were sad, yet she smiled. "And you'll think back to this very moment and say, 'why was I such...a dipshit.'"

"Ha! Wow, dipshit? Really?"

"Yup."

"Okay."

She could see the wheels in Jackson's head turn, and for a second, she hoped something would click, but nothing did, and she watched as he slowly got up from the bed and walked over to the closed curtains. "No, no! Jackson don't—" she yelled as he forcefully ripped them open, sending a blinding torrent of light into the room making Reece dramatically hiss. "What is your problem? It's Sunday, right? Go to football!" Reece swept her hair from her face and looked up at Jackson who just continued to smirk at her, his green eyes glowing.

"Fine, but you have to get up too. Seize the day, all that shit."

"Ha, sure, whatever you say. Have a good game, and Jackson...?"

"Yeah?"

"Fall in love."

Jackson stood still for a moment, his eyes latched onto hers, replaying her voice in his head. He loved the sound of her voice, sometimes riling her up on purpose so he could listen, and for a second, Jackson humoured the thought of falling in love just because she said it.

But the fantasy quickly passed, and it was only moments later before Jackson was pushing the window wide open, letting in a gust of cold wind and darting out the room.

"Jackson!" Reece called angrily after him, standing on her bed, letting the covers drop from her legs, and reaching from the edge to the window to pull it closed.

Just then Jackson burst back into the room, shouting, "Arise!" once again and grabbing Reece by the waist and throwing her back down on the bed, leaving her flustered and whiplashed.

RECKLESS

"Shit, shit, shit!" River gasped, frantically trying to remove the green paint from his eye.

The low roar of clattered chatter could be heard from downstairs, and River felt himself getting anxious that he might miss out on vital seconds of the party. He had only been in the bathroom for 5 minutes, and yet the walls were already lashed with green, and a sick-like residue coiled around the sink's drain. Looking into the mirror, River was quite impressed with his efforts; ignoring his burning bloodshot eyes, he managed to turn himself into quite the convincing 'Beast Boy', and he smiled, looking down at his black and white baseball tee to which he had ironed on felt letters spelling 'Meat is Murder'; quite fitting for the vegetarian.

Zasha was notably less impressed as she stood watching from the bathroom doorway, loudly munching on a plate of chicken nuggets, dunking each piece into a vat of tomato sauce. River had been so preoccupied with his costume he hadn't noticed Zasha standing there and jumped a little when he did.

She was wearing opaque tights underneath a black swing dress that hung loosely from her thin frame, her collar bones slightly showing through the material. He looked at her neck, noticing the gold chain hanging from it and the gold cross pendant sitting on her chest. A crimson flower crown nuzzled into her baby brown hair, which was pulled back into a small bun, letting the bathroom light shower her face in a golden haze. River looked at her lips, slightly parted and sweetly brushed with a pink gloss, and finally drawn to her bright blue eyes; he was nothing less than transfixed.

He gulped, now more self-conscience than ever, wondering how someone can be so effortlessly pretty, and he tried to think of a smooth way to tell her that before—

"Why the fuck are you green?" she laughed, leaning her shoulder on the door frame, one leg crossed over the other.

River stood illiterate as if the perfect page had been ripped from his spine. "It's Beast Boy...From Teen Titans," River explained.

Zasha tilted her head, confused.

"He's the little green boy," he reiterated, but still with no luck, he showed her a saved image from his phone for reference, to which he was met with an "Ohhhhh," before she walked away unamused, chicken nuggets still in hand.

Left feeling a little rejected, River followed her downstairs, keeping a fair few step behind.

The change in atmosphere was jarring as River made his way down the stairs into the pool of loud darkness at the bottom, knocking into two shadowy figures on the last step.

"Hey!" a girl yelled, backhanding River's leg aggressively,

"Sorry!" he squealed, making one last effort to stretch over them onto the ground floor, and turning back to see Nora and Will drunkenly swigging Jack Daniels from the bottle. Dressed as Mia Wallace and Vincent Vega, River took a second to recognise his flatmates under the cheap wigs but was thoroughly impressed when he did.

It was only around 10pm when River returned from a Scribbler's committee meeting, but it was obvious he was well behind on the drunken shenanigans already. (Scribblers was a Creative Writing Society River led, ask him about it, he's very proud.)

"Hey, Will! Loving the costumes," he said cheerily, looking back at Nora, who was still scowling from her brutal attack.

"I know, right!" Will chuckled. "Got these from the costume shop on Botanic."

"Good get! Have you guys seen Reece?" River asked nervously, looking through into the lounge at the collection of strangers and their stranger dates.

"Right behind you, man," Will smiled, pointing to Reece's room. Nodding, River turned and tried to pull the door handle, but it was locked. Confused, River hesitantly knocked with his pointer knuckle and was instantly met with a, "Who is it?" yelled from the other side of the door.

"Uhh, River?"

A metal bolt clicked, the door swung open, and a small hand pulled River into the room, the door swiftly locked behind him. Startled, River laughed, "Bloody hell, Kid!" as he studied Reece's costume.

As part of a group, Reece decided to go as 'Raven' from Teen Titans, a demon-human hybrid; quite fitting, actually. Reece stood in front of River, a dark purple hooded cloak draped over her petite frame, her shiny black hair waving down to her waist. She was wearing a black leather corset under purple harem pants tucked into leather combat boots, giving her at least 2 extra inches of height. She was still tiny, which made River laugh even more as he looked down at her serious face. She wore a purple diamond between her deep eyes, and her lips were painted black.

"What's wrong, Kid?" River asked more seriously this time, familiar with Reece's dramatics by this point; he took no shock when Reece swung her cape around her shoulders and started pacing the room; it was all very amusing to watch.

"Well, to start, I'm not nearly drunk enough, but more importantly, McManus is out there saying 'we need to talk,' and Al won't leave me alone, and did I mention I'm completely sober!" Reece collapsed on her bed, back of hand over her face, her short legs barely reaching the end.

To fill you in, Al was a friend of Nora's who had been staying with them in the flat for the past week or so and had taken a strong liking to Reece when she got drunk and kissed him in a bar a couple nights ago. But had not so much taken the hint that 'drunk Reece' and 'sober Reece' are two very different people, and just because whispering Spanish complements in her ear worked the first time does not mean it's a given the next. And as for McManus, well, you know.

River took a second to think about her dilemma. "I'll be back," he said, quickly leaving the room, the door closing behind him.

Lying in the harsh light of her room, Reece thought about those words, *we need to talk*, and she could feel the sickening butterflies rise through her chest, and in that second, the thought of drinking made her gag. Just then, the door swung open, the handle knocking loudly into the wall.

"That was quick!" Reece laughed, sitting upright and looking at Jackson stood in the middle of the room, the door closed behind him. "Oh," she said softly, smiling ever so slightly.

"Well. What is the craic?" Jackson beamed, dressed in a fake moustache and Italian football shirt, with the Italian flag that usually hangs over his curtains tied around his chest like a cape.

"Firstly, hate this," Reece laughed, gesturing to the moustache that made Jackson look like a foreign paedophile.

"What! I look incredible, and you look—" Jackson looked down at Reece sat on the end of her bed, the tight black corset laced in the front and fitting all the right places, "Uh-huh," he held back, distracting himself with things around her room, playing with the Sumo Wrestler stress ball on her desk.

"Ha, great," she whispered as she stood, encouraging Jackson to turn back around and face her,

"No, I mean, you look—" he paused once again, pulling the hood away from her face and looking straight into her eyes. "You, uhh—should definitely undo some of *this*!" he teased, pulling on the lace at her chest and laughing as she immediately grabbed his hands to stop him. "No, you look–"

"Right, so I've got vodka and peach schnapps!" River yelled excitedly as he burst through the door, choosing to ignore the uncomfortable faux hair on Jackson's face. The three of them stood still for a second, "Did I interrupt something?" River asked mockingly.

Another second of silence passed before Jackson screamed, "Goal-latzo!" and ran out of the room, the Italian flag floating behind him, leaving River poignantly confused.

"Italian football player," Reece explained, "pass the vodka."

In Flat 6, things were a lot more intense. The lounge was filled with strange faces, most of whom were Nora's foreign exchange friends that even she had trouble introducing but had no issue governing the liquor table.

The DJ's table was proudly set up in the corner facing the kitchen. Behind stood Amy's boyfriend Callum, a tall hipster-looking character wearing an ugly Hawaiian shirt, unironically, and bopping his shaggy hair to the equally hipster music. I think Declan Mckenna was playing. Amy stood unimpressed beside him, arms crossed with a bottle of rosé wine in one hand, it must have been half empty at this point, but you couldn't tell from her sour face.

Damian sat patiently on one couch, waiting for a girl called Isobella, who said she'd "be right back" to come back, but it had been over 20 minutes, and he had started to doubt her return.

Jackson seemed to be having a better night as Damian watched as he led a 'sexy ninja' and 'sexy nurse' upstairs to his room, glancing back to give Damian one last cheeky grin before disappearing.

The night was young, and yet Damian felt a stagnant weight on his chest, and the Rockshore wasn't helping.

It must have been around 11pm when a completely blitzed Reece and River came wandering through into the neighbouring flat to rescue Damian. Seeing him sat alone, Reece pulled him from the couch excitedly, exclaiming, "Damian! Come see this!"

As relieved as ever, Damian held onto her hand as she pulled him through the crowd back to Flat 5 and into the lounge, occasionally stopping so he could take a sip from an Amaretto bottle she scored from her travels. The liquor was sweet on his lips and a delightful palette change from the dry beer he had been nursing.

Stopping abruptly in front of the black leather couch, Reece, Damian, and River watched in awe as four of their close friends locked lips in a kind of rotating sushi bar fashion, going from one friend to the next in a widely uncomfortable rhythm. Damian looked horrified as Phil pulled away from Chloe's kiss, eyes glazed over in a way that can only be described as haunting.

"Hey, man!" Phil loudly slurred, pulling himself from the couch to wrap both arms around Damian's neck.

Phil was a fairly tall boy, with straight greased black hair and square-rimmed glasses; he had a large smile and dark eyes.

He was normally seen wearing patchwork shirts, colourful pants, and corduroy jackets, but tonight he was wearing a well fitted white shirt and brown leather waistcoat, and Reece wondered whether he finished work late or whether he had actually dressed up this year. Either way, this was the best Reece had seen him look in a long time.

Phil took a step back, admiring Damian's costume, "And you must be Robin!" he chuckled, identifying the burgundy letterman jacket with the iconic 'R' stitched to the chest and oval black mask around his eyes.

"Ahh, someone finally got it!" Damian gasped, a small smile breaking across his face.

Now looking at Reece, Phil smiled even more as he greeted, "...And Raven," confidently.

"Aw, you big nerd, come here," she laughed, hugging him tightly around his waist, holding him just long enough to smell Chloe's perfume before pulling away to sit on the couches' armrest, breaking up Lewis and Betty, and offering them both some Amaretto.

River, who had not been that close with Phil in the previous year, too outstretched both arms to give Phil a friendly hug to which Phil joyfully fell into and squeezed. Phil was not one to turn down a hug, especially from River, who Phil at that moment explained, "...Gives good hugs!"

"Thanks, Bud," River cooed before turning his attention back to the manic couch scene. "Now, what's going on here?" River laughed, but there was a hint of fear in his voice as he locked eyes with Chloe; a small plump girl, with small spectacle glasses and a sex drive that could be felt from a mile away; and shuddered.

"Ha, just a bit of fun, isn't it?" Phil leaned in between River and Damian; his back facing the couch; whispering, "You know, I'm actually starting to like Chloe. What do you think?" Phil's question was met with wide eyes as they both pointed a finger to the couch, gesturing to Chloe, who had gone from sitting alone to sitting on Lewis's lap in a matter of seconds. "Well." Phil sighed, "... That's just another girl who's rejected me." After that, Phil left the lounge, the others not catching up with him until later that night.

Back on the couch, Chloe pulled away from Lewis's lips, licking her own and asking, "Lewis...Have you been drinking Amaretto?"

Reece's ears pricked upwards at the question, bottle in hand.

"Yeah, why?" Lewis slurred.

"I thought you were allergic to nuts?"

Just then, both Reece and Lewis started to panic.

"You're allergic to nuts!" Reece yelled, frantically trying to read the back of the bottle and panicking further when the words wouldn't stay still. "I can't read!"

Lewis dived to the floor, looking for his bag; he knew he had packed his EpiPen, but the room was dark, and he had a lot of compartments.

Chloe reached for her phone, ready to dial 999; Betty, drunk and unaware, left to find Phil, and River let out an awkward squeal type laugh, the one he does when he is undeniably uncomfortable before turning to Damian instructing, "You're a doctor! Help him!"

"I'm not a doctor! I study biological science!" Even during the frenzy, four heads slowly turned to face him, all dead behind the eyes as if to say, "Really...now?" to which Damian nodded, noticing that specifics weren't important right now.

"Right, I found it!" Lewis gasped, EpiPen in shaking hand. "Right, Reece, you did this to me, so you have to stab me," Lewis laughed a little when he said this, perhaps too drunk to be mad.

"What!" Reece screamed, her hand now shaking too.

"It's easy, slide the button up, and aim for my leg...Try not to hit a vein."

"Are you insane!"

"Now, Reece!" Lewis shouted, holding out the pen.

Reece grabbed the pen with fear-induced eyes and passed the bottle to Damian, who began reading the back. She leaned over Lewis, trying her hardest not to focus on the jockstrap between his legs as part of his 'Clockwork Orange' attire.

The rest of them watched as she pushed back the slide revealing the needle, ready to puncture, and brought down her hand and—

"Wait!" Damian screamed, stopping Reece just inches before Lewis's skin. "Guys, it's almond flavoured liquor... There's no actual nuts in this."

A moment of pure silence passed as the tension was released from the room in one swift swoop. Reece slowly lowering her hand, sliding the needle back down into the pen.

"Well, thank fuck, for that!" Lewis exclaimed, pulling his curly blonde hair over his head, laughing. Chloe was the next to join, giggling to herself and throwing her arms over Lewis's shoulders in relief.

River and Reece couldn't help themselves and too started to laugh with Reece giggling, "So, what would have happened if I injected you?"

"Well, with the amount of alcohol he's been drinking, you could have given him a heart attack..." Damian exclaimed, hand behind his neck, massaging the tension out of it.

Another moment of silence swept across the room as the seriousness of the situation settled in before Reece teased, "Who's the doctor now?" laughing hysterically and joined once again with the others in an uproar of immature giggling.

Jackson lay on his bed, the fake moustache long gone. The two half-dressed girls lay either side of him, turned over his chest, each with a leg over his.

Hayley, as described the 'sexy ninja,' ran her long fingers through Jackson's hair, her lips so close to his ear, her tongue grazed him with each word. He stared at the tight lycra stretched over her flawless frame, eyes gliding past the red ankle warmers to the perfect arch in her back. Hayley was a pretty girl with a wide white smile and sultry eyes, but he didn't notice nor care.

The black cherry Yankee candle burned next to the bed gave the room a sexy flicker of light, the red wax projecting rosy hues onto the white walls.

Maeve, the 'sexy doctor' lay scowling as she watched Hayley curl her leg up Jackson's torso, watching her tongue caress the side of his face. Maeve began to slip her hand beneath Jackson's shirt, but still unable to draw his attention, declared, "You know what I've always wanted to have?"

"What's that?" Hayley whispered.

"A threesome."

Both Maeve and Hayley giggled, exchanging a flirtatious look and then both looking towards Jackson to see his reaction.

This was the only time I can recount that Jackson Seth Tsang was speechless.

Unable to believe his ears, he spluttered a cough, throwing his hand over his mouth and apologising, which only made the girls giggle more.

"It'll probably never happen though, Maeve..." Hayley teased, now sitting upright over Jackson and facing her friend.

Maeve too sat up, looking down at Jackson, "That's a shame..." her soft whisper was intoxicating, and Jackson could feel his eyes roll to the back of his head as he lurched forward and kissed Maeve, his lips hard against hers, and both hands tight around her waist.

Excited at first, Hayley watched in amusement, unzipping her bodysuit just enough to be 'unintentionally alluring' and pouted her lips seductively. But after a while of being ignored, Hayley became annoyed and made a point of turning to lie back on her stomach, pulling out her phone to 'text.'

Jackson then noticing Hayley's disengagement, pulled away from Maeve, who seemed unimpressed by this, and tried to seduce Hayley by running his fingers over her cheek and turning her over to face him.

It was just then that a burley 6" 4 rugby player burst through the room. "Have you seen Ava?" he growled, unaware of the events that were to transpire on Jackson's bed.

"Uhh...No, sorry," Jackson answered, his voice coated in frustration.

"Have you seen Ava!" The boy yelled once again.

"No! Now get out." This time, Jackson leapt from the bed to forcefully remove, who he would later find out is Mason, aggressively shoving him out the door and locking it behind him. The girls sat up on the bed, looking awkwardly up at Jackson, who was trying desperately to forget the past 30 seconds ever happened, but it was obvious from their faces the mood was gone.

"Hayley, can you pass my phone?" Maeve asked, pointing over to the pink iPhone on the windowsill,

"Sure," Hayley replied, turning quickly to grab it but knocking over an open bottle of Port in the process, and watching blankly as the red liquid spilled over the white sheets. "Oh, I'm sorry!" she pleaded, scrambling off the bed, leaving the bottle to empty out in waves.

Jackson stood open-mouthed at the door and watched as Hayley and Maeve tiptoed towards the exit, heels in hand, the irony not lost on Jackson as he unlocked the door to let them out, too angry at Mason to be upset about the sheets.

It was now approaching the early hours of the morning, and between the two flats, the number of conscious to unconscious was dropping fast. Nora had taken some guy no one knew up to bed, leaving her Spanish friends to disband, Will had crashed early upstairs, and Amy and Callum had made their way to Ollies, a nightclub in the centre of Belfast with Matthew. River and Zasha could be seen deep in chat at the bottom of the stairs, and Damian was consoling Phil in the kitchen.

Reece watched from the lounge in Flat 6 as Hayley and Maeve stumbled down the stairs and left out the front door;

Jackson defeatedly following after them and into the lounge and sat expressionless beside Reece, fist clenched. "I heard what happened..." Reece whispered, giving Jackson a slow pat on the back.

"What the fuck? Already! How?"

Reece gestured to Mason, who was standing beside the kitchen laughing to a bunch of guys she didn't recognise.

"I'm gonna kill him," Jackson growled, scowling so harshly he could feel a vein pop in his forehead.

Reece's full lips curled into a gentle smile as she brushed her fingers through his hair. "Ahh mon ami, you're gonna be okay."

Jackson turned to look at her and couldn't help but smile. "It's kinda hot when you speak French, y'know."

"Si." Reece grinned, watching Jackson's eyes roll.

"You're a fuckin' idiot," he laughed, unclenching his fist and slapping the fake moustache back on his top lip. "The game continues!" he announced, running back upstairs to retrieve his cape.

Left alone, Reece sat on the cold couch, listening to the soft sound of Clairo playing in the background, her eyes gently closing, and for a minute, everything was peaceful again. Until –

"Hey Reece?"

Reece opened her eyes to the sight of Alex McManus standing over her, his tall frame casting a shadow over her body. "Hey," she said, her voice so soft you could sleep on it.

"Can we talk in your room?"

"Okay."

Alex extended a hand to Reece, and he led her through to the neighbouring flat into her room, passing Jackson on the way, who shot her a worried look. Reece sat shyly on her bed; Alex respectively next to her. The silence was deafening.

"So... I'm dressed as 'Slater'..." he began, looking desperately at Reece, who only stared back blankly. "Y'know, from 'Dazed and Confused'? You got me the Tapestry remember?"

Reece's lips pinched together as she side glanced, as if to say, "I have no idea what you're on about," but she did. She remembered everything. She remembered watching the film with Alex because it was his favourite, she remembered how much she hated the lack of plot, and how Alex's love for coming-of-age American films was adorably pointless... She remembered spending hours picking that tapestry out and how nervous she was to give it to him. "Sorry, terrible memory," she sighed. *Liar*.

"Oh," Alex looked down, disheartened, "well anyway, I just wanted to say that I've missed you, and I'm sorry for—"

"Look, Alex..." Reece paused. Looking into his deep brown eyes and thinking to herself, she must be crazy. He was the most handsome boy she had ever seen; he had the type of face you could become addicted to. The richest eyes she had ever gazed into, and the brightest smile, with his hair like bitter coffee, gorgeously waved over his ears, and when he spoke, in that hushed husked Dublin accent, she was spellbound. But none of that mattered now. "When we were in Dublin, before you left for Amsterdam, I told you, I loved—"

"I know, I just—"

"And you made me feel so stupid for saying it, you told me you didn't care, and you let me get on that bus with nothing more than 'have a nice summer'?"

"Listen, I—"

"And then while you're away, you didn't text, you didn't take the time to call, and when you finally did, it was to say you 'forgot you had a girlfriend'" Reece's eyes began to sink in tears as she continued sobbing, "and now you have the nerve to say you 'miss me'?"

"I do miss you! It was a mist—"

"It wasn't. And I don't blame you." She wiped away the tears, her voice breaking ever so slightly, "I'm just over it." With that, Reece left, leaving Alex head-in-hands behind her.

Running through the scattered crowd, Reece bumped into Alfredo, who had been standing by the stairwell between the two flats.

"What's the matter, Chica?" he comforted, holding Reece tightly as she sobbed.

"Nothing, I'm okay."

"No, you are not. You are crying. You look beautiful when you cry, but this is still sad."

Reece laughed, trying to choke back her tears; she noticed she was crying into a vast red material; pulling away, she realised Al was draped in a red sheet that reached the floor. Through her sobs, she asked, "What's your costume?"

"I'm your period!" Al laughed, brushing Reece's soft hair behind her ear and watching as a smile broke across her face until she was also laughing.

Damian watched from the bottom of Flat 6's stairs; an empty bottle sat beside him. Jackson was also leaning on the wall next to Damian, and they both stared emotionlessly.

"I'm sorry, man," Jackson said after what seemed like a while. With no reply, he comforted, "There's tonnes of birds here, need a wingman?"

"Do you?" Damian asked right back, silencing Jackson for an extra second, and in that second, they saw Reece pull down at Al's collar, wrapping her other hand around his neck to kiss him, with him smoothly placing one hand on her waist, and the other at the small of her back.

Damian could feel his eyebrows pinch together and set deep into his face, watching as Alex strode past them and out the front door, with that same look, purposefully knocking into Al as he did, causing the two to pull away.

Slowly turning to face Damian, Reece's head was tilted in worry. Damian looked angrier than she had ever seen him; little did she know it would be days before he would speak to her again; and before she could ask, an uproar of shouting and screaming could be heard from the top of the stairs.

"Yuergh!" Mason thundered as he threw some guy over the bannister and down the steps, causing Damian and Jackson to leap out of the way as the boy hit the bottom. Painfully, the boy scrambled to his feet and ran down the stairwell and out the front door. "Don't you ever fucking come back, or I'll fucking kill you!" Mason yelled, venom in his tongue. "Fucking prick!" he yelled once more, stepping heavy-footed down the stairs.

"What happened?" Reece asked, pinned to the back wall, eyes in shock.

"Mother fucker, tried to steal Will's phone. Stupid prick didn't see him in his own room."

"But who was that guy?" Damian joined in, subconsciously pushing his sleeves up to his elbows and clenching his fists.

"The guy's name's Luigi, dickhead's only 16, but he knew someone else here and was apparently invited. He—"

"Mason!" Will called down from the top of the stairs; panic in his voice. "He took my wallet!"

"Im'a fucking kill him." Just as Mason turned back around, Damian had raced down the stairwell and out the door. Reece,

Jackson, and Mason watched through the stairwell window to see Damian sprint down the street towards the Spar until he was out of sight.

"Should we phone the police?" Jackson asked.

"Well, I'm high as a fucking kite, so fuck that!"

"You also assaulted a minor..." Reece added under her breath.

"That too."

It was dark in River's room, the kind of dark you're drawn to, where each shadow had a silver lining, and each fallen fairy light caught a golden spec in your eye. The air was warm, yet the sheets were cold. Zasha lay on her back, one arm stretched out underneath the crisp pillow and the other hand laying open by her side.

River lay next to her, in the dark, tracing his soft fingers over her palm, feeling every crease in a delicate glide. He played in smooth circular motions, sometimes daring to stroke up her arm. There were no words exchanged, and perhaps it was better that way. The party's light humming could still be heard, but River was no longer afraid of missing out. This was better; this was serene. He looked down at her, studying the contours of her face in the dark, looking at the curve of her button nose, and the shape of her jaw and down to her neck, even in this light, he could see how soft her skin was but refrained himself from touching it.

They lay like this for a while before they heard a scream in the bathroom next door. River tried to ignore it, but Zasha leapt up out of bed to see the commotion, leaving River in the dark.

"What is it?" Zasha asked Reece, and a girl called Rebecca, standing outside the bathroom door, watching as the toilet bowl erupted with water onto the blue tiles. "What the fuck!" Zasha exclaimed, stepping over the puddles and seeing a large hole in the basin, the missing cement piece discarded across the room.

"I don't know!" Rebecca cried, "I came to use the toilet, and it was already like this!"

"It must have broken earlier; someone just didn't realise and flushed it," Reece added, looking down at the river of toilet water pooling around the floor, and stopped herself from retching.

"Well, who the fuck done it?" Zasha cursed but was only met with blank expressions.

Damian, who had returned from his run and had heard the noise came running up the stairs.

"Zasha, what's going on?" he asked, still out of breath, but Rebecca answered all too quickly.

"Someone broke the toilet and left. I think it was one of Nora's weird friends. A bunch of them came up here and then left about 10 minutes ago."

Reece looked at Rebecca, shocked, brows pinched together as she tried to recall the event.

"Fuck's sake!" Damian grieved, "the ones waiting outside for a taxi? I passed them on the way up."

"I think so."

Aggressively grunting, Damian turned back down the stairs in a powerful sprint, and while he was intently watched, Rebecca quickly grabbed something from the bathroom floor and held it behind her back.

"Where the fuck is he going?" Zasha laughed, finding Damian's hero complex vastly amusing.

"I think he's going to chase down the Spaniards... He likes to run now," Reece answered, still in shock.

"Well, I'm going to make a sign for the bathroom door. Make sure to tell everyone to use the small toilet instead."

"Good idea." Reece watched as Zasha went into her room to find paper and pens and then focussed on Rebecca, who was staring seriously at her. "What's wrong?" she asked as Rebecca revealed the Amaretto bottle from behind her back and gave it to Reece. It was empty. "Why do you have this? I left it on the..." with wide eyes, Reece realised what had happened, "oh, shit."

A beautiful sign was made for the outside of the door, and I wish I could say that people read it before they used the broken bathroom, but this was not the case. Lewis, for one, having to mop the floor at 3 in the morning after a minor mishap, and Will not realising either as he crawled on all fours to throw up into the bowl. Needless to say, that did not end well either.

River and Zasha laughed at the events of the night as they nuzzled back into place. This time with Zasha playing with River's hair while lying with her leg wrapped over him. The night could have ended perfectly here, that is, if a drunk and crying Damian hadn't have stumbled into the wrong room after his second run of the night and fallen dead asleep at the bottom of River's bed. Funny at first, but somehow the fairy lights didn't do the same for the sparkle in Damian's eyes, and the loud globial snore of his throat did more than enough to kill the mood.

VAIN

The quiet purr of the morning breeze whistled through the open front door and hummed against the windows. The floors were sticky and at parts still completely wet from pools of drinks spilled, and the padding of small cushions sat in heaps around the lounge. Lewis's epi-pen lay broken in the middle of the sticky floor, and more bottles and bottle caps than you could care to count were scattered over both couches, the stairs, and every spare surface. It was a mess.

Al was the first to wake, still cloaked in his 'period red' sheet; he rolled off the end of the couch and straight onto the floor. Perhaps too eagerly assuming he would crash with Reece that night, he hadn't put much thought into where he would sleep, as his dedicated blow-up air mattress in the spare room or 'sex room' was all too quickly shot-gunned by two others at the party: later leaving behind stained sheets and a bloody pillow.

The couch was wet and cold, and as he hit the floor, Al thought that it couldn't get that much worse. Al was a pacifist, one of those hippy-dippy, peace be with you, smoke a joint and stay breezy type characters, but even this was too much for the Buddhist to handle as he immediately went to work, sourcing a black bin bag from under the counter and filling it house party debris.

In Reece's room, Reece woke up, alone, to the sound of bottles clanging together as they collided in the bottom of Alfredo's bin bag. The wringing sending a shock through Reece's body as she jolted upright out of her sleep and out of bed. Despite her incoordination that night, she had managed to change out of the leather into a large cotton work shirt, which had been buttoned up incorrectly, and had a large rip that led up to her ribs. She did manage to put on a small pair of shorts, and her brother's rugby socks that she had stolen the last time she visited home, which she wore like tights, and her hair, as per usual, was a mess.

Hazily wandering into the lounge, Reece stood in the doorway as she watched Al look up from the floor and smile as he caught her gaze.

"Ahh, Chica! You're awake!"

"Unfortunately," Reece smiled, confused. "Why are you cleaning?" she asked, with just enough admiration to encourage the continuation of said cleaning.

"Because it is a mess Chica! You can't live like this; it is not good for your soul."

"My soul?" Reece laughed as she pulled out a Corona bottle that had been wedged between the cushions.

"Of course!" Al got up from the floor and walked over to Reece, gently taking her hand so he could kiss it. "Your soul is important to me."

"Right, but like, how everyone's soul is important to you," her voice cracked a little as her hand pulled away from his.

"No, just yours."

"You've only been here a week..."

"Feels longer."

"Uh-huh." Her head tilted slightly as she looked up at Al, more confused than ever, eyes widening as he took the bottle out of her hand and leaned in closer.

"Listen, Chica, I was thinking. We should go on a date, just us."

Reece gulped, taking a small step back into the corridor. "You know, I would! But, uhh, I have work today!" she said, backing up into her room, Al following intently.

"Aw, that is a shame. When?"

"Like—now."

This was a lie, of course, but this didn't stop her theatrically searching around her room for her work shirt and tie and clumsily pulling crumpled black trousers over her shorts.

Al, who had respectfully turned around so she could change, smiled to himself, finding Reece's bizarre behaviour oddly amusing. After a while, he turned back around to see Reece fully dressed in an unwashed white shirt, tightly fitted tie, and one small black pump in hand. Al slowly walked over, holding the tie at the knot and slowly pulling it down until it hung loose in the centre of her chest.

"It looks better on girls like this," he spoke softly, wrapping his hands around her waist and pushing her gently towards the bed until the back of her calves hit against the frame.

"Al, I have to—"

"Shhh," he hushed as he pulled her shirt untucked on both sides and placed his cold hands against her skin. "Lock the door, Reece. Work can wait," he whispered, his r's rolling.

"Look," Reece said, laughing a little at the pre-emptive irony, "I take my job very seriously, I can't be late." Quickly

69

moving Al's hands from her waist and grabbing the other black pump on the floor she had spotted while Al was trying to be sexy, she added, "Also, I don't want to," before running out the room into the stairwell and bumping into Jackson as she clumsily pulled her shoes onto her feet.

"Where are you going?" Jackson laughed, looking down at her, noticing the flush in her cheeks and the ratted black tangles in her hair.

"I uhh—" Reece went to speak, but as she did, she could hear Al leave her room, "I'll explain later!" she yelled, brushing past Jackson and running down the stairs and out the door, one shoe still in hand.

Laughing to himself, Jackson let her go. Watching through the glass as she struggled to put on her shoe mid-run and disappear around the corner. Like most, Jackson had learned that it's best not to ask in times like this and just accept that a girl like Reece will always be in a world of her own. However, he ended up putting two and two together when he walked into Flat 5 past Reece's room and saw Al patiently waiting in the doorway.

"She was late for work," Al explained, his lips forming a slight smile.

"Uh-huh," Jackson sighed before making his way up the stairs.

In River's room, things were calm, serene. Zasha lay close to River, his warm breath humming against the bridge of her nose, and her lips, slightly parted, only inches away from his. The fogged-up glass beside the bed hid the morning birds singing morning songs and the tiny droplets of dew collected on the windowsill.

Still lying curled up at the end of the bed, Damian wrapped his arms around Zasha's ankles, like an anchor, overtime pulling Zasha further and further away from River. Now, I'm not saying the poor boys a cock-block, but there's a metaphor in there somewhere.

Jackson stood in the doorway, silently watching, more confused than anything else. He had come to check on his friend who had hooked up with a 'sexy devil' in the 'sex room,' but River's open door drew him in.

Jackson knocked loudly against the frame, causing River to purr himself in consciousness, stretching his arms above his head and sit upright in bed. Taking in the room, River's heavy eyes scanned the sheets, at first smiling as he saw Zasha was still lying next to him, stroking her hair behind her ear and pulling the fallen covers back over her shoulders. It was then, as he struggled against the blanket that he realised Damian was still in the room, like a newborn pup cradled at the bottom of the bed, coverless and cold.

River laughed as he realised, he had no memory of Damian ever being there. It took a second before River even considered looking up at Jackson, who had been standing there for some time now, and when they did finally make eye contact, it was as awkward as if they were strangers. "Well, hello!" River coyly smiled, mid-yawn, and eyes half-open.

"Uhh, hey. I was just checking on—"

"Looking to join?"

Jackson let out a high-pitched laugh, the kind of one I warned you about, the kind that could send jolts through your spine and wake you up from your sleep. Which is what it did; both Zasha and Damian shot upwards in bed, hands-on head and eyes squeezed together as if that would help.

"Well fuck," Jackson winced, looking directly at River, who had not changed expression, before darting out the room.

Sighing, Zasha wiped the smudged eyeliner from her cornea and flattened the back of her hair, trying to make sense of the bedhead before rolling onto her stomach to face River once again, both mirroring each other's soft smiles.

Like a slow fade, Damian dissolved back into the sheets and began snoring instantly.

Running his fingers through Zasha's hair once again, River whispered, "So, I was thinking today we should bake, watch movies, chill... cuddle."

Zasha's eyebrows pinched together, and her smile sunk into her chin.

"Cuddle?" she asked, her voice husked.

"Umm, yeah. Like what we've been doing?"

A second passed before Zasha let out a spiteful breath of laughter, "River, I don't know what you think this is, but we're not like 'together'." Now sitting upright so that she could look down at River's face, which had contorted into a mold of perpetual fear, she laughed once more, "Like I'm sorry, but fuck, we just slept in the same bed; that doesn't mean anything, even Damian's here!"

"I know we're not *together*, but you have to admit, there's been more than just sleeping together."

"What the fuck does that mean?"

River gulped, remembering now how talking to Zasha was like playing minesweeper. "I just mean that we've—"

"We've *what*, River?"

"You know, had momen—"

"Moments!" Zasha snapped. "We haven't had moments River, you can't just latch on to any girl that spends time with you."

"Look, I'm —" Before River could finish, Zasha had thrashed herself out from under the waves of covers and walked towards the door. "Dude, I'm sorry!" he yelled after her as she slammed the door and thumped down the stairs. Leaving River's eyes wide and stunned, with a pounding weight on his chest, he knew to be an anxiety attack.

Once more, Damian came to. "River... what are you doing in my room?"

On the other side of things, the air was calm, undisturbed. Al had made his way over to Flat 6 with a full bin bag, costume long gone.

Amy had returned from staying at Callum's, raced upstairs to fetch her keys, and had left for work all within a minute, passing Al in the corridor with a "What the fuck?" in regard to him sweeping.

This was normal for Amy. To leave, I mean. In fact, at the end of the year, 'Amy's absence in the flat' was quite the topic.

Upstairs, Will lay awake, staring up at the IT poster by the foot of his bed, pillow curled around both sides of his head. His walls were occupied with various cult classic posters and some anime film no one knows. The room, much like Will, was the obvious stereotype for any film student. A MacBook pro constantly charging, with oversized print tees on the floor, and once again, like talking to the boy about the importance of sleep and self-care, actual broken records hung on his door.

Will was also still in his costume from the night before, the Vincent Vega wig now lopsided and the stray hairs tangled in between the chain of the ugly 'moon stone' necklace around his neck, which he said promoted healing but really looked like a hard third nipple under his shirt.

The windowsill sat just inches from his face, the wet sludge from the open vent oozing in streaks down the glass. The stench of mould was foul and did nothing to help his gag reflux at that particular moment.

Drunken flashbacks from the night before faded in and out like episodes, and he couldn't help at cringe for the most part. Losing his wallet was the least of his worries when he remembered how he danced to 'Uptown Funk' in front of multiple girls. Will's head began to pound, and the sound of Nora's bedroom door swinging open and heavy footsteps beating down the stairs didn't help either.

Nora's room was the smallest of Flat 6; she could just about fit a single bed and small bedside table which she filled with random trinkets from her European travels. Her 'closet' took the shape of a thin metal rail at the foot of her bed which she crammed excessive amounts of knitted sweaters and bootlegged trousers.

Opening his door, Will saw Nora across the hall leaning against the bannister, looking over and watching.

"Morning!" Will sang, walking over to Nora to give her a cheerful hug and pleasantly surprised as his hands ran over the soft silk nightgown she was wearing.

Nora laughed, "Hey, Will."

"Torres, was that a boy leaving your bedroom?" he teased, looking around to see the back of Nora's head in matted tangles.

"Yes, that was Marco, he's from Barcelona. He's here for ERASMUS."

ERASMUS was a 'studying overseas' program run by Queens. Students would only spend one term abroad.

"Very nice. I love a man from Ba-th-alona!" he sang again, making sure to really hiss the 'th'.

Laughing some more, Nora shook her head, eyes pinned to the floor as she tucked a lock of hair behind her ear. "Yeah, he's a lot of fun."

"Oh, I bet—I might have to call up Marco myself."

"Heh, shut up! What do you mean?"

"I mean, I love you, dude, but you sounded like a deep-sea creature. Might have to start calling you 'Whale-Torres!'"

"That is disgusting!" Nora shrieked, looking as horrified as you can imagine.

"Heh-heh, I bet it was."

Just then, Jackson's door opened, and Jackson stood in front of the two dressed in blue, football boots in hand. "Did I miss the meeting?" he smirked, looking Nora up and down, also appreciating the silky pink apparel.

"Nah, man, just discussing Nora getting it 'awn' last night," Will cheekily chirped seconds before the back of Nora's hand smacked into his chest.

"Oh yeah. Can you be louder next time? It's really hard for me to masturbate with a cup to the wall." Jackson's face was stern; this was the first time the mention of sex didn't send him into ecstasy.

"Heh—fuck you, Jackson," Nora playfully scolded before rolling her eyes and returning to her room, locking it behind her.

Jackson stood with Will for a moment before whispering, "I felt like I was their third."

Light-filled Wills eyes as he remembered another event of the night. "Well. Three is a *crowd*. Right Chief?" he toyed, placing a patronising hand on Jackson's back which was instantly shrugged off.

"Mason can go fuck himself," Jackson spat, huffing down the stairs and out the door. Obviously, a sensitive topic.

A couple hours had passed when Reece called Will on his way back from the bank.

"Hey-yo, Reggie!" he sang.

Reece could hear his smile from the other end of the line. "Yo! Where are you right now?"

"Uhh, on Botanic, I'm coming back from the bank."

"Oh right...Why?"

"I had to cancel my cards; my wallet was stolen, remember?"

"Oh my gosh! Yes, I remember I'm so sorry, dude, that sucks."

"It's alright. There's no money in it. I'm just pissed he got my QFT voucher. But yeah, what can I do for you, dude?"

"Fair. Can you meet me on Fitzroy? There's an alley behind 119. I need your help."

Fitzroy was a street close to the flat on the Holy Lands' border, known for its multiple bomb scares and an underground brothel.

"Uhh, sure, I'll see you in 5."

"Sweet."

As he said, Will turned up 5 minutes later to the dingey alleyway behind 119. The ground was coated in a breadcrumb of glass, and several smashed pumpkins lay like corpses on the path. Hundreds of papers were also scattered. Some lay in heaps, others wavering through the light breeze. There were also coloured highlighters dotted around, a few pens, and a colourful striped binder and folder that had been shoved into a recycling bin.

Trying to make sense of it all, Will called out to Reece, who was facing the end of the path, her back to him. "What happened here?"

"Someone went into my room and stole all my Film notes," she said plainly.

"What? Why? That's so random!"

Reece turned slowly towards Will. In her hands, she held a bright yellow notebook and a small carved pumpkin. It was Will's.

"Is that mine?" Will laughed, walking over to take it from her.

"Yeah. I just don't understand, there were laptops, phones, wallets, *your* camera in my room! Literally, everyone left stuff there. Why the hell would someone steal a folder with some coursework in it?"

"I don't know," Will spoke softly as he looked down at her. The calm wind wavering through her wavy hair as she stood in the middle of the hollowed street, the sound of the rustling papers crisp to the ear. It was all too cinematic.

"Y'know, this would be a perfect shot. Can you wait here while I go get my camera?" he teased, and for the second time that day, he was met with the back of a hand being slammed into his sternum. This time a little more forceful than the last. "Ow!" he yelled, taking a step back.

"Sorry! I didn't know that was going to be that har—can you just help me, please?"

"Fine. How did you even find this stuff?"

"The guy who found my diary rang me; all my details are in it." Reece flipped to the first page of the yellow book, showing Will.

"Ahh. Well, aren't you glad you did that!"

"Yeah, who wouldn't want to spend time picking up soggy paper and pumpkin chunks from a dark alleyway?"

"That's the spirit chief!"

Between the two of them, they managed to find every scrap of paper, pen, and other stationary item from the alley. Pushing it deep into a large black bin on the corner of their building. Walking back tiredly back up the flights of stairs into the flat, Will paused for a moment before entering.

"What is it?" Reece asked, head tilted.

"Bro, what are you wearing? Where have you been?"

Looking down at her crumpled shirt and tie, Reece grinned, "The library."

'Flaherty's Portrayal of the Inuit Culture' being her highest-graded paper to date.

OBSESSIVE

The amber hue of the autumn season wasted into an icy glaze in the later November days. The air was the type of cold that burned, and even inside, the flat would cover up with blankets, beanie's and hot whiskies to battle the temperamental boilers. Covered in pasta sauce and overpriced red wine, Reece pulled herself up the stairs and into the lounge of Flat 5.

River and Zasha were sitting side by side on the black leather couch under a soft yellow blanket. Zasha's hair was scraped back into a bun, and a red tint of tomato sauce was brushed across the corner of her lips. River's long coarse hair looked wet, with both their eyes were glued to their screens. It was obvious they hadn't moved all day.

"Hey, Reggie!" Zasha yelled in a cheerful tone.

River adding, "Hey, Kiddo!" peeling his eyes away from the episode to look up at Reece.

She was wearing a black and grey chequered short-sleeve shirt and a short black apron tied around her waist like a gun-belt. Her hair pulled back into a loose pony.

"How was work?" he asked.

Since her first year in University, Reece had been working at an Italian restaurant on Botanic as well as her recruitment job. It paid minimum wage, her boss was terrible, and the kitchen staff was full of pervs, but she got free food, which seemed to make the above all okay.

"Work was awful. Janet—*my boss*— made some girl cry for being a few minutes late. Borris—the other boss—screamed at me when I forgot the dessert forks and made me stay late, and some kid ran into me with a bowl of bolognaise, and somehow, I had to apologise and take money off their bill. But! Some old guy said I looked cute in the uniform and gave me a £10 tip." Taking a deep breath after the rant, Reece slumped down into the opposite couch.

"Men are the worst," River sneered, his face forming a grimace.

"Yeah."

"At least you're getting tipped, I mean, for the sexual harassment," Zasha added sarcastically.

Softly laughing, Reece pulled her hair out of the bobble and swung her legs over the armrest so she could lie across the leather. "How are you guys doing anyway?" she asked, head turned towards the two.

A moment of silence passed before Zasha answered, "We're fine, just been watching F.R.I.E.N.D.S all day."

"I also made chickpea and butternut curry, was really good. I crushed it!" River beamed but was quickly shut down when Zasha explained, "It was fine."

"And I appointed my new Vice President for Scribblers! Her name's Jo, she's wonderful, and we have set up a writing workshop for tomorrow."

"Oh, sweet," Reece said, pulling out her phone from her apron pouch. "What's her last name?"

"Sawyer,"

"Damn, that's a cool name!"

"Right? She's American." From Portland, Oregan, to be exact.

"Oh! She's super cute," Reece revelled, looking down at Jo's profile photo.

Jo was a short girl with fair brown hair and large blue eyes. She had small thin lips and dotted freckles across her nose.

"Yeah, she's really pretty," he agreed, catching Zasha's look of disdain from the corner of his eye. "She's not my type, though!" he trilled; his head turned away from Zasha to the floor in embarrassment.

"Anyway..." Reece hesitated, seeing the wheels in Zasha's head turn green, "anything new with you, Zasha?"

"Yeah! I've been talking to Alex—Sorry, 'Warner,' and I'm meeting up with him tomorrow tonight to give him back his stuff."

I should explain. During 'first year,' both Reece and Zasha dated boys called Alex, this became confusing very quickly, and so to distinguish them since the break-up, Reece started calling them by their last names. This caught on and became the norm inside their friendship group.

Reece looked concerned, her eyebrows pinched together, and the top corner of her lip pointed upward. "I thought you gave him back all of his stuff weeks ago?"

Zasha's face reset. "No. I gave him back a hoodie. We went out for 10 months Reece, there's going to be more than a fucking hoodie."

"I get that, but why wouldn't you just give him all of his stuff back in one go?"

The answer seemed to click as soon as she asked it out loud, and Reece instantly began texting Damian, who was in his room upstairs.

"What are you saying!" Zasha screamed, now standing up from the couch and looking down at Reece, who had now turned upright.

"I'm saying, maybe you're giving his stuff back in chunks, so you have excuses to see him."

"What the fuck? What the fuck! You're making me sound pathetic!" Zasha began pacing around the room, turning back every so often to see the look on Reece's face, but it was unfazed; Reece continued to sit calmly on the couch, watching her strut around the lounge with the frequent curse.

Barely a minute had gone by before River's phone vibrated in his hand, and he abruptly got up and paced out the room.

Waiting for him to be out of earshot, Reece insisted, "I don't think you're pathetic, Zasha, I think you loved him and seeing him move on hurts like hell, especially when you haven't."

Hearing this, Zasha stopped and turned towards Reece, venom in her veins. "He still has feelings for me, Reece!" she spat.

"What?"

"I know he does! Because you can't go from loving someone to never wanting to see them again!"

"You can when you're hurt, and Zasha, you hurt him. And I'm your girl, you know that. But I'm not gonna pretend that what you did wasn't wrong. And he did some horrible stuff too, which just shows you guys were toxic together, and if he asked you to leave him alone, Zasha, you have to let him go!"

Tears began streaming down Zasha's face, which she pushed away with the cuff of her sleeve, her hand formed into a tight fist.

"What the fuck is wrong with you, Reece? What the fuck." She paused for a moment before sobbing, "If you loved McManus the way I love Warner, and he moved on, I would never say to you what you just said to me."

Her words struck a nerve in Reece, and her cheeks began to flush red and hot, and she found herself choking back tears before saying, "Maybe, but I'm only telling you this because I'm your friend, and I want to see you happy. If you still want to meet up with him, I won't stop you. But if you need me to drop off the stuff instead, I can do that too." Saying this, Reece finally got up from the couch, untying her apron and throwing it down into the corner of the seat, leaving Zasha alone.

"I never asked for your fucking advice—or help! So just stay the fuck away from me!"

Upstairs in Damian's room, Damian and River sat on opposite ends of the bed, with Reece cross-legged on the floor in the doorway looking up at them both. Zasha's cursing as loud as ever through the floorboards.

Damian's room was the furthest from the stairs, and directly above Reece's; a quaint square bedroom with a polished dresser and tv stand, to which he hoarded his flat screen like a troll with treasure; and when entering his room, there was always a black bin bag in the corner next to a large cylinder of Protein Powder which he took religiously before and after going to the gym.

Looking around the room, waiting for the dust to settle, River began counting the mass volume of printed photos pinned to Damian's wall in neat rows. He counted 72.

Damian, trying to make small talk, still angry with her, asked Reece about work which she replied with a less angsty version than before and in turn asked about his day.

As usual, Damian spent the day in the library, working on a microbiology paper I won't even try to explain. But, as I recall, had something to do with sea algae, and then he went to the gym. Reece could tell it was a back and arms kind of day as Damian was holding a dripping ice pack to his shoulder, obviously needing to refreeze it, but the soggy sheets beat the alternative of going downstairs.

The three of them waited in silence for some time until they heard the front door open, and slam shut. The coast was clear.

"So, what the hell was that all about?" Damian asked, his gaze flicking between River and Reece.

"Reece overstepped with a Warner issue, and now Zasha's pissed," River explained bluntly, looking down into the mattress.

"Um, I'm sorry. I *overstepped*?" Reece asked, taken back.

"Yes, dude. *Overstepped*, it's not your place to tell her that she can't give her ex's stuff back when it's obvious she's trying to be done with him."

Hearing this, Reece's face settled into a smile. "Do you know why they broke up?" her voice was soft as if singing a child to sleep.

River thought for a moment, "Yeah, um, they were in Budapest together over summer for that festival thing. They hadn't seen each other in months, and he broke up with her after sleeping with her. Like I said, men are the worst. And you should be supporting her right now, not taking his side."

"Did she tell you that?"

"Yeah."

"Okay, well what she didn't tell you is that they weren't even together at the festival, they had broken up months before then, but they still had the tickets, so they decided to go together as friends. They did hook up, but that was before Zasha had told him she had already slept with another guy since they got there, and so did he—*with another girl I mean*— and that's why they ended it for good."

"Oh," River sighed, his cheeks warming in embarrassment.

Damian just looked puzzled. "Well then, why did they break up the first time?" he asked, reaching for his Mimikyu plushie and holding it in his lap.

"It doesn't matter, but just so you guys know, I'm her friend, and friends tell each other when they're making a mistake." Getting up from the floor, she smiled a last time before leaving the two alone in the room and going back to hers.

Some more silence passed before Damian handed over the toy to River, saying, "Listen, I don't know what happened downstairs, but you know you can talk to me about anything."

River didn't respond. He just continued counting the photos on the wall with an addled expression, his head tilting more and more as he counted, *44...45...46...*

"Like, I know she comes across as harsh, but she means well!"

...49...50... "Who, Zasha?"

"No, Reece. Shes' got a point, I think—"

"Of course, you'd think that." *52...53...*

"What does that mean? I'm just saying she's right. I—"

"56!" River gasped, eyes wide and head swivelled round to the back wall like an owl.

"What?"

"56 Photos Damian! You have 72 photos on your wall and fucking 56 of them are of Reece!" Damian immediately looked angry, his fists burying into the sheets.

"They're group photos! We live together, of course she's going to be in a lot of them!"

"This is a shrine!" River let a high pitch squeal and threw both hands over his mouth to stop the ugly sound. "Oh my god, this is wild! It's a shrine!" Like a child, River continued to giggle under his palms, staring at Damian and watching the fire burn.

"It's not like that, I—"

"Yes, it fucking is. I swear if there's more than 10 of just the two of you, I—" River began scanning the walls, and within seconds, he had counted 7.

"River, just stop!"

9...10...11...

"Please just drop it!"

13...14...15...

"Look, I didn't mean to—"

17...18...19... A genuine look of worry passed over River's face as he tallied the last few. "Oh, Buddy," he whimpered, now holding the toy close to his chest.

With defeat written all over his face, Damian asked, "How many?"

"22. How long have you—"

"Since first year."

"But she was with Alex first year, I—"

"I know."

"How bad?"

"Bad." Damian was a man of few words, and this was the first time River had seen him struggle with a girl problem, and Damian's ex liked to be lathered in yoghurt.

"I don't know what to say," River cooed, leaning over to wrap his arms around Damian and rest his head on his shoulder. Within seconds he could feel the jolts of resisted sobs.

"And I know it's stupid because we live together, but I thought when she broke up with Alex that I had a—" the words lodged in his throat like starch.

"Well, Bud, you know what she's like, maybe it's just that, you guys are friends, and you live together, she would never cross that line."

"You say that, but I've seen her with Jackson, she—"

"First of all, Jackson's a piece of shit, and Reece knows that."

"But I see them together, and they're always flirting, and going places together and—"

"Second of all, I'm convinced Amy and Jackson have a thing."

"Why's that?"

"Why do you think he's even living with us in the first place? None of us knew him before this year, and Amy only fought for him to be here because she fancies him" —he paused for a second— "look, all I'm saying is there's a reason why Callum doesn't like him."

I think now is a perfect time to explain something about Amy. As juvenile as it sounds, Amy 'fancying someone' is as common as, Will reciting movie quotes, Nora playing the 'foreigner card,' or Reece forgetting where she left her keys, ergo, practically continuous. And the 'Amy fancy' as coined by Reece, has evolved into a simple explanation for when you are attracted to someone, for any reason at all: their looks, voice, the way they crack open bottles, or in this case, being under the same roof. Nevertheless, it's fair to say Callum was not a fan of the 'Amy Fancy.'

"Maybe, I just don't know what to do. I still can't bear to be in the same room with her after the whole 'Al thing.'"

"Aw, dude, you can't hold that against her. She doesn't know...Who does know?"

"Jackson, Will, and now you. You can't tell anyone, though, if she finds out—"

"I'm not going to tell, okay Bud? But I would suggest taking down a few of these photos...maybe like...30."

Damian pulled away, softly laughing, his eyes red and filled with tears.

Looking down at him, River laughed with him, grateful that Damian could open up to him like he did and grateful that all this distracted him from his own problems for a second or two.

Hours had passed, and most of the flat were asleep, with Zasha being the only one still out. Being as quiet as she could, Reece crept up the stairs and into River's room; the soft hue from the fairy lights fading from under the door told her he was still awake.

"River?" she whispered, standing at the foot of the bed.

He was sat upright under the covers, his face lit by the dimmed screen of his laptop. The faint smell of mulberry stagnant in the room. Approaching December, his mother had sent him a Christmas care package, only a few packets of treat-sized pretzels left unopened.

"Hey Kid, what's up?"

Reece climbed onto the end of the bed and pulled a spare blanket over her lap and around her shoulders, her back pressed against the cold wall.

"I need to tell you what happened," she whispered, and she did.

Zasha and Warner hooked up at the start of 'first year' on a whim; he was currently seeing 3 other girls, one of whom was an ex from Manchester that he would occasionally fly back to see. When Zasha found out about the other girls, however, she made him choose. Being won over by her spicy, exotic nature and pretty face, he chose her, and they celebrated their exclusivity with a next day trip to Amsterdam, as you do, and for the next couple of months, they were inseparable.

At one point, Warner ended up moving his bedframe down the street into her building in Elms so they could live together. Of course, Alex still kept a blow-up air mattress in his own room for nights when they needed some space or Zasha wasn't in.

Now, River knew the prologue, being in the same circles as Alex and Zasha, it was pretty hard to miss the milestones. What few knew though, and Reece had the privilege of knowing; being Warner's flatmate, was that often enough at early hours of the morning, the two would be up, screaming at each other. Either Alex had taken too long to text back, or Zasha had lost her temper and overreacted, or the gluten-free pasta didn't taste as good as the normal pasta. You get the drift.

But there was one night, in the spring of that year during a film formal at the Crescent that topped the lot…

It was Maytime, the flowers outside Sycamore 5 were blushed in full bloom, and the grass was just firm enough that Zasha's stilettos were only partially stuck in the soil. The taxis were just starting to arrive when Warner met Zasha at her side, wrapping his arm around her waist and leaning over to her ear to whisper, "You look amazing, Zaz," taking the two empty rosé bottles from her hands and throwing them into a nearby bin.

"Aw, thank you, babies, you look so handsome." Zasha pursed her lips for a kiss but pulled away after only a moment, "Alex?" she asked, "you're wearing black?"

Alex looked down at his suit and back at Zasha, her eyebrows furrowed together.

"Uhh, yeah, you don't like it?"

"It's not that I don't like it. I just thought you knew I was wearing blue, that's all," her voice was laced in frustration as she looked down at her dress. It was a navy blue A-line with a sweetheart neckline. It fitted her well and showed off her angular frame. She wore her hair up in a romantic bun, and silver jewellery hung from her neck.

"Oh," Warner started, feeling guilty that he had switched suits when his mum had called to say he looked better in black last minute. "Sorry, Zasha, I can go change!"

"No. It's fine," she insisted, keeping it to herself that she disapproved of his sudden outfit change. After all, it was a special night, and it would not be ruined by something as trivial as—"It's not like everyone knows that black and navy look shit together!" she spat, leaving Alex on the grass to talk to the taxi drivers, informing them that a few still haven't arrived.

Back in the flat kitchen, mutual friends and their dates downed the remaining bottles of wine, Will being sure to sneak in a small bottle of vodka in his blazer pocket and Amy assessing whether she could conceal a bottle of Jack strapped to her thigh before giving up and handing it to her boyfriend Callum who had not said a word since pre's started.

Others in the kitchen, unfamiliar with Callum, tried to start a conversation but had lost motivation after a minute of monosyllabic small talk.

"You don't have to be here," Amy insisted, standing up from the couch and straightening her dress. Amy was wearing a silver sheen fitted gown with a deep-v neckline and a high split up the thigh, her eyelids painted a sparkling cyan in an attempt to match Callum's navy suit.

"Well, I'm not gonna let some other guy take you to this thing, am I?" he mumbled, now standing next to her, his eyes perusing around the room at the male contenders.

"*Other* guy? You mean Jackson?"

"I didn't say, Jackson, did I?"

"He didn't want to go, you know that."

"You shouldn't have asked him!"

"You didn't want to go either!"

"And now I do, so can we just get this thing over with, please." Callum, continuing to sulk, left the kitchen with Amy following frustrated behind him, hiding her face from a few others who had been listening, Will and Reece being 2 of them.

"To an unforgettable night!" he cheered, raising his glass above Reece's head and slowly lowering it when he realised, she couldn't reach.

"Hear hear!" Reece laughed, clinking her own glass to his and downing her vodka and coke, which, being poured by Will, was a respectable 50/50 ratio. "Okay, wow," she laughed, "I am blown away, Sir, and not only because you look dashing in a suit!" she teased, appreciating Will's tailored three-piece that gave the 'busboy' a more 'red carpet' feel.

"Why, thank you, my dear, and may I say you look ravishing yourself." Will winked, throwing his arm around her shoulders and escorting her outside. As they waited for the others to gather, Reece could see McManus running over from Chesnutt (the group of flats next to Sycamore).

"Hey! Sorry, I'm late!" he called, his thick Dublin accent masking any leeway to scold.

"You're alright, mate," Will cheered, patting him on the back and dramatically sighing. "Well, you sure do make the rest of us look bad, don't ya? Sorry Reece, I tried! But your boyfriend here's got me beat. I guess I have to hand you back now."

The three of them laughed as Will walked off, swinging his blazer over his shoulder and jumping into a taxi with Amy and Callum.

"What a guy," McManus sighed, taking Reece's hand in his and leading her into a spare taxi.

As they drove off, the two could see Zasha walking hastily ahead with Warner running after her, calling, "I said you looked amazing! Just get in the taxi!"

"No!"

Later at the Crescent, the sun was just beginning to set, and sweet-smelling cherry blossoms shed pink petals over the few on the patio. Reece stood looking down at her small white heels, nipping the points together nervously as McManus stood in front of her under the floral arch.

It was a warm evening, the sun showering her in a golden light, and catching the green pigment in her eyes, the slight breeze weaving through the waves in her dark hair. Alex took her hand, and as they stood together, a slow song began to play from inside, luring others around back into the hall to dance and leaving the two alone.

McManus took a moment before he spoke, looking down at Reece, at her sun-kissed face, where the powder had rubbed from her nose, leaving it rosy. He looked down at the dress she was wearing: a satin black baby-doll, cinched at the waist, that hung petitely above her knee. Alex could tell she was nervous. He watched amusingly as she would look at him for a second, then down at her shoes, then biting her lower lip.

"Reece?" he whispered, reaching for her other hand. Still, in silence, Reece's dark eyes fluttered back up to meet his gaze, the flush in her cheeks deepening. "Do you remember how we met?" he asked, a devilish smile growing on his face.

Confused at first, Reece answered, "Uhh, yeah, backstage at the Player's show."

McManus laughed a little. "No, well yes, but like how we really met?"

Reece thought for a moment, "You walked me home after one of the shows...and I—"

"You gave me your number and said you'd be expecting a call."

"And you called, we went out—"

"I took you to see the Christmas lights—"

"Well, I mean, you dragged me blindfolded into a dark alley and told me to trust you—"

"It was romantic!"

"It was terrifying!"

"You looked so beautiful." He paused "...You are beautiful." McManus smiled, pulling her closer until her hands were wrapped around him.

"I bet you say that to all the girls," Reece teased; her nerves finally calmed.

"No, just you."

Looking up at him, Reece could see the amber lining around him from where the sun was beating down behind, the sunlight escaping through the cracks in his thick hair and light caramelising his eyes into dark toffee. It was in this moment that Reece knew she was in love with him, she had been unsure before, but this, in this moment, she knew. "Hey Alex, I—" but before she could say anything, Will sauntered through the courtyard doors, eyes wincing at the beating sun.

"Ah Reggie, my good fellow," he charmed, swaying a little too much to blame it on the music. "Amy's inside looking for you."

"Oh, okay, thanks." Reece smiled, turning back to McManus, saying, "I'll be back," before running inside, tapping her hand on Will's shoulder as she left.

It was a couple of minutes before Reece found Amy standing next to the foyer's large glass pane. The window curved around the south side of the building and overlooked the hotel parking lot below. Amy's long thin fingers were pressed up against the pane when Reece joined her at her side, now to looking down at the ground below. "Should we do something?" Amy said abruptly, her voice pained with more frustration than concern.

"I don't know."

Reece silently watched as she saw Zasha shout and scream at Warner. Even from so far, Reece could see that they were both crying. Alex was standing with both hands in his hair, pulling at the roots, and Zasha, utterly distraught, ripped off her heels and threw them at Warner from the other side of a parked car. The two were like this for some time.

At points, it would seem the dust had settled, but then the riot would start back up, with Warner occasionally trying to walk away and Zasha running to rip him back.

"Does Will know?" Reece asked, noticing where Amy's fake tan had streaked and left striped ripples down her leg, to then realise how white she looked standing next to her.

"Yeah, he said I should get you though."

"Huh." This puzzled Reece. For some time, both Will and Reece had been on either side of Warner and Zasha's antics and up until now, had dealt with things together.

"He said that this is our night, and he's not going to let their fucked-up relationship ruin it," Amy added, her face emotionless, as it usually was.

"Uh-huh," Reece murmured once more, eyes widening as she watched Warner walk away one last time, and Zasha left screaming to the point she collapsed on the gravel. Seeing this, Reece quickly turned and left the foyer, running down the grand flights of stairs into the entrance hall, her shoes also off by this point; she moves quicker footloose style.

Meeting Warner at the front doors, she instantly wrapped both arms around his back and squeezed, her heels hitting into him slightly as she held them in her left hand. It took a moment before he hugged her back, and his face contorted as he tried to hold back more tears; they weren't alone in the entrance hall, and Warner wasn't one to make a scene...intentionally.

"What happened?" Reece asked, looking up at Warner, watching a bead of sweat drip from his forehead to his nose.

"I uhh—she's just having a bad night," he sobbed.

What had happened was that Warner had told Zasha he needed some time alone, that he loved her, but perhaps living together after being together for 2 minutes was crazy, and he needs his own room back. And we all know how these talks go—

"You want to go on a break!" ect... However, for these two, those conversations don't comply with the "We're in public, let's talk about this later" unspoken rule.

"Oh," Reece sighed, nodding slowly. "So, what now?"

"Let's just...Enjoy the rest of the night. I missed starters. There's no way I'm missing dessert." He smiled, sturdily holding out his arm so Reece could link it; they met up with the rest of the table, having from then on, a pretty amazing night—

"Couples fight, Reece. I don't think Zasha throwing her shoes is a deal-breaker," River interjected, closing the lid of his laptop so that he and Reece were sitting in near darkness.

"I'm not done."

The rest of the evening had passed, Warner sat alone at the table enjoying every last crumb of his chocolate cake, Reece even saw him lick the plate at one point, and she smiled remembering how much Zasha hated chocolate before McManus twirled and dipped her, making a comment about what a terrible dancer she is.

"I don't dance!" she laughed, grabbing firmly onto his arms to steady herself after she rolled over on a heel confirming McManus's theory.

At the other end of the dance floor, Amy and Callum stood side by side, both shifting awkwardly as if they were strangers, and Will, seeing this, tried to pull Callum into the middle but failed and resorted to raving alone—

"How long is this story?" River interrupted once more with a slight chuckle. Now adjusted to the dim light, his face dropped as he could see Reece's large eyes darken and angrily morph, her top lip pointing in the corner and her fist clenching into the sheets. He was instantly uncomfortable and only now remembered why he found this small person so unnerving.

"Sorry..." he pleaded, motioning with his hand for her to continue and seeing her face instantly lift into a pleasant pose, her voice singing with child-like enthusiasm.

It was only in the very early hours of the next morning that Warner saw Zasha again; coming back after the formal while the others went clubbing, he retired to his own bedroom. Throwing his tie to the corner of the room, and suit jacket over the orange plastic chair, also making sure to put his phone on charge, which had been dead for some time. His room was bare since he had been living with Zasha; he had moved all his belongings to hers as well, leaving only a poorly pumped air mattress and a single thin sheet he used as a blanket. He told himself it was like coming back to a budget hotel, which seemed to make it better.

Warner lay on his bed in the dark, staring up at the shaded walls, his mind whirring, when a bright light from his phone shone at the ceiling and began vibrating aggressively. Sighing, Warner leaned over to look at his screen, and within seconds his heart sank so deep into his chest he couldn't breathe. Over 30 messages came through, all from Zasha, and as he read down, he felt he could throw up.

Where are you?
Pick up your phone!
Why are you ignoring me!?

He continued to read.

Alex I'm sorry
I just love you, the thought of ever being apart from you just hurts so much.
IS YOUR PHONE OFF!?
WHY DID YOU TURN YOUR PHONE OFF!?
I said I'm sorry, can you just come home now?

Throwing his head into the sink, Warner began to retch.

I swear to FUCK Alex if you don't pick up, I'm going to kill myself!
Alex!
I MEAN IT!
Alex I'm at the bridge
If you don't reply I'm going to jump
I will jump and kill myself
Alex please!!
PLEASE!!!!!!

A stream of similar texts continued to filter through, and Warner, failing to purge, took his phone and ran to Reece's door, pounding his fist against it, screaming, "Reece! I need you! I need you now!" Hoping and pleading, she had come back early. "Please!" he cried, tears flooding down his cheek. "Please open up!"

Just then, from back down the hall, Warner heard a wringing smashing sound of broken glass. Others on the ground floor who had heard began pouring out their rooms, gathering outside his door. Callie, a short, plump girl who roomed opposite Warner was the first to inspect the room. Like Reece and Will, she knew well of Warner's and Zasha's relationship and had, up until this point kept quiet about her concerns.

Walking into his room, Callie stepped into a pool of wine that was pumping out a Rosé bottle on the floor. A gust of wind spoke through the broken window, and shards of glass travelled in the spirit and collected around her feet. Warner's bed shimmered where smaller pieces had landed and caught the light of the hallway, and the faint sound of the campus siren could be heard leaving reception. By now, Warner had joined Callie in the doorway and stood in silence as he watched the bottle spit out the last of the Rosé.

Callie also stood in silence for a moment before turning to face Warner, saying, "get rid of that crazy bitch."

Reece paused in her storytelling, watching the wheels in River's head turn.

"Wait, I'm confused."

"About what?"

"So, someone, what? Threw a bottle of wine through Alex's window?" River stumbled, eyes twitching, trying to process the information.

Reece laughed, "*Someone?*"

"Well, how do they know it was Zasha?"

"Ha!" Reece laughed again, throwing her hands over her mouth, grimacing, waiting for a second to then continue, "Elm's security found her lying in the middle of the road, she confessed straight away."

"Well, at least she—"

"Alex's parents filed a restraining order against her. She had to appear in court to testify that it was an 'accident' which is bullshit. She almost dropped out of Uni and spent like a week sleeping on the couches at reception."

"Oof," River winced. "That's fucked up, dude."

Reece nodded, "Yeah, Queen's also forced her into counselling, and she had to pay for the window, which is fair, but still."

"Still," River sighed. There was a heavy weight on his chest, the same discomfort he could imagine Warner feeling all those months ago, and yet as he sat there, in the early hours of the morning, where the sun was just starting to filter through the blinds, and the room didn't seem as dark, he couldn't help but think, *I'm not Alex though, and Zashas changed.*

Reece looked defeated for a moment, watching a comfortable smile curve on River's face; she knew there was not much else she could tell him.

"Well." She stood up, dropping the blanket onto the bed, and leaning on the door frame, attempting to speak in a yoda-esque voice, saying, "Heed my warning, young Sky-Walker!"

River looked appalled, "That's not— Reece, that was genuinely awful."

But she just laughed, with lit eyes and a full smile.

And as she turned to leave, River called out, "Thank you... for telling me."

Reece paused for a second, smiled, and said, "Zasha is... loyal, fearless, crazy, but unapologetically so. She can be fun, and wild, and caring. But she can also be harsh and violent and stubborn and selfish."

"I know."

"I'm just looking out for you."

"Why would you need to, though? Nothing's happening between us."

Reece tilted her head, smiling caustically as the sun had risen just enough for Reece to see the dark red bruise on River's neck. "N'night."

MISTAKEN

Jackson sat in silence, back pressed tall against the chequered seat of the train. He had managed to snag a table seat; being the kind of thin that he could disappear sideways was his advantage when darting past the geriatric. Every so often, he would squirm or reposition his legs; these cubicles were not made for someone as tall as him, and he could feel the leg cramp loading in his joints.

"Eurgh," he sighed, looking across at Reece, who sat comfortably opposite him, her short legs resting perfectly on the seat next to him. Her eyes were squeezed shut; she also hated trains; the travel sickness was sometimes so bad she had to carry plastic bags with her in case she needed to throw up on the move. "You, okay?" Jackson asked some-what concerned.

"Mm-hm," Reece nodded slowly, twiddling her thumbs underneath the table, "are we close?" They were close; perhaps one or two stops away from Helens Bay when she asked, and the stops to and from Belfast came at rapid intervals.

"Yeah, get up," Jackson instructed, waiting for Reece to gather her bag and follow her to the train doors. Dressed once again in formal waiting attire, Reece jumped from the train onto the platform and started to run down the street. Jackson dressed similarly, walking at a moderate pace beside her. "Why are you running?" he laughed, seeing her already out of breath; it had been 20 seconds after all.

"We're late!" she yelled; her voice exasperated.

"No, we're—" Jackson looked at his phone. She was right. Their shift was starting in 15 minutes and the walk from the platform to The Old Inn was over a mile long, all uphill. "Fuck it, who cares if we're late."

Reece's run' transitioned into a brisk walk as she turned back to look at him. "I do!"

"Why?" Jackson could see Reece beginning to fluster and her eyes double in size. She was doing that thing with her face that made it impossible for parents to say no.

"You care too much," he growled, a little annoyed with her tactics, before reaching for her hand and running, pulling her firmly along.

There was a chance they could have been on time if Reece hadn't stopped to take a photo of a group of lambs on the side of the road, knocking on a whole 2 minutes to their ETA as she attempted to lean over the fence to stroke one, and got her hair tangled in the barbed wire.

"You're a fucking liability," Jackson laughed, unwrapping a few of the looser strands.

"I'm not a—"

"A fucking child," he continued, still smiling as he unhooked the last lock, grabbed the back of her collar, and pulled her back onto the pavement.

"I didn't know my—"

"Just walk."

They walked, mostly in silence, to the Old Inn, only a couple minutes late.

The Old Inn was a Tudor-styled building, with large stained-glass windows and a beautiful courtyard laced with water lilies and white roses. Although the Inn had an open restaurant and bar, Jackson and Reece usually worked the large functions below ground. Anything thing from birthdays to corporate events to weddings.

Tonight, was a wedding reception; Reece's favourite event, the menus are set, the speeches are wonderful, and the drunk uncles are generous, the perfect shift when you're broke and in need of an ego-boost.

Jackson, however, liked working any and every shift at The Old Inn; the majority of the staff consisted of newly turned 16-year-old girls who would fawn and flirt and giggle when he walked into the room, if only they were tipping guests.

"You're late," a loud, deep voice boomed from the kitchen the second Jackson and Reece entered. The rest of the staff, already aproned and name-badged, stood in rows keenly staring. A few younger girls giggling as they saw Jackson in his fitted shirt.

"I am so sorry, we—" Reece started but was interrupted as Jackson took a step-in front of her saying, "We just need two seconds, Mike."

Michael was a large man, both in height and width, with a dark beard and receding hairline. He was dressed in a dark grey suit and red tie.

Michael exhaled, clenched his jaw, and pointed over to the counter where the last two-name badges were left, and two of the aprons were folded on the counter. Being the last ones in, Jackson and Reece were left with the half-sized aprons, which on Jackson fitted like a mini-skirt; they were both dis-coloured and without pockets.

Seeing this, Michael growled but continued, "Trey, I want you at the bar. If I see you anywhere other than the bar, I will not be pleased."

Trey, a fairly older staff member with an unshaven beard, and pooka-shell necklace, nodded, grabbed a couple trays from the side, and walked to the bar.

"Kimberly, Chloe...You, you, in fact, all of you—" Michael commanded, gesturing to a click of blonde girls, "...are all on food, if you can't carry three plates at a time, raise your hand, I—"

Eight of the ten girls shyly raised their hands, all wide-eyed and petrified.

"Good Lord," he growled once again. "Well then, I want you all moving at twice the speed. Am I understood? This is a professional function; I want each course served and collected in fifteen minutes. Do I make myself clear?"

Ten girls all nodded their heads like dolphins waiting for their next instruction.

"Jackson, I want you on white, Reece on Red. This is a small wedding, so remember there are only twelve cases of each. If you run out, I want to be notified immediately so I can add to their bill. Reece, you know how to serve wine, yes?"

"Uh-huh," she nodded; smile pinned to either side of her cheeks.

Unimpressed, Michael grabbed a bottle of red cooking wine from the pantry and a small wine glass from the sink. "Show me," he said abruptly, his brogue accent making the instruction a little harsh.

Catching Jackson's smirk and Kimberly's "Oooh!" Reece shook her head, laughing a little as she pointed out, "Well, first, that's the wrong type of glass. Red is large," she said, taking a large wine glass from the shelf and placing it firmly on the counter. She then gestured to be handed the wine and holding it from the base, began pouring into the glass, keeping her left hand behind her back and turning the bottle anti-clockwise from a 3-inch drop. After a second or two, the glass had been filled a quarter of the way, and she was instructed to stop, but she carried on pouring.

"I apologise for doubting you," he smiled coyly before turning, "Jackson, do you also need to demonstrate your abilities, or can I presume you can pour into a cup without spilling?" Without waiting for an answer, he flicked his wrist to reveal his watch; the way all men in movies do; and exclaimed, "2 minutes until service! You two, at the bar, now!"

Reece was the first to leave, waiting until Michael had turned his back to take the glass of wine, finish it, and leave the glass in the sink, running out the door as soon as she did.

Jackson, watching this, laughed and called after her, "Since when can you do *anything?*—" but the sound of the heavy door closing after him muffled his voice.

The staff left in the kitchen slowly surrounded the hot plate, taking their time to double up on cloths over their arms and jumping out of their skin when Michael screamed once more, "I said twice the speed!"

Downstairs, the small, marbled bar pointed towards the large hall. Inside, the guests were seated at large round tables that were dressed in beautifully bunched beige cloth and ivory white tulle on the trim. On the tables themselves, small easels holding photos of the bride and groom were positioned next to a winter bouquet inside a metal birdcage. There were also silver votives dotted around the sides, lit and smelling of cinnamon—December weddings.

While Jackson scanned the room for attractive bridesmaids, Reece stood and watched him do so and was surprised when she found herself jealous, scrunching and then un-scrunching her face when she realised her face was scrunched before distracting herself with an empty gravy boat on the counter.

"I would crawl on broken glass to hear that girl fart through a microphone," he said, the sides of his grin touching his ears.

Reece, who had become used to Jackson's sense of humour, sighed, took her first bottle of red, and began circling the tables.

Trey, who was in fact not used to Jackson at all, looked appalled, his mouth turning upside down like a fish. "Dude— no," he heaved, abruptly turning to frantically polish glasses out of Jackson's eye line.

"Ha!" Jackson laughed again, finding Trey's reaction wildly amusing, before taking a bottle of white and following Reece's lead.

All courses were finished within the hour, clear up being the most tedious for the bartenders as they then had to serve tea and coffee to every guest, running back up and down the endless stairs to refill the pots every couple of minutes. Carrying the tea/coffee cups in itself was a challenge, as they had to be served the same way a dish would—plate, saucer, then cup and teaspoon, perfectly balanced on top of each other.

Michael stood in the corner watching the staff wobble to and fro between tables, struggling to keep the teaspoon from flying off the edge. After a moment, he ended up making eye contact with Reece, who had managed to hold three sets of each in her small hands, and he nodded approvingly.

Jackson, who had been going around with a coffee pot, also saw this and made sure to cross paths with her so he could whisper, "Stop trying so hard, you know you'll be fired by the end of the week," in her ear.

"Oh wow!" she laughed, looking up to catch his wink before he turned around the next table. Little did she know, he was right.

After coffee, the guests cleared while the staff broke down the tables and set up the floor for speeches and dancing. It only took a couple minutes, and then the food staff was set free while the bar staff finished washing and polishing the glasses with the policy "You can go when you're done."

Perhaps an hour later, the guests were back on the floor, some dancing, some fiddling through their speech notes, rehearsing their punchlines, and laughing to themselves when they hit it right. Trey was long gone by now, leaving Jackson and Reece behind the bar unsupervised, which is always a bad idea.

Within seconds of his leave, Reece had sourced a cocktail shaker and was experimenting with different spirits behind the bar, mixing in fruit juices and coating the outer edge of the glass with sugar while Jackson ran upstairs to see if the cake was left unattended. It was.

"Chocolate or lemon?" he asked, holding two small napkins filled with cake behind his back. Reece looked at him with slight offense.

"Ah, right." Jackson laughed, "Like I had to ask," before handing her the chocolate slice.

"Two flavours? They fancy," Reece chuffed, handing Jackson a pink-looking drink with pieces of strawberry sliced onto the rim amongst the sugar. Jackson took it, looking down into the glass, swirling it around before he pleaded.

"Nahh, im—" and was then handed a pint of Smithwick's red ale that she had poured earlier. "Now this. This fucks," he purred, tightening his eyes like a lucky fortune cat.

As they drank and ate, the band started to play Chris Young's 'Who I am with you', and the bride and groom stood and walked onto the floor hand in hand and began to dance.

"Come on," Jackson whispered, taking the glass out of Reece's hand and putting it into the sink.

"Why?" she whispered back; he didn't respond; and she followed him out the back door into the parking lot, wedging the door open with a brick. The yard was empty, enclosed with utility sheds and large black bins, and as they stepped out, it began to rain.

"What are we doing? It's raining!" she laughed, both hands on her head, attempting to shield herself from the downpour. Still, in silence, Jackson walked to the car park centre and outstretched his hand.

"*M'lady,*"

"*M'Lord,*" Reece responded, taking his hand and positioning his at her waist, and wrapping both arms around his neck.

"Did you like the reference?" Jackson beamed, finding the height difference hard to manoeuvre and deciding to hold her up instead.

"I did!" she exclaimed, laughing loudly as she was picked up like a ragdoll.

The reference was from Reece's favourite show 'Community'; Jackson had thought Reece reminded him of Annie, but since the only character he related to was Jeff, he decided to keep that to himself. (Watch the show.)

The two danced for some time, badly, and in the rain, with Reece screaming loudly at points to "Put her down!" but he didn't listen and continued to waltz around the carpark. But after about a minute, the charming rain evolved into an angry storm, and the two started to shiver.

"Wanna run it?" Reece shouted over the wind.

"Fuck's sake."

Back in Flat 5, Amy and Will lay on their backs in the upstairs corridor, both staring up at the moulding ceiling. The hall was dark, and the floor hadn't been cleaned since they moved in, but somehow this kind of moment was necessary.

"I'm just fucked off," Amy moaned, readjusting her hair to lay smoothly on the rough carpet.

"Ahhh," Will sighed loudly, his breath white and cold. "What has the man done now?" he asked, his smile punched into his cheeks and his fingers intertwined on his chest. It had been a while since Will had heard anything positive about Amy's boyfriend Callum, which was odd since all Will could think was that he was a 'swell guy.'

"He's just being a bit of a prick really," she started, her face deadpan. "So, I was over at his yesterday, waiting for him to get changed or whatever, and for as long as I can remember he's had this yellow Hawaiian shirt hanging over his bannister, but—"

"Man with taste," Will teased, lifting his head slightly to see Amy laugh a little.

"Ha, well—but when I was there yesterday, the shirt was gone. I didn't think anything of it because it's a fucking shirt and—"

"Shirts tend to get worn."

"Well, yeah—but then one of his friends posted a photo of them all at Parlour, at one of those 'shit shirt' parties, right?"

"Right?"

"And he's standing there with his mates, and some girl is in the photo wearing his shirt—"

"His shirt? Like the exact shirt?"

"Yeah, like obviously I was curious, so I asked him about the shirt, and he just said he 'lost it' but wouldn't tell me where. It just really pissed me off." Amy's rant sounded like a newscaster reading the teleprompter with little enthusiasm, monotone, and emotionless. "And I lost my fucking toothbrush! Did I tell you?"

Will shook his head.

"Right, so you know how I went to Auschwitz with my parents?"

Will sighed, and nodded, his eyes rolling. By now he had heard many times of Amy's trip to the most depressing place on earth. Auschwitz, surprisingly being an upbeat topic for the girl.

"Ha! Well—while I was there, I got this recycled toothbrush, and—"

Will looked sick. "A *recycled* toothbrush...from Auschwitz?"

"Yeah, it's made from bamboo and everything—"

"Ohh!" Will exhaled, a smile of relief brushing across his face.

"And I bring it here, and a few days later, it's gone."

"That's uhh—"

"I bet you that Luigi guy stole it, I—"

"The guy that stole my wallet?"

"Yeah! I—"

"I doubt it, Amy," Will chuckled, slowly shaking his head once more.

"It was a nice—!"

"Shhh." Will lay there thinking for a moment, completely forgetting about the dental hygiene side-rant. "Why are you still with him again?" he asked blatantly, really trying now to think of the last good thing Amy said about Callum and coming up blank.

"Who? Oh! Well—" Amy began laughing, the kind of laugh that her leg shot upwards every couple of 'ha's. "I'm not a bitch or anything, but it's too close to my birthday to break up with him now. And then it's Christmas—"

"In it for the gifts I see, I like it!" Will chuckled, finding this very amusing.

"It's not like that, I just—"

"You just said!"

"I was joking!" Amy wasn't joking. She had actually put a lot of thought into when was the best time to break up with Callum. It would be sometime between Christmas and December 30th, plenty of time to collect all expected gifts but then be single just in time for New Years' so she would have an excuse to hook up with a stranger at midnight and not be called insensitive which of course she was.

Amy and Will continued to argue over the term 'gold-digger' for quite some time when they heard the front door open and quick light footsteps up the stairs.

"Oh, hey guys!" Reece beamed, standing at the end of the hallway, pools of water forming at her feet from where her thick hair dripped onto the carpet. Her white shirt was completely soaked through, and she began frantically blinking to try to dissipate the droplets on her lashes.

While watching the pool spread near her hair, Amy threw herself upright and pushed herself back against the wall, so she was facing Reece. "Hey, where have you been?" she asked, watching as Will also sat up and repositioned himself towards Reece.

"Just at work, me and Jackson had that wedding remember?"

Amy's face dropped for a second, mocking, "What the fuck? What wedding?"

Startled by Amy's tone, Reece glanced at Will for guidance.

"Yeah, you guys have that recruitment job, right? At The Old Inn?" he chimed, nodding subtly at Reece.

"Oh, right," Amy sighed, blushing a little.

"Yeah, it was such a pretty wedding! There were white and yellow flowers and tiny birdcages, and the cake was amazing—" Reece began to ramble, now joining the two on the floor. "But yeah, t'was good. Where's Damian?"

"Boys in his room," Will sang, shaking his head, pretending to be disappointed.

"Yo, Damian!" Reece shouted, and within seconds the gnome's door opened, and a puzzled-looking Damian stuck out his head.

"Someone say my name?" he asked quickly, looking down at the three of them on the floor and smiling. "Been swimming?"

Reece laughed and motioned for him to join the pack, Amy shifting over to the right so Damian could fit in the circle. Damian was still in his pyjamas from the night before, as the group knew he had an exam coming up, so he had been skipping class to catch up on work.

"How's it going, Chief?" Will asked Damian, slapping a palm on his back and rocking affectionately.

"Yeah, not too bad, not too bad. I've missed a fuck tonne of classes already but should be okay."

"Ah, I have faith in you man, when's the exam?"

"Next week Monday, so no partying for me-ee," he whined, rolling his r's and singing the last 'ee' sound, in a slightly racist Indian accent, a 'bit' he would do when he felt sorry for himself. His head hung for a moment, and the others stayed silent.

The bathroom light was broken and would occasionally flicker, and the rumble of the storm outside whirred at the floorboards giving the hall a Belfast' tumbleweed' experience.

A couple more moments passed before Reece chimed in once again, "So, what's new?" to Will.

"Amy's a gold-digger!"

"Fuck up, I'm not—"

"Ha! Why?" Reece's eyes lit up excitedly.

"She won't break up with Callum until after Christmas..." Will explained, smirking as he saw Amy cross her arms in a huff.

"But," Reece stated, "you hate him."

"At least you're not ruining Christmas for the poor guy," Damian added.

"Look, all I was said was that I'm going to wait until I—y'know, get my presents to—"

"Oh my god, Amy!" Damian looked appalled, eyes wide and slack jawed.

"Ha, well—I've been with Callum for 4 years, I think I deserve—"

"Oof!" River laughed through the crack in his door before stepping out to glance down at the circle on the floor. He looked like the headmaster at a boarding school, pushing his fake round glasses up the bridge of his nose and tightening his thick chequered robe around his waist, book held under his arms against his ribs. "I mean, I respect it, but oof." River's grin melted like honey into a more confused expression as he stared at the four wide-eyed children at his feet. "What's wrong?" he asked, a little scared.

He looked at Will first, who didn't respond but had a smirk on his face that stretched from one side to the other.

Damian also kept quiet, jaw still ajar, but now his eyes were pinned to the patch of carpet in front of him.

Amy scoffed in disbelief, pulling her t-shirt over her mouth in an attempt to muffle the sound.

"Reece... What's going on?" he asked once more, checking behind him in hopes it was something on the wall.

"Dude, who gave you that!" Will finally screamed, pointing to River's neck where the bruise had doubled in size and was now a noticeable hickey on the side of his artery.

"Well fuck!"

JEALOUS

"Right...Okay, I'm gonna do it!"

"Then do it—"

"I'm gonna do it!"

"For fuck's sake, just do it!"

"If you shout at me, I won't be able to!"

"Reece!"

"Fine!"

With a surge of adrenaline, Reece wrapped her arms tightly around the ball, bent her knees, and pushed off, running straight across the lounge floor, screaming loudly and off-key. Jackson, who was standing at the other end of the room, laughed and ran towards her, grabbing her by the shoulders and throwing her down onto the floor, pinning both her wrists into the red rug and watching as the ball rolled away.

"What kind of scream was that?" he laughed, seeing her face go red and her upper lip curl.

"That wasn't a scream! That was a war cry!" she growled, now squirming under his grip.

"Pathetic." Jackson smiled. "Try again."

"Eurgh." After being pulled to her feet, Reece let out a frustrated sigh before reaching for the ball once more and walking back to her starting position, Jackson also returning to his place at the other end of the lounge. He watched intently as he saw Reece straighten her grey jersey vest over her chest that had become skew in combat, and brush her hair back over her shoulders. This wasn't a game anymore. The sofas had been pushed back to either wall for maximum 'pitch space' and all obstacles were removed from her path.

Jackson looked at her face and watched her large doe eyes sink and lock with his, the room so quiet he could hear her every short breath.

"You ready?" he teased, cracking his knuckles out in front of him.

"Are you?" she quipped back, tilting her head ever so slightly and faintly smiling, her eyes still latched on to his.

"Let's go."

With that, Jackson took a large step towards her and reached for the ball, eyes wide as he watched Reece sidestep his advance and leap onto the arm of the sofa and run across the leather towards the end of the room, screaming as she did, and jump from the second arm, only to be pulled mid-air back towards the cushion and aggressively pinned down once more. Jackson couldn't help but laugh as he held her, breaking her arms away from the ball and leaning over, so his face was just inches from hers; his feet still firmly on the floor.

"Better," he smirked, holding her down tighter as she thrashed against his grip.

"Get off me," she snarled.

"Ha! Reece, you really are shit at this."

"Let me try again!"

"Hmm,"

Reece could feel Jackson's breath on her nose, and although only moments had passed, she found herself unable to keep eye contact and continued squirming wildly. "Jackson, let me go!"

But he didn't, he just chuckled and continued holding her down.

"Look, I'm going to end up hurting you, and then you'll cry, and it'll be awkward, and then I'll hug you, and you hate hugs, so it'll just be you, mad, being hugged, which will make you madder, and then we won't be friends, and then I won't have anyone to practise rugby with and then—"

"You done?"

Reece took a big breath in, "No—and then—"

"You can't hurt me!"

"Yes I—"

"Just think about what you would do if this wasn't me. I'm just a guy, I'm stronger than you, I have the advantage, what would you do?"

As she laid on the couch, her body pressed deep into the cushions, she thought for a moment, glancing at the space between her hips and his.

"Well?"

Just then, Reece rolled her knees to her chest, rocked her hips backward, and wrapped her legs around his waist, squeezing them hard against his ribs.

Stunned and slightly winded, Jackson let go of her hands and jolted upright; Reece still latched on like a koala around his body, her arms now clasped together behind his neck. "Well," he repeated with shortness to his breath. "What's next?" he whispered, his hands now resting on the small of her back.

There was silence as the tips of their noses gently touched, and their chests pressed up against each other. Reece could feel his heavy heartbeat pound against hers, and as he breathed, her body rose and fell with his.

"Well, I would—"

Just then, the lounge door flung open, the metal handle slamming into the white wall and causing a small dent in the plaster. At first, Will looked shocked, his mouth open as he dropped his backpack to the floor and eyes as wide as ever. But after a second, like butter, his expression melted into a smirk, and he waltzed forward.

"Well, well, well, must be something in the air it seems," he chuckled, watching as Reece frantically unwrapped from Jackson's torso and dropped onto the carpet; with Jackson taking a little longer to react, there was a brief moment where he was still holding on.

"Hey, Will!" Reece beamed; her breath stretched thinly over her words as she walked over to Will to give him a less intimate embrace.

"Hi-yo Reggie, what did I walk into here then?"

"I was teaching her how to tackle," Jackson chimed in, his face flustered and obviously embarrassed.

"Well, I sure have missed a few training sessions, then haven't I? Coz' I haven't been taught how to do *that* yet!" he teased, hands-on-hips, looking down at Reece with a smirk the size of Saturn.

"Pfft! Well...Looks like you need a new coach because—" she started, but halfway through catching Jackson's slow shaking head, her voice fizzled into an awkward giggle.

"That's alright Reggie, I have Jackson here to teach me!" Will yelled, running towards Jackson and jumping into his arms, wrapping his hands behind Jackson's neck like a bride. However, the unexpected force of Will's leap threw Jackson backwards, and they both ended up on the opposite sofa, Will still sat romantically in his lap. The two began laughing loudly, and within seconds had moved onto the topic of Indie Bands and the song 'Sweater Weather', still in this position.

Taking this opportunity to leave, Reece silently stepped out of the lounge and into her own flat, passing Amy at the top of the stairs. "Oh hey!" Reece beamed, looking up at Amy, who looked less than happy to be back at the flat.

"Oh, hey," Amy said plainly, her face struggling to form a smile.

"How was work?"

"Shit. Were you with—?"

"Oh yeah, Jackson and Will are in the lounge."

"Great."

Amy's lips formed a sour line as she manoeuvred her large handbag up and over Reece's shoulders and strode past her and into the lounge, with Reece ducking a little and running on through into her room.

"There she is!" Will cheered as Amy entered. Amy looked exceedingly tall from the couch, her long legs stretched for miles, so much so that her leggings seemed thin across the distance.

"What the fuck?" Amy laughed, seeing Will cradled in Jackson's arms, all of a sudden feeling lonely.

"Well, we were just rein-acting Reece and—" as Will began to tease, he could see what was the start of a smile on Amy's face, fade, her mouth pouting ever so slightly. "I just wanted a cuddle!" Will finished, talking in a child's voice and dramatically squeezing Jackson around the waist.

"Okay, I'm done," Jackson laughed, throwing Will off his lap into the seat next to him and leaving the room, Amy's eyes following him out the door.

Will saw this, and a weight of guilt began forming on his chest. He liked drama, friction, and meddling in things he shouldn't, but this was different. This was sadder.

"You found your toothbrush yet, Amy?" he asked, an 'on-screen' smile aired on his face.

"Huh?" Amy's head darted back to meet Will's smile, and she appreciated the change in topic. She sighed, slumping down into the sofa, the bag still in hand, and said, "No. Fuck's sake. It was a really nice toothbrush! Did I tell you it was—?"

"Wooden?"

"Eco-Friendly, yeah."

"Many times."

"Ha! Well—it was! I got it in Poland, when I went to Auschwitz."

"I know."

"I loved that fucking—"

"How's Callum?"

"Huh?" Amy let out a short breath, eyes wide and eyebrows raised, a slight red hue basting her cheeks. "He's fine! I think we're going to be okay."

Her voice was laced with white lies, and Will could feel the heaviness on her heart from the other side of the room, but still, he replied, "I'm glad," and after a few seconds—"who knows! Maybe he'll get you a toothbrush for Christmas!"

"It's on the list."

121

A couple hours had gone by, and by now, Flat 6's lounge was almost full. Jackson had returned from upstairs and was now sitting relaxed with his tall back against the arm of the couch; Amy sat arms folded on the other end, turned slightly to face him. Will hadn't moved from earlier but now had Reece's legs resting on his lap, and she lay with her back across the seats and head resting on the bridge of the arm.

They were laughing, most likely about something stupid, but the tension from earlier had seemed to fade, and Amy too found herself laughing at a few of the jokes that were passed around. Nora was there also, humming to herself in the kitchen corner as she made herself coffee in a pink metal coffee pot on the stove, it whirred and screeched and was incredibly rusty, but she swore it's the best cup she's ever had.

The air was warm from the body count, and there were just enough cinnamon tea lights dotted around the windowsills by Reece to mask the scent of sweat from Jackson, who, after leaving the lounge earlier, had played a couple hours of football and hadn't showered since. Amy had also tried to make the living room festive as she decorated the surfaces with old Christmas ornaments her Grandmother gave her and placed a small fern tree on top of the shoe rack that was recently acquired from an alley and placed near the door.

"So, how are we going to do this?" Jackson asked, looking straight across at Will.

"Uhh, I don't know. Pull names out of a hat?" he answered, looking over at Reece for approval.

"We could always do it online. There's an app that emails you the name of the person, although with budget, deadline reminders, that kind of stuff," she chimed in, now looking at Amy.

"Why would we do that?" Amy said plainly, talking to Reece though not taking her eyes away from the wall behind Jackson's head.

"Dunno. So, you don't accidentally pull out your own name and have to redraw."

"Oh, guess that makes sense."

"That sounds cool!" Will cheered, taking out his phone.

"Nah, that's so much effort. Let's just write the names out," Jackson laughed, walking over to the wooden table in the far end of the room and reaching for a pen and paper. He began scrawling instantly, and within seconds had ripped the names from the sheet and folded them over, grabbing a bowl from the counter and throwing the pieces in. "See? Done," he declared, now standing in the middle of the two couches and gently shaking the names in the bowl about.

"Huh..." Reece sighed, her hand gesturing to Jackson to hand her the bowl; he did and watched intently as she took every name out and unfolded the rips. Will also turned to face her as her eyes lit up, and she began to laugh.

"What?"

"Jackson, you wrote Nora's name twice!"

"Ha! No way!" he screamed, his smile pointing up towards his eyebrows as he took the two pieces of paper from Reece's hand and saw his mistake.

"Fuck's sake Jackson, you had one job!" Will said, laughing loudly.

Nora, who had kept quiet for most of this, also chimed in at this point, teasing, "You're such a fucking idiot, Jackson," and waiting for him to turn around before she cheekily winked.

"Yeah, yeah. You all can fuck off. What's this app's name then?"

"I'll do it." Reece continued to giggle as she downloaded the app and plugged in all the names, "Should I wait for the others?" she asked but was all too quickly answered when Damian paced through the lounge door, quiet as a monk.

"What's this?" he asked Reece, looking around the room and being pleasantly surprised at the gathering.

"Secret Santa!" she answered, swinging her legs back around to make space for Damian in the middle between herself and Will.

"Very nice, very nice."

It wasn't long before River, and Zasha too, entered the lounge. They had just returned from a 'Soak' concert held at Limelight, one of the main student clubs in Belfast, and funny enough, they returned home soaked. It was raining outside, and Limelight was a good 20-minute walk away.

"Hey, Zasha!" Amy finally cheered, now sitting upright, holding out her arms for Zasha to fall into screaming, "Aw, Amy babies!"

"Well, how was it?" Will asked River, who had been standing awkwardly at the door, his black denim dungarees patchy with damp spots.

"Aw dude, so good! Their set was beautiful, and they played one of my favourite songs!" he chanted, walking to the centre of the room and casually wrapping his arm around Zasha's shoulder. "I'm so glad we went," he cooed, leaning over to kiss Zasha's cheek but stopping just inches away as he felt 6 pairs of eyes laser into his skin. In a panic, he froze, his lips now sealed shut, and his words lodged deep in his throat.

Zasha, also noticing the audience, roughly pulled away, shrugging his arm away and taking a large step towards the kitchen.

"What are you doing?" she screamed, a slight laugh in her pitch.

"I, I don't know—" River's eyes were twice the size, and he began frantically scanning the room in hopes of finding someone who hadn't seen.

Once more, he met Reece's gaze, and without words, she motioned for him to sit on the arm of the couch next to her before announcing, "It's ready! Everyone, look at your email! You've been sent the name of your Secret Santa, obviously don't show, tell or hint anything! The swap is on the 18th, a day before Will and Nora leave, so we should all still be here. That cool?" The swift change in topic encouraged murmurs between the flat as they hustled to open their emails, most covering their screens with their palms.

"Thanks," River whispered in Reece's ear, smiling through his red-hot cheeks.

"Course."

It wasn't too long before most of the flat had left again. River had plans to teach Reece and Damian how to make cinnamon rolls, which, of course, meant Reece and Damian watching Brooklyn Nine-Nine and waiting for cinnamon rolls.

And Zasha, Nora, and Will had slowly filtered out the lounge, all claiming to be tired, leaving Jackson and Amy in the living room alone. It had been a while since the two of them had hung out by themselves, and it's fair to say there was a chill in the air.

Jackson had tried to break the ice by playfully knocking Amy's foot with his, and bringing up mutual enemies that he 'would do' but only out of hate, and when that didn't work, he continued to sit in silence, watching Amy play with her phone out the corner of his eye. "Well!" Jackson sighed, "I would say 'night', but we live together, so I don't have to."

"Why is it so fucking awkward between us?" Amy exclaimed, stopping Jackson midway off the couch and causing him to fall back into place. Stunned for a moment, Jackson murmured at a loss for words.

"What do you mean?"

"We're different. You don't talk to me anymore; we don't hang out. So, what's fucking changed?"

Jackson, having a moment to adjust to the situation, casually brushed her remark off, claiming, "Nothing's changed, Amy."

"Yes, it has! You never want to do anything with me. You're never free anymore—"

"Amy!" Jackson stopped her, "we live together, we don't need to plan things, you wanna hang out? You can knock on my door and ask me."

Amy let out a frustrated sigh as she threw her hands down, her phone slapping against the leather, but before she could respond, Jackson continued, "You're the one with a job, you're never here, you have a boyfriend—who hates me by the way—"

"I am here! Not like you would notice..."

"What?"

"Oh, come on, Jackson, you spend every spare second with Reece. When you're not fucking flirting, you're going out together or fucking wrestling of whatever the fuck you guys do. Tell me, Jackson, are you two fucking?" As the words left Amy's lips, she inhaled sharply, holding her breath at the top of her lungs, wincing in suspense.

"Me and Reece? No! We're friends, that's all!" he shouted, now pacing angrily up and down the room.

Hearing this, Amy could breathe again, now watching him as he walked.

"Is it jealousy?" he asked, pulling up his black sweatshirt sleeves to his elbows.

"No."

"Then what is it? Because I haven't changed." Jackson looked down at Amy's thin face and watched as slow tears fell from her eyes. "Why are you crying?" he asked, his voice now softer.

"If it wasn't for me, you wouldn't have met anyone here, and now—" The cuff of her sleeve brushed across her face as the words became heavy in her throat. "You like her more than me," she finished, burying her head in her hands, refusing to look up.

Hearing this, Jackson stopped in the middle of the room, back turned, and took a deep breath in. "It's not like that, Amy. We're still good, I just— me and Reece have become good friends, we work together, we watch the Rugby, and she's good banter, that's all." Jackson slowly walked to the end of the couch and sat beside her once again, the palm of his hand gently resting on her knee.

This was the first time he had seen Amy cry, well, from something he did, and the sobbing made him increasingly uncomfortable, but she was right. If it wasn't for Amy, Jackson would be living on his own or with his mother and her boyfriend, the thought bringing the taste of sick to his mouth. And because of Amy, he was able to meet Will, and Damian, and Reece. Yes, they were annoying students, but they accepted all of his flaws and sometimes even laughed at them. He knew he owed a lot to Amy, even if they had drifted apart.

"So... You would never—?" Amy asked, tears finally dried and now looking at Jackson, her eyes a little swollen and red. Jackson thought for a moment, desperately looking for a way to turn this situation around.

It was a few moments more before Jackson laughed, shook his head, and said, "Come on, Amy, you know I would never be with someone like *her*!"

The two laughed out loud, this answer seeming to satisfy Amy as she began apologising for her outburst, blaming it on insecurities and her bad day at work. Utterly clueless to the fact that Reece had been listening from the other side of the door when she came only a few seconds before to retrieve her phone she had left on the couch.

"Oh."

CHILDISH

It was cold outside, the kind of December chill that lay stagnant between black ice and snow. The kind of cold that made it hell to take your hands out your pocket to call a very sleeping Zasha to open the door. Shuffling his docs, Phil stood, freezing outside 82 Rugby avenue, every so often jumping up and down to encourage body heat and frustratingly kicking at the front door.

"Fuck's sake, Zasha," he grunted through closed teeth, rapidly breathing through the gaps. It had been a couple months since Phil was at the flat, and he had been nervously hoping that everyone had forgotten about his PG-three-way with Betty and Chloe. They hadn't.

Minutes had gone by, and Phil had accepted he could very well die that day when Zasha finally opened the door. Her hair was matted and sticking up in places gravity missed, and her silky yellow vest top was so skew Phil could see her polka dot bra.

"Hello, babies!" Zasha yawned, wiping the sleep from the inner corner of her eye and throwing her arms around Phil's shoulder.

"What's the craic?" Phil asked, breathing cold air onto her neck and smiling because she smelled of strawberries. She always smelled of strawberries, strawberries, and smoke.

"Ehh, not a lot. I just woke up," she answered, shivering a little and walking back upstairs, forgetting to lock the door.

"Ah! I can see that."

Entering the flat, Phil was instructed to sit down while Zasha made tea. They had plans to rehearse a script for class, but Zasha rarely did anything before tea. The two chatted for some time, discussing the 'subtext' of their characters, with Zasha arguing that the 'kiss scene' at the end of the script was merely a suggestion, and Phil equally determined, argued that it was needed and to rework that scene would be an insult to the playwright.

"It's just weird!" Zasha was shouting when River entered the room, making every effort to avoid her gaze as he blushed in flames. "Isn't it?" she asked, directing her attention to River, who had attempted to walk straight in-between the two on his way to get cereal, thinking that would work.

"Uhh... 'isn't it' what? Hey, Phil."

"Hey, River! What's the craic?" Phil asked again.

"Nothing, my dear, as per usual. How's the rehearsal going?"

Phil gritted his teeth and side glanced at Zasha, who was still waiting on River's answer, pouting her lips and running her foot up and down the side of her shaved legs.

"Phil thinks we should kiss!" she blurted out, eagerly studying River's reaction, and then turning to look at Phil, who was so caught off guard he coughed up a bit of tea onto his shirt.

"Fuck, Zasha. Context!" he defended, now too, watching River shift in his steps, and open a cupboard door, 'looking for cereal' but intently blocking his face.

"Well, I mean. If it's in the script...You guys do drama. Surely this isn't a surprise."

Zasha scoffed, finding River's answer extremely frustrating.

"Yeah, I mean, professionals do it all the time," Phil included looking at Zasha with large, scared eyes.

"Fucking fine then, but don't you dare stick your fucking tongue in my mouth!"

"Fucking hell, Zasha. Of course, I wouldn't do that!"

"Fuck me dead, dude!" River expelled, now settled and willing to show his face hovering over a bowl of Weetabix Minis. The room was once again silent, and River didn't know whether he should stay or leave. He could see Phil was now extremely uncomfortable, and he watched as Phil readjusted the length of his chequered sleeves over and over and stuck between tying his lengthy black hair back or leaving it down.

Zasha also looked undecided as she pretended to re-read parts of the script and make notes, but really, she was thinking about kissing Phil and whether he had dry or wet lips, but both made her squirm.

Many a moment passed of this inner monologue when Reece walked into the room, dressed absurdly. All three heads turned as she entered, all three exceedingly confused. "Oooh, River, is that 'minis'?" she asked excitedly, running over to look in his bowl and having to stand on her tiptoes to do so.

"Uhhh, hey there, Kid, what's the get-up for?" he chuckled, motioning to the fitted shirt and suit jacket, but she just laughed mid 'bowl-retrieval' and ran over to Phil to give him a hug.

"Hey, Poppet!" she gleamed, leaning over and squeezing him tightly.

"Hey, Reece! I second River's question, why are you wearing that?" he asked, now pointing specifically to the purple tie that hung around her shoulders.

"Is that mine?" River laughed, now noticing the tie too.

"It is indeed," she confirmed, slumping into the couch next to Phil, her oversized nylon trousers brushing across the dirty floor.

"Reggie, what the fuck?" Zasha asked, tired and so obviously not in the mood for anyone's drama, bar her own.

"I'm getting into character!" Reece explained, "dress like a detective, think like a detective!"

"Why the fuck are you a detective?" Zasha sighed, making a point to slurp the last drop of tea from her oversized striped mug.

"Because I tried sleeping and I couldn't! I need to know who has who for Secret Santa!"

"Aw, you guys are doing Secret Santa!" Phil beamed, thinking about how he can convince his own flatmates to do it also.

"But you were the one that said—" River began.

"I lied! I can't deal with not knowing. It's stressing me out!" Reece confessed, slumping deep into the couch and hitting her forehead with the back of her hand.

"No one's going to tell you," River continued.

Zasha adding, "We're not fucking children!"

"Well, I hope not!" Reece laughed, Phil after a second laughing also as he got the joke.

"Fuck's sake, Kid."

"I'm sorry! I won't tell anyone. I just need to know!"

"I respect that," Phil concluded. 'I respect that' being one of his many catchphrases, that, and 'fair do's like.'

Taking a second to hate everything about Reece's childish incentive, River sighed, paced across the room with his cereal, and motioned for Reece to follow him.

"We should leave them to rehearse," he said, a thin coat of authority to his words which made Reece get up from the sofa and follow him out the lounge and up the stairs into his room.

"So, who do you have?" Reece spurted out the second the two reached the room.

"I'm not telling you, but I do need to—"

"Do you have any ideas for them?"

"Eurgh, not in the slightest," River scoffed disgustedly, falling back onto the end of the bed and looking Reece in the eye.

"So, you have Nora or Jackson," she said plainly, her face unflinching but inside revelling as she saw River's face contort into shock.

"What?" he asked, confused, laughing a little, but more out of awkwardness than anything else.

"Well, you scoffed."

"So?"

"There's only 2 people in the flat you would dread buying for, and that's Nora because you think she's stuck up and know nothing about her, and Jackson—" she paused for a second; like a child pouting with wide eyes; noticing the subtle quiver in his top lip and watching as he pressed his palms together between his knees, continuing "which as I'm saying this...I *know* you have Jackson. You think he's a perverted narcissist."

"I mean— I *do*, but I don't—"

"Yes, you do."

"What? This is so stupid, I don't have Jackson, and you should stop trying to guess. You'll just ruin it for everyone else!" The room was quiet for a second. River looking mildly frustrated sighed, sat up straight, grabbed both ends of the tie around Reece's neck, and began tying them together.

Reece, waiting for River to finish in the slight chance he might strangle her, stood in silence, her face innocent like a kitten before—

"You do have Jackson—"

"I don't!" he did, and it bugged him more than anything that she knew. "Look!" he sighed again, this time louder, like a father talking to his 'vegetable-refusing child.' "I need to tell you something, and I need you to be calm..."

River proceeded to tell Reece; while having his eyes pinned into the corner of the room; that last night, Zasha and he slept together for the first time. It wasn't planned, in fact, it only happened because Zasha had gotten drunk and stumbled into his room at 3 in the morning, stripping off at the end of his bed and lying directly on top of him, shouting "Let's do this!" with River taking little time to analyse the pros and cons of the request.

Now, I've hinted at R-Rated *happenings* in the flat before, but I'm not prepared to go into the dirty details of that night, at least, not without consulting my therapist, but let's just say they both showered afterwards, and haven't mentioned it since.

Reece, for the first time in a while, was speechless. She, like the rest of the flat, had only just wrapped her head around the pairing, and they all knew this would end badly.

"I'm happy for you..." she lied; she was terrified, but the shock made it difficult to think straight.

"Thanks, Kid."

Meanwhile, downstairs in the lounge, Zasha and Phil were having an almost identical conversation, with Phil being a little more animated.

"You what!" he screamed, throwing his hand over his mouth. "Oh, Zasha."

"I know! Bad, bad Zasha," she teased, only now realising her bra was on show and subtly fixing the fabric.

"Well...Was it, y'know, good?" he asked, extremely uncomfortable but trying his best to seem unphased.

"Uhh, I don't know. Can't really remember it, is that bad?"

"Oh, Zasha," Phil repeated, a veil of sadness in his Irish country spoken words.

Hearing this, Zasha laughed, scoffed, and argued, "It's just sex, Phil. And I just bet River is going to make a big deal out of it."

"Well, I mean—"

"Eurgh, I bet he's up there, fucking, telling Reece everything. I bet he's already planning to get my name tattooed on his arm or— fucking, arse." She continued to describe to Phil how having sex in Uni was like giving someone your 'card,' meaningless, and no-one cares if they don't call. To which Phil nodded his head to in silence, but only out of fear.

A while later, River and Reece re-joined the others downstairs, and within seconds they all knew, they all knew.

A couple hours later, and a couple confessions down, Reece was closer to solving her Secret Santa puzzle. She had managed to wrangle Will into a statement when he foolishly implied that he wasn't sure if his Secret Santa would be in the country, so he couldn't risk ordering anything, which Reece deduced, "...You have Nora," and Will spent the afternoon in a mad silence.

She also managed to work out that Nora had Will when she walked past her room and heard Nora on the phone say, 'Necesito que Will reciba un regalo para–Secret Santa...' But the others were going to be a challenge, she hadn't spoken to Jackson since *that* night, and she really didn't want to talk to Zasha right now. The next victim was Amy.

Reece found Amy in Flat 6's lounge, sitting at the broken table in the corner, charging her phone in the nearest port. She was wearing baby pink corduroy trousers and a white ribbed crop top, and although Reece was dressed like she raided her Fathers' closet, the summer attire was equally as odd. "Hey, Amy!" Reece radiated a warm smile, knowing full well she was about to be hit with a disdainful, "Hey."

"What'cha been up to?" she asked, sitting opposite Amy at the table, twiddling her thumbs in front of her.

"Fuck all, really" —Amy paused— "me and Jackson were supposed to be going on a drive, but I don't know where the fuck he is." There was a moment where Amy made eye contact, just long enough that Reece knew there was a message being sent, but not long enough to know what the message was.

"Oh, do you need me to call him?"

"Why would I need you to—"

Reece pointed to Amy's phone charging on the floor, at the black screen with the red charging symbol.

"Oh, no thanks."

Ignoring this, Reece pulled out her phone from her inner coat pocket and called him, Jackson picked up in seconds, and Reece was instantly stressed by the loud whirring wind through the line. "Yo!" she shouted into the mic.

"Yo!"

"Where are you?"

"Was out with Sonny, coming back to the flat now. Why, what do you need?"

"Oh, nothing, was just asking."

"Okay, uhh, me and Amy were gonna go somewhere if you wanted to come?"

Within seconds the room was filled with hot rage, and the air was stale and choked. Reece looked up at Amy through her brows and gulped. She could tell Amy was clenching her jaw and watched as she straightened her back and slowly leant against the wooden chair, awaiting her response.

"No, that's okay! I have a shift at Scalinis tonight, so—"

"It's *Scalini.*"

"What?"

"You said 'Scalinis' it's *'Scalini.'*"

"So?"

"So? It fucking frustrates me, you always call it 'Scalinis,' and it's wrong."

"You're so odd."

"Right, fuck off, and I'll see you later."

"Shweet-shweet." Reece placed her phone face down on the table. "He'll be back in a sec."

"I heard." Amy knew how she sounded. In those brief moments of silence, she replayed her voice in her head and winced at the harshness, but it was either that or tears, so she tried something else. "What are you wearing?"

And for the 3rd time that day, Reece explained her theory on 'detecting,' and for a slight second, Amy looked amused. "Oh yeah? How's that going?"

Seeing Amy's faint smile, Reece happily sighed, "Pretty good, speaking of...Did you know Damian's favourite game is Skyrim?" Reece looked closely at Amy's face, but it was unmoving.

"Okay?"

"And that Zasha is starting a collection of large mugs?" Amy looked unimpressed. "Or that River is obsessed with bees?"

"Really?" *Bingo.*

Reece's smile grew as she continued, "Yeah, I didn't know this before because we were never really that close, but the dude loves bees. Have you ever seen his earring?"

Amy looked up, trying to recall whether she had before admitting, "No, I don't think so."

"It's actually pretty nice. I think it's gold...or gold plated."

"Probably plated."

4 down, 3 to go. Reece hung around Flat 6 until she heard the front door open, and Jackson yell,

"Who the fuck left the door unlocked!" before she nipped out of the room and into her own flat.

Amy adjusted her car seat, pulling the lever underneath to slide all the way back and pull herself back into place. It was her car, no one else ever drove it, yet it never felt right until she had done this. Jackson squirmed uncomfortably for a second as he, too, readjusted his seat so that his knees were not so close to his chin; it was obvious a small person had been in the seat before him.

"Yeah, sorry about that, ha," Amy chuckled awkwardly, just above a whisper.

"It's cool," Jackson replied, biting the inside of his large cheeks and looking around the inside of the car, eyes landing on the Yankee Candle air freshener hanging from the mirror, reading 'new car smell' and laughing to himself as he scanned the MacDonald's packaging by his feet. Clumps of cat and human hair around the gearbox, thinking *that's not going to help* before realising that they had been in the car for a few minutes now, and yet the car was still in park. "Are we gonna—"

"Oh right!" Amy exclaimed, caught off guard as she was fixing her hair in the mirror. Jackson began to laugh loudly at Amy, watching as she now in a panic, fiddled with her keys in the ignition and pulled out onto the road, once again missing the one-way system signs and heading into oncoming traffic. At first, she felt embarrassed, yet the infectious sound of his laughter melted the ice, and she found herself also laughing as she dodged an angry woman in yellow fiat, shouting, "Read the sign!"

After about 20 minutes in the car, they found themselves at Belfast's outskirts, at what Jackson called 'The Secret Beach'. Not because no one knew about this beach, but because Jackson *thought* no one knew, and therefore very proud to introduce Amy to the beach everyone else referred to as 'Ballyholme' in Bangor.

As they sat in the sand, just metres away from an old swing set that slowly creaked in the wind, Amy ran her hands through the sea soil, shivering as the cold grain fell through her fingertips. It wasn't late, yet the sun had already begun to set and was casting a golden hue across the water. The air was cold, so cold that Amy had already started hallucinating about her 5ft hot water bottle that was patiently waiting for her for when she returned. Still, she was worried that if she complained, Jackson would want to leave, and so she put all her effort into shivering as little as possible.

Perhaps if Jackson had been paying attention, he would have seen the goosebumps appear on Amy's bare arms and maybe would have offered his jacket, but instead, he was focused on finding a video to share with Amy that he found hilarious but would have undoubtedly made her scoff.

"Yes!" he screamed, leaping from the sand to stand over Amy, pressing play and handing her his phone. "This is the only thing I ever want to talk about again!" he exclaimed.

Amy watched the video, eyebrows burrowed deep into her face. The video showed Ed Sheeran and another artist free-style rapping about Nandos; only amusing to a certain degree, and yet Jackson couldn't stop himself from dancing and singing along. Breaking character ever so often to laugh childishly and catch Amy looking up at him completely unimpressed. When the video ended, Jackson waited patiently for her reaction.

"What the fuck, Jackson?"

"What! How can you not like that? How can you not appreciate the artistic brilliance of Ed Sheeran, 'Example' and Nandos!"

"Because it's fucking stupid."

"Nah mate, if I never see another thing in my life, I—" he stopped, sighed, and resumed his place on the sand next to Amy. Once again, the two sat in silence, both waiting for the other to say anything, and Amy hoping it wouldn't be dumb. "Y'know, me and Sonny used to come here all the time."

"Yeah?"

"Yeah, only to fuck about, like. Like this is the place where I smoked weed for the first time, ha."

"I thought you didn't smoke weed?"

"I don't, well, not really, not since that first time. It just makes me feel fucking sick, but we would do other things too, like, if you've ever seen any of Sonny's old YouTube videos, they were filmed here. I've been in a few, but not for ages since he's a cunt."

"How?"

"Like, he just thinks he's fucking, professional or whatever, he doesn't really make time for me anymore." Jackson paused, realising how vulnerable he sounded before adding, "...But it's fine, I've got other friends, just a bit shit y'know?"

"Other friends like Reece?"

"Like Reece, Will, Harry, Damian...You."

Amy took a deep breath, inhaling the crisp sea air. In the few minutes they had been there, the sun had sunken beneath the horizon, and they were now sitting in the dark, yet the deep shadow of their hands just inches apart made her heart skip a beat.

"Here," Jackson whispered, finally noticing the slight shake in her body and taking off and passing his coat.

"Oh, thanks." Amy smiled, her heart now beating fast as she wrapped the corduroy sleeves around her shoulders. "Jackson?" she asked, turning slowly to face him.

"Yeah?" Jackson now turned inwards, unable to clearly see her face, but he could feel her warm breath airing on his mouth.

"Do you think, if we didn't live together, we would—" she paused, hoping she wouldn't have to say it out loud.

"We would *what*?"

"Y'know..."

"Not really."

"We would get togeth—"

"Amy," Jackson stopped her. "We're friends, I could never... Not with a friend. That's something I've always said to myself."

"But I—"

"And you have a boyfriend."

"So, you're saying you've never even thought about it?" Amy's voice cracked ever so slightly as she felt her throating burning down the tears.

"No, course I have! But like, not seriously. Like, you know I fancied you when we first met—"

"You did?" Amy knew he did, yet in this moment, she just needed to hear him say it.

"You know I did. But then we became friends, and you started seeing Callum, and that's just how it is."

"But if I wasn't seeing Callum… And we weren't close. Just based on looks, would you?"

"Would I fuck you?" Jackson's eyes lit up so much, they became flashlights, and his loud laugh a siren in the dark.

"Well?" Amy pushed. "It's not a hard question, like if I was single, I would fuck you. It doesn't mean I like you."

"It doesn't?"

"No! Just means I'm not a fucking pussy to admit it. I would fuck you like I would fuck any other fit guy."

At this, Jackson became stunned, processing all that she was saying and feeling incredibly arrogant, so much so that he seemed to blur over her question and focus solely on the words *fit*.

"Oh, my fucking god, will you just admit it!" Amy shouted over the waves, throwing herself up from the sand and standing over Jackson, who, following, also stood.

"Amy, you don't need me to tell you you're hot! That's what Callum's for!"

"That's not what im—"

"Yes, it is! But I can't do this with you!"

"Why not!"

"Because me and Callum used to be friends!" Jackson, mid yell, paused for a moment, his voice lowering. "Whether I'm his or not, he's still *my* friend. So, I can't be the one his girlfriend goes to when she needs an ego boost, and I can't be telling her what I would do if she was single. That can't be a conversation we have."

With that, Jackson pulled away, walking with hands in jean pockets along the coast, leaving Amy to crumble behind.

With streaming tears, she ran to her car and sat in the dark, head resting on the wheel, not caring whether her sobs would beep the horn, and she waited.

The journey seemed to take longer on the way back home, the silence maliciously stretching out the minutes into hours, and both Jackson and Amy could hear the clock ticking. When they finally arrived back at the flat, and the car had been parked neatly outside the door, the two sat yet again in that cold parallel universe of theirs, where they each waited for one to break the stillness.

"Hey, Amy..." Jackson smiled, all anguish and confliction finally settled back down into a playful report.

"Yeah?"

"Oi you, are we gonna bang though? No, I—want some fuckin' Nandos!" he sang, laughing at himself and laughing even more when Amy reacted with a "Jackson!" and hitting his arm with the back of her hand. "Ha! It's just too brilliant!"

"Get out of my car!"

He did. "Y'know..."

"What?"

"You're not ugly Amy, you could put more effort into your appearance, though."

"What!"

CARELESS

"**We** are such virgins." Jackson pointed out, talking mainly to River, who had been patiently waiting cross-legged on a wooden stool, a glass of Ruby Red Port in one hand, and small recycled notebook in the other, a pen also resting behind one ear.

Sitting on the couch to his right, Zasha, Reece, and Phil sat cosily under a large blanket, sharing a bottle of Echo Falls and not so subtly swaying.

On the opposite sofa sat Jackson, Will, and Damian, who had made sure to distance themselves a little more obviously and were each holding a very separate drink. Will and Jackson sticking to spirits, and Damian, a bottle of Pino, which he sipped nervously after Jackson's 'virgin' comment.

"Right, my dears, we begin… with Will and Damian." River spoke softly, his voice so airy you could whip it into soft peaks. "You both wake, on either side of a large room, to the flicker of nervous candlelight seeping from under your door. You hear voices from the other side, but you cannot make out the words.

From the window, you can see the early morn beginning to bolster, though you can only see sky. You know it to be around 3am. Frantically, you search yourself for any remaining belongings from…that night. Will, the only things you have on you are a chipped wooden sword and a golden amulet around your neck… You—"

"So, I'm naked?" Will interrupted, eyes wide and mouth turned downward.

"No. You are still wearing your armour and cloak. I meant more those are the belongings you have on you."

"Ahhh. Gotcha."

"Damian! The only thing…Apart from your clothing, you find is the spiked glove on your right hand and an empty satchel. You do, however, realise when you stand that the few gold coins you kept in your boot are still there."

"Awesome!" Damian almost hissed excitedly, finishing his glass and pouring another, catching Reece's pouting glance from across the room and handing her the bottle too, with River continuing…

"You both try to stand, yet the floor beneath you wavers, and you find it hard to keep your balance. You realise quickly that you are on a ship. Looking around, you notice a small desk in the corner, covered in dusty letters. Taking a step into the darkness, you see a pair of bright eyes. You do not know you are staring at each other. What do you do…Damian?"

All heads turn to face Damian, who instantly felt panicked in the sudden spotlight. "Oh, urm. I don't know," he mumbled, his palm squeezing the neck of his wine bottle. "Escape?"

Others in the room began to laugh, Phil specifically who had played Dungeons and Dragons before, finding his answer particularly amusing.

"Well, I don't know! I don't really get how the game works."

"Okay, that's fair. Maybe I didn't explain it as well as I should have," River admitted. "So, how the game works is the 'Dungeon Master'—me, narrates a world that the players—you guys, exist in. It's pretty basic in the way, like, you can sleep, and eat, and talk, but what makes the game interesting is the characters you guys have made. So, like, Damian, you're a high elf, right?"

"Yes, Fenwick the High Elf of Zanbar."

"So, you have ties to the monarchy of the realm, so your character might act more entitled or serious. You also might be one of the wealthier characters and more likely a lot older."

"Well, I've written on my sheet that I live a 'comfortable lifestyle' because that's what the book you gave us said."

"Yeah, 'comfortable' in-game terms means you're pretty well off. You rolled quite well for gold as well, didn't you?"

"I think so. I have 45 gold pieces on me right now."

"Yeah, okay...I will say, though when you wake up, you only find 15 gold in your boot."

"Oh."

"Yeah. You'll have plenty of chances to get more, though. Don't worry."

"I get all that, but I don't get what we are supposed to say when you ask us what to do." Zasha jumped in, wriggling under the blanket to stay warm.

"Okay, good question." River smiled at Zasha before turning back to Damian, saying, "...So, in this situation, you wake up, you don't know where you are, you probably want to get out of this room—"

"Yeah, so I want to escape."

"Don't you mean...Jump *ship*?" Will sang, holding for applause and being disappointed when he was met with blank unappreciative stares instead.

"Yes, but it's not that simple. You have to describe exactly what you do to escape—"

"So, like, do you open the door? Do you talk to Will's character? Or do you want to investigate the ship first!" Phil chipped in, a little eager to get the ball rolling. Jackson, however, was happy Damian didn't understand, as he too had no idea what was going on.

"Right, okay...So, where was I again?" River sighed but continued smiling softly.

"Would you like me to start again?"

"Yes, please."

"Okay, you begin..."

From this point, the game seemed to progress quite smoothly, excluding the odd interruption of jokes being made at Phil's expense and the sound of the fridge door opening as Zasha grabbed another bottle. In fact, up until the meeting of Phil's and Reece's character, River would have described his first campaign as 'a dream'.

"What do you mean I can't stab him?" Reece laughed, swaying ever so slightly. "I take out my sword, and I stab him."

"Why do you want to stab me?" Phil cried, both in laughter and confusion.

"Because you're in my way."

"Oh, so it's a non-lethal attack?"

"No, no. I want to kill him."

"Right, but you are aware you guys are on the same team?" River explained, head tilted, and left hand reaching for his glass of port.

"My character doesn't know that. He's just some weird dragon boy to me."

"I see her reaching for her blade, and I introduce myself!" Phil shrieks, catching Reece's look of disappointment. "Hello! My name is Bloodwin the second, I am a descendant of the infamous golden dragon, and I am here to help you escape!"

"...And find the Paladin known as 'Jackson' who rumour has it, has a massive dick! Ha!" Jackson screamed, now bored as his character had yet to make an appearance.

Hearing this, Phil puffed the wine in his mouth out his teeth and sprayed the floor in front of his feet. "I say those words exactly!" he wheezed, rubbing his shoe into the carpet to hide the damp.

River, looking frustrated at them both rolled his eyes, sighed, and rolled his eyes again, saying, "...Well *Tatiania*, you now know the 'dragon boy' to be a powerful descendent of a dragon deity who promises to help you escape...and lead you to the Paladin you are trying to find...Who is supposedly... well endowed...And called Jackson..." River sighed once more, turning to Jackson. "Could you not have thought up another name?"

"Nope."

"Yeah, I stab him," Reece confirms, a look of disgust now permed into her face.

"Roll for an attack."

"Wait! No, I stab *her*!" Phil squealed.

"You can't do that, I said first."

"Well, can't I anticipate your attack and attack first?"

"What, are you psychic?"

"No, but I'm part reptile, I have quick reflexes!"

"That's not how—"

"He makes a good point," Jackson interrupted once more, Will nodding from across the room and Zasha fake snoring to make a different point.

"Normally, I wouldn't make an argument for reflexes in combat unless there was a modifier involved, but I like your thinking, Phil," River said, feeling quite chuffed that his players were starting to think creatively. "Even though *technically* it was Reece's turn. I will allow you to roll for initiative. Whoever rolls higher can attack first."

"What!"

"Remember Phil, your 'dex' is pretty high, so you get to add a +3 to your roll."

"This is stupid."

Despite his +3, Phil rolled pretty badly, causing him to whine, "Fuck, I roll badly." Before Reece's equally disappointing natural 1 on damage.

Over-zealous and a little impatient, River decided to speed things up, informing the two that the 'answers they are looking for' lie with a prophet inside the castle, which, if they wanted to find, had to leave right away, as footsteps are 'quickly approaching' up the stairwell.

"What do you do?" River smirked, flipping to a page in his book titled 'The Prophet from Zanbar' and tilting it away from Phil's eye line.

"Well, I—"

"I push Bloodwin out the window."

"What!"

"Reece, you are in the top of a castle tower. That's at least a 30-story drop. How are you going to survive that?"

Reece thought for a moment, "I use Bloodwin's body as a landing."

"Ha!" Jackson laughed loudly.

"Fuck me!" River shrieked, also laughing.

"Uhh...Can I not object to this, please!" Phil pleaded, now turned towards Reece.

"Nope."

"Alright...Phil. Make an opposed strength check." He failed, and his character was indeed pushed out a 30-story window and used as a landing pad.

If you're wondering how they survived, they didn't. Both Reece and Phil were on death saves for the next two rounds and would have been dead for good if Zasha's little Halfling hadn't been snooping around the castle grounds with health potions and an enchanted flute.

"I don't like this," Zasha whined.

"What do you mean?" River asked, trying not to sound too disheartened.

"It's just so boring. All my character does is heal, and his name is stupid."

"You named him Joe! And you also only picked healing spells. As a Bard you could have picked charming spells like 'Hideous Laughter' or other illusion spells."

"Yeah, but like, they're not good for fighting."

"Why did you choose to play a Bard then?" Phil asked, hiding a yawn under his sleeve.

"How am I supposed to know Bards can only do shit stuff!"

"Okay, guys," River stopped. "This is why I told you to read the Player's Manual I bought. It goes through and explains each race and tells you what they are good and bad at. Like Bards aren't supposed to be beefy, and they are actually pretty interesting to play if you know them well. Like Zasha, you haven't used any of your inspiration points," River explained, though he could see he was talking into an empty chamber. "Never mind."

It wasn't too long after this Zasha decided she was tired and left for bed, instructing River to join her after he had finished his 'little game'.

After about an hour of playing, and I have no doubt River orchestrated it this way, Jackson was finally asked to introduce himself after the rest of the group bumped into his character trying to trade 'the service of his penis' at a troll bridge.

"I hear it's massive!" Phil yelled, once again being met with River's scornful stare.

"Right, Jackson, after deeply offending the troll woman, she casts you away. When you turn, you notice an odd group of people watching you from behind the thicket."

"Can I roll to investigate? Like if they are good or evil?"

"Yeah, course, so I would say that's actually 'perception.'"

Jackson rolled the blue dice onto the floor, the loud sound of the dice against the wood rocking Damian's face off the palm of his hand and back into consciousness. "I got a 17... That's with my +2 perception modifier."

"That'll do it. So, I'm going to say you perceive the group as passive. You don't notice any weapons drawn, and a few of the group seem pretty young, even from where you are standing. You doubt they would be aggressive."

After arguing with Jackson about the appropriate amount of penis jokes, the group finally all came together in a single quest to find a different prophet on the other side of the map, since all players had unexplainably ran away from River's obvious instructions. "You come into a clearing in the woods, and Will, uhh, *Slayer*, would you say you're walking more towards the front of the group?"

"Uhh… yeah, I think so."

"Great." River smiled coyly as he reached for the dice and rolled onto the book in his lap, covering his score with his other hand. The whole group went silent as they nudged to the end of their seat, hoping to catch a glance at the number. After noting something in his notebook, River looked up and smiled wider. "Does a 23 hit?"

The room gasped.

"Who? Me!"

"Uh-huh."

"Uhh…Since my armour class is 13, yeah, I think it does!"

Rolling once again, this time in the open, River's fingers released the blue dice onto the floor, watching them curdle into a 2 and an 8. Will looking increasingly stressed.

"Okay, so while you are walking *Slayer*, out of the darkness, you can hear what you assume is heavy breathing coming out from a nearby bush. Yet, when you walk closer, you see these piercing yellow eyes, and before you can shout for help, a large monstrous black wolf leaps from the shrub and pins you to the ground.

Its long claws at first digging into your shoulder, causing you 2 points of damage, then you cry out as you feel its jaw clamp down into the side of your neck, causing you another 8 points. You can feel your neck bleed out in waves, and you have just enough energy to scream out to the others behind you…*Slayer*, how many hit points do you have left?"

Will, in shock, scrambled for the page in front of him, "Uhh…I started with 16."

"Cool. Mark off 10, and everyone, roll initiative."

What was planned as a minor detour and easy feat within minutes had turned into a player bloodbath. With a measly 12 hit points, the black wolf tore through the group effortlessly. At first, finishing off *The Slayer* with another slash to the throat, then gauging Fenwick's ribcage in an opportunity attack, a play River had warned the group about countless times.

After this, River began rolling with disadvantage, just to balance the odds, though it didn't help.

Reece's *Tatianna* rolled another natural 1 on her attack and shot herself in the foot with an arrow, causing her to fall prone, and was finished off by the wolf a round later.

Phil also rolled incredibly badly, barely scratching the wolf with his leftover cantrips after he had used all his spells trying to cross the bridge without paying. It cost 1 gold.

Jackson, funnily enough, was the only survivor out of the group. Choosing to run in the opposite direction until the battle was over, causing River to give up completely, ripping pages from his notebook and making a discard pile at his feet.

"Welp. I think that's a good place to end tonight's session," he sighed.

"Yeah, cause we're all dead," Reece mocked through gritted teeth.

"Can't we just call that a practise round?" Phil pleaded. "And we can all think of better characters for next time? Ones we actually like!"

River paused for a second, noticeably uncomfortable. "A lot of work went into this campaign, dude," he explained. "It's going to take me a while to make up another one."

Phil blushed at this, feeling guilty. "Aw man, yes, of course! Fuck, I'm an idiot! You just let us know what you want to do, no rush at all!" Phil kept his eyes pinned to the floor, shaking his head so that his long black hair swayed below his chin, covering his face.

"No, I don't mind! It just might take me a while if you guys don't mind waiting a couple days?"

"Yip! That's perfect! I have stuff to do for class anyway, so..."

River nodded slowly; his lips sucked into the middle as if he was waiting for something.

"Did we do it right?" Reece asked after many moments of quiet.

"Do it *right*?"

"Yeah, like, did we play the game right?"

This made River laugh as he shuffled the crumpled notes on the floor with his feet. "Okay, so, here's the thing..."

River then went on to explain that even though you can't technically play the game...wrong, you can, however, ignore obvious plot devices and go on an unprepared side adventure that River was completely unprepared for. A sweep of embarrassed realisation came across the room as the players understood that they did indeed play the game wrong, Phil then suggesting once again to 'continue the sesh' at a later date.

"But, but I didn't get to—" Jackson whimpered, watching the four of them file out the lounge.

"Sorry, dude. We'll pick it up again when Amy can play too."

"And Nora."

"Eh," River smirked, turning to Reece and patting her softly on the head. "Night, Kid, you did great."

"Thanks River, that was cool."

With the others gone, Reece and Jackson sat momentarily in silence. They both listened quietly to the sound of Damian's rapid footsteps up the stairs, and the slow, heavy footfall of

River's after him. Phil could be heard shouting up the stairwell a final "Goodnight," and Will couldn't be heard at all, apart from the gentle notch of his bedroom lock.

Jackson looked at Reece for a second. He looked at her nose, how it turned up ever so slightly at the end, and the smooth straight line of her jaw, and how her dark hair fell over her shoulders curling at the ends; she must have finally brushed it. She was wearing a dark blue camisole, sitting just low enough for Jackson to notice the winged bones of her clavicle and it made him...nervous.

"Why do you have to be soo..." he paused, meeting her large eyes with his.

"So, *what*?" she asked softly, her lips remaining ever so slightly parted.

Jackson took a deep breath. "...Never mind."

"Hmm," Reece mumbled, before asking, "want some?" holding out her glass towards Jackson.

"Oh! Uhh..." Jackson's face began to contort, an uncontrollable twitch sparking in his top lip.

"What is happening here?" Reece laughed, gesturing with her five fingers to the spasm on Jackson's face. "You don't like wine?"

"No, it's not that, it's just—" he paused, taking a moment to gulp. "You've drunk from that glass..."

"So what?"

"So...I can taste you—"

Reece choked. "Uhh...You can *what*, now?"

"Taste you!" Jackson explained, "I can literally taste when someone has—"

"Why would you say it like that? Gosh, Jackson!"

"What?" Jackson took a second, "Oh! I see what I did there, ha!"

Reece's face reset, her face blank as she waited for Jackson to stop laughing to himself, it took a while, but eventually he stopped wheezing, and continued, "As I was saying! I can taste when someone else has drunk from the same glass, it's like a bitter, sour—"

"You can taste saliva."

"Yeah—but don't say it like that—"

"Worst. Superpower. Ever!"

"Ha—ha," Jackson teased, looking at Reece and holding his smile until she smiled back, and the room once more fell into a comfortable stillness.

"...So, what are you getting Zasha for Secret Santa?"

"What? How did you—"

"I didn't, until just now."

"Reece! You liability!" He shook his head, smiling, "What are we gonna do with you?"

"Hmm. Love me, feed me, never leave me." Reece got up from the couch and began walking to the door, "... N'night, Jackson."

"Wait."

She paused, turning back.

"Do you wanna stay up with me and watch 'The Legend of Korra'?"

Reece was exhausted, wine-tired, and she knew she should just go to bed, and yet, she found herself walking back towards Jackson, nodding her head slowly.

"Well, come on then," he insisted, pulling her hand down with the rest of her into the couch so that she was lying across the leather in front of him; his body fitting in behind her. Reaching around her to turn on the laptop that was sitting on a small coffee table in front of the couch and surprising himself when he let his arm stay wrapped around her afterward, pulling her closer into his chest as he did.

As if by instinct, Reece pulled the blanket lying crumped at her feet up and around them, nuzzling the back of her head into his chest. Neither of them said a word for some time, yet no attention was being paid to the episode either. Instead, they both just lay there, as close as they've ever been, only being able to hear each other's slow exhaled breath.

"Jackson?" Reece whispered.

"Yeah?"

"Are we cuddling?"

"Just watch."

KILLJOY

River woke that morning, cooing into consciousness like a baby woodland creature, nose twitching as he brushed away Zasha's fair hair that had floated into his face. She looked so peaceful, he thought, looking at how one hand lay flat underneath her cheek and the other outstretched above her head still holding onto a cup of tea from the night before, the sun lacing the side of her golden face and pink lips, she looked angelic.

Lifting the blanket just enough to see that he was completely naked and looking over to see so was she. River couldn't help but beam before tucking the blanket in and around Zasha's small frame and waiting, hands in lap for her to wake.

It wasn't long before a gentle knock on the outside of River's door knocked Zasha out of her sleep, and like a rusty hinge, she straightened her back against the wall.

"Hmm?" she mumbled, taking in the room and realising the duvet had dropped to her waist and jolting it back up around her neck. River, however, was happy to hint at the affair, comfortably tucking the blanket in at his sides, singular chest hair showing and all.

"River…You up?" Reece whispered from the other side of the door.

"Yeah, Kid, come on in."

Uneasy at first, Reece opened the door and stood at the end of the bed, eyes wide as she surveyed the event that so obviously occurred, and catching River's smirk as he realised, she did.

"Oh, hello, Reggie Babies!" Zasha yawned, leaning forward for a hug then deciding against it as once more she realised, she was naked.

"Is this a bad time?" Reece asked plainly, eyes catching the glimmer of a shiny pink wrapper on the floor and another on the windowsill behind River's head. "Maybe I should wait until—"

"No, Kid, it's okay. What's up?" River asked, grabbing a fluffy yellow chick toy from under the covers and handing it to her. It was an Easter gift his mother had sent to him the previous year in Elms.

"Aw, I love this duck!" Reece babbled like a child, squeezing its soft head with her small hands and then squeezing it some more under crossed arms. "Zasha, I actually wanted to ask you if you have your Secret Santa sorted yet?"

Zasha instantly let out a disgruntled moan, rolling her eyes and responding, "Fuck no, kill me dead."

River watched as Reece lit up once more, like a bulb behind her eyes.

"Aw, no, Reece! Just don't!" he pleaded.

"Then cover your ears!" she responded bluntly, now excitedly focussed on Zasha, who was still not aware of what was going on.

Hating but obeying, River squeezed both hands over his ears and turned his head away, thinking to himself that this was Reece's most annoying quality.

"Do you want me to spy on Damian for you?" Reece asked Zasha, a childish twitch in her smile.

"What? Why would you—"

"Well, you have him, don't you? It was either him or me, and I know for a fact I'm easier to buy for."

Surprisingly, Zasha let out a sigh of relief, finally relaxing her shoulders and slumping a little into the mattress. "Yes, so much, yes! The boy is fucking— I don't have a clue on what to get him!"

"Well, he's not *that* hard to buy for—"

"Yes, he is! He doesn't even read! I tried snooping around his room for ideas, but it's empty!"

"His room?"

"Yeah! Like what the fuck! He has no interests at all!" It was at this moment that both Reece and Zasha had realised something quite strange. "Have you never been in his room before?" Zasha asked, a faint laugh in her voice.

Reece thought about it again, and she hadn't. In the brief moments where Damian would open and close his door, she had obviously seen inside his room, but she had never stepped inside, and she didn't know why.

The moment of silence and realisation sent both Reece and Zasha into hysterics, causing River to finally uncover his ears, asking, "What did I miss?"

"She's never been in Damian's room!"

"Oh, Bud," he ached, head tilted.

"I don't know what it is! I think it's just his room is soo…"

"Boring?"

"Uninviting!" she corrected, now feeling a little guilty.

"Well, is he in now?" River asked, only now noticing the condom wrapper on the floor and clenching his jaw.

"Yeah, he's there, think he's studying though...Might just go in, stand there for a sec and leave."

"Good idea."

"Also, Reggie! *You'll*...?"

"Ha! Yeah, I got chu'" Reece turned to leave, but just before she did..."Hey guys?"

"Yeah?" Both Zasha and River chimed.

"You might want to open a window...It smells of sex in here."

Both a little stunned as they watched Reece turn and flee through the door and both now giggling, Zasha got up and out of bed, letting the blanket drop behind her.

"I have a better idea," she toyed, taking River's hand, checking the coast is clear, and leading him into the bathroom, locking the door behind them.

The sound of her voice behind the door jolted Damian's hand on the mouse, causing him to close a critical tab.

"Eurgh!" he panicked, "...yeah, come in."

The door opened, and Reece stepped inside, seemingly nervous but smiling anyway. "Hey," she beamed, looking at Damian sitting cross-legged on his bed surrounded by papers, books, and stationery.

He was wearing a tight-fitted Gym-Shark tracksuit and a blue bandanna tied around his unnatural black hair. It had only been a month since Halloween, but most of the flat had expected the dye to fade. It was obvious Damian was stressed. He had let his beard grow past 'a stubble,' and the black bin bag in the corner of the room was overflowing with junk wrappers, his tub of protein powder packed far away.

Reece looked around the room, something was...off.

"Are you okay?" she asked, her voice soft as silk.

Damian, obviously flustered, took a second to respond, looking back up at Reece and noticing how the black wave of her long hair contrasted against her red lips and couldn't help thinking of how his little brother Rory would say she looked like Snow White. Another thing that he noticed was how she wasn't wearing pyjamas for the first time in a long time; whether she had a class or not, Reece was always seen in loungewear apart from the few times she decided to go to work.

In fact, she was dressed quite normally, black fitted jeans, a chequered blue shirt tucked in, and her hair obviously brushed, all of which distracted Damian from her initial question for some time.

"No, yes. I'm fine!" he finally answered. "A little stressed, but what can you do-oo!" he sang awkwardly.

"Well, what are you working on?"

"Ha. Well." Taking a deep breath and swivelling his screen so Reece could see, he began pointing at a long list of protein names shown on an excel spread. "So basically, for this assignment, I'm looking at the collection of proteins found in the human blood—which are on this spreadsheet—and I'm going through and learning the characteristics of each and every one and categorising them by function."

"Oh," Reece's pitch peaking. "That doesn't sound too bad."

"There's over 300 of them."

"Oh."

"Yeah, not fun. Very tedious work."

"So, what is that called? Like what is the name of the assignment?"

"Well, the title of my report is 'A Bioinformic analysis of the plasma proteome of Mastocytosis patients'." Damian could see the wheels in Reece's head begin to turn, watching her eyes as they shot upwards as she tried to process what he just said, mouthing the title as she did.

Moments passed before she looked back down, sighed, and said, "You need a break. When is this due?"

"Not for weeks."

"Great, you're coming with me to Subway."

"I *am* coming with you to Subway," he confirmed, smiling wide and lifting his trainers from the floor.

Less than 5 minutes had passed before they were outside Subway, looking at the 'sub of the day' deals on an outdoor billboard. Perks of living so close to Botanic.

Botanic was always beautiful, even in the cold December days where black ice lay thick against the street, and bus benches were glazed with dew, and the streets were bustling with students, bikes, and old women walking tiny dogs. It was the smell of botanic, the harmony of every culture's food smells, and the strong scent of flowers and greens from the gardens at the end of the road. And the aroma of strong coffee foaming in waves as you past Starbucks and Clements, and that smell being overpowered by the one druggy on the corner: an unbeatable atmosphere.

It was here, in the queue for a sandwich, that Reece leant over to Damian; words laced with mischief; and got her final Santa.

"Hey, Damian?"

"Yeah?"

"Have you got your Secret Santa's present yet?"

"I have actually! I went to Dunnes the day after we got the names."

"*Dunnes*, huh? So, you've got a girl?"

In between ordering his ham and cheese on Italian, Damian gasps, "What? Why would you think that?"

"Because it's a clothing and home store, what guy wants a candle?"

Jackson. Jackson was the type of guy to ask for a candle, and Reece knew that, but she also knew Damian didn't know that...And that River had Jackson.

"Fair play. Alright missy, I *do* have a girl. But you don't know which girl!"

She did. In fact, these questions were meaningless.

"Well, I know who has Zasha, and I know who has Nora, so you've either got me or Amy."

Damian's face dropped as he swiped his card along the machine and sat down. Reece taking a little longer as she had ordered meatballs, and they were out. Picking the table furthest from the door, Damian sat, unable to unwrap his sub.

"So, you might as well tell me," Reece teased, sitting opposite, already a meatball down from the time she paid.

"Nope. I guess you'll just have to wait and see like everyone else." Feeling strong about his answer, Damian nodded as if to say, "And let this be the end of that!" before reaching for a bite and stopping when—

"You know if you don't tell me, I'm going to know it's me, right?"

Damn, she was annoying. "Well!" Damian freaked, huffing publicly and pouting just a little, "Well, that's too bad because I have Amy!"

Amazing. A coy smile wrapped itself across Reece's face, and for a while, she didn't mention the names at all, that is, until they were back at the flat, about to part ways into their own rooms. "...You know *I* have Amy, right?"

"Oh, for fucks sake!"

NAIVE

The streets were dark, the tall blinking lights giving off little to no orange hue. The streets were empty, even at around 2am, the prime 'walking home' time. And the streets were cold, releasing icy breath from the ground into the black space above.

As the two of them sat there, on the pavement, their legs stretched out into the hollow road, close enough that their shoulders leaned against each other but purposely looking straight ahead, time seemed to stand still.

Out of the corner of her eye, Reece could see Jackson's hand gripped into a tight fist by his side, his jaw obviously clenched, the sound of his teeth slowly grinding, sending shivers down her spine.

He was wearing a bright yellow Carhartt sweatshirt, one of his favourite brands, that now had patches of damp beer soaked into the fabric, and she wondered how long it would be before he noticed his brand-new shirt was ruined.

Reece loved the colour yellow; she had always thought that it was impossible to ever feel lonely around the colour yellow, but in this moment, she was heartbroken to be proven wrong.

Jackson had noticed the slight open and close of her mouth as she had tried to speak but couldn't find the words. Her small hands gripping onto the cuffs of the jacket he had wrapped around her, telling himself that he "Hated wearing jackets anyway" and getting frustrated that he found the way it draped over her small frame cute. He could still see the bottle green top she was wearing, the colour brilliant against her honey skin, and the deep scalloped hem enticing against her chest.

As they sat there, the gentle breeze had brushed her hair forward so he could no longer see her face. That made it easier.

"You know, me and Damian aren't always going to be around to protect you," he said, now turned inwards, hands finally relaxing.

"I know," she whispered, a single tear slowly falling down her cheek. Quickly brushing it away with her finger, she turned towards him, tucking her hair back behind her ear.

Jackson looked into her eyes, her large dark eyes, watching her pupils expand into them until they were a void. And suddenly, all the frustration he had been holding onto dissipated.

"Jackson, I'm—"

Jackson then wrapped his arm around her, pulling her into his side, subtly smiling as he felt the weight of her head on his chest. "I know."

Earlier that night.

Dear Friend,

River began typing, his long, elegant fingers dancing on the old typewriter stacked heavy on his desk—the sound of the rusted keys clicking rat-tat-tat beneath his fingertips in melodic synchrony.

It's been far too long.

I hope this letter finds you well, wherever you find yourself these days.

Venice, was it? Or Vietnam, the destination from which you last wrote me?

Forgive me, I have kept all your letters in too safe a place, I cannot retrieve them.

Regardless, I do not doubt your life is far more thrilling than mine.

River paused, looking towards the bird-crap-stained windows and pretending not to notice, taking in a deep theatrical sigh. "Oh, Emily," he whispered, a shroud of sadness in his words.

You see, Emily was an old friend of River's. He had met her on his Christian Mission trip to Cambodia when he was 18. He spotted her on the coach, sitting a couple of seats ahead, and had noticed her long mousey brown hair that curdled over the cushion and the elf-like point to her nose when she turned her head.

She was a tall, slender girl; with enough freckles, that they could have been caused by fallen petals in an autumn storm, and her eyes were deep and blue. He had thought her the most beautiful girl he had ever seen, with her adorable, gapped teeth and collection of mismatched jewellery hanging from her ears. And as he sat there, River could remember thinking how insane he must be to share the same air, let alone talk to her.

However, to his luck, Emily was also a kind girl, taking pity on the lanky loner on the back of the bus and inviting him to sit next to her, unknowingly becoming the object of River's affection for the greater part of 3 years...

Now, River claims it was never *that* bad, and we can choose to believe him...that is, if debating cutting off a chunk of your hair and giving it to a girl in a locked box doesn't count as '*that* bad.' But this was different. He was better now, over her in fact, he had Zasha, which is more than any one guy can handle, so for the first time in a long time, when he wrote 'friend', he truly meant it.

As he typed, River could see the shadow from the sinking sun creep up the page, he had been sitting there for some time, yet with all the sighing, he had only managed to write a couple more lines.

I am seeing someone, the girl I told you about.
Zasha,
I hope you will meet her someday, you would enjoy her tenacity and love of literature,
She, like you, becomes lost in Pushkin and Tolstoy,
I try, but as you know, Eyre and Austin keep my heart full.

River sighed once again, looking at the classic Pride & Prejudice edition resting upright against a framed character piece of 'Raven,' thinking back to when he had read Reece the first chapter, and she had fallen asleep by the fifth page; he missed Emily; he needed more highbrow friends.

It was the late afternoon when River signed his name at the bottom of the page; in pen, like a contract; and enveloped it. Pressing a dried daisy into the wax seal and hiding the letter in his top draw, on top of the many other letters he had written but hadn't yet sent.

It was then that River heard Zasha's distinctive knock from the other side of the door and braced himself. He watched as she pushed the door open with her hand, the other resting suavely against the frame.

She was wearing loose-fitted blue jeans with a golden silk vest tucked into them. The colour was brilliant against her skin, and he could see the brush of freckles across her petite chest. He gulped a little and wondered if she noticed.

"Are you coming out tonight?" she asked, quite bluntly, staring back down at him as he sat knees pinched together on the stool by his desk, noticing the food stains on his quilted robe that had been there for some time.

"Uhh, I hadn't really given it much thought," he gulped again.

"Well, Reece and Damian are going to Lavery's, but her work friends are going to be there, and I can't be asked. So, I'm probably going to Filthy's with Phil and some drama people. You in?"

River was hesitant to do either. He had heard stories about the people at Scalini and wondered why Reece would even consider going out with them, and well...The drama people were all insane, insane, and dramatic, so both options looked bleak.

"I think I'm just going to stay in tonight, Zasha, but if you change your mind, I can cook for you?" He smiled innocently, standing from the stool to wrap his long arms around her shoulders and being more than embarrassed when she pulled away.

"Why are you so fucking boring?" she snapped, taking a step back into the corridor.

"Cooking could be fun! We can get wine, look through recipe books, you can put on F.R.I.E.N.D.S..."

"Yeah, I think you should know, you're better at baking than you are at cooking, no harm an' all."

River looked crushed; Zasha watched as his eyes doubled in size and his nostrils flared, the warmth in his cheeks glowing red. "Zasha! You can't just say something like that! That's so rude."

"Why is it rude? You want to cook, I'm just telling you, I prefer your baking. Don't be a little bitch about it."

River threw his hands up in the air, as if to say, "I'm done!" but he wasn't. "Zasha, I've cooked for you so many times. If you didn't like the food, why didn't you say?"

"Because I was out of curly fries, and it's cold outside."

"Oh my god!" River gasped, wanting to storm out, but she was still blocking the exit.

"I don't see what the problem is." She continued, "Like the other day you made this ugly pasta thing with purple stuff, and you went *on* and *on* about it, and it was horrible. Sorry, but I'd rather go out and get pissed than stay in and eat shit."

"You mean the pan-fried eggplant! That was one of Gordon Ramsey's recipes!"

"Who?"

"Oh my god!" he huffed once again; his breath stretched thin. River could feel himself getting worked up, and the fact Zasha still looked unphased did little to calm him down.

"Look, me and Reece are pre-ing downstairs. Come join us when you stop crying." With that, she let out a bitter laugh and left to go downstairs, leaving River completely frazzled and rethinking his 'plan b' as a MasterChef contestant.

Downstairs, both Zasha and Reece were giggling mercilessly.

"The purple mush?" Reece wheezed, a hysterical tear rolling down her cheek.

"Exactly! Like what am I supposed to do? *Eat* the purple fuck?"

"'The purple *fuck*,'" Reece repeated, unable to breathe through the laughter. "It did look like baby-sick, but hey! Beats having to cook, right?"

"Fuck no, I can cook!"

"You can?"

"Fuck yes, I can! River never lets me because he's a fucking-entitled..." Zasha thought for a second. It was moments like this she knew she should have paid more attention when learning the language. "...Entitled...He can just go wipe it up his ass!"

Reece choked, the vodka she had been drinking shooting straight to her brain. "He can *what*?"

"Wipe it up his ass! I don't care anymore if he—"

"Zasha, what are you trying to...do you mean, 'he can go fuck himself?'"

"That too! I—"

With that, Reece let out the loudest laugh she had done in a long time, throwing a hand over her mouth and burying her face into the black leather couch, her shoulders jerking up and down as she tried to swallow the hysterics.

"What!" Zasha shouted through winced eyes, looking at Reece's small, paralysed frame on the couch.

"That's not how—" Reece tried once again to speak, but the words were bubbled in her giggle.

By this point, Damian had also walked into the lounge, the laughter drawing him in from upstairs.

"What's going on?" he asked Zasha with a confused smile.

"I don't know! I just said River could 'wipe it up his ass'!"

"You *what*?" Like a canon, Damian too found himself curdled on the floor laughing at Zasha's poor choice in words, and after that, it wasn't long before Zasha realised her error.

"For fuck's sake, Zasha!" she cried to herself, joining Reece on the couch and laughing into her shoulder.

"That is the best thing I've ever heard."

A couple hours later, and more than a few drinks down, more of the flat had convened in the lounge, River, still robed, stood in the kitchen corner making 'White Russians' with Reece, trying to measure out Baileys and being thrown off course when Reece free-handed the vodka. "You can't just—!"

Will had also come in from Flat 6; holding a packet of Rich Tea biscuits he had pilfered from Amy's side of the kitchen cupboard; joining Damian on the sofa and trying to converse over Phil's rendition of 'Moon River'; he had brought his guitar and was not shy to ballad at will.

Singing along, badly and out of key, Zasha sat cross-legged on the floor, sipping from a bottle of white wine, ever so often checking her phone. "Nawh! Amy has to work tonight, so she's staying up with Callum in Lisburn!" she yelled as Phil took a breath between "Oh, dream maker" and "You, heart breaker."

"Aw, dude, tell her to call in sick!" Will protested, crunching a cookie between his teeth and watching the crumbs scatter over his lap.

"What about Nora?" Damian piped in, not really caring but taking a moment to sound torn-up.

"Pfft, fuck knows. Probably out fucking Marco." Zasha scoffed, the room settling into silence.

Things had been on edge between the two for quite some time. Zasha hated how close Will and Nora had gotten over the last couple of months; especially since they had yet to recover from their fight on move-in day, and well, Nora thought Zasha was a bitch, and was glad her loud sex kept her up at night. A genuinely toxic pairing.

"Torres is upstairs editing, she's got that video essay due tomorrow," Will explained, after many moments of quiet.

"...Yeah, ours isn't due until next week, right?" Reece asked, noticing Zasha's frustration and trying to sway the subject.

"It is indeed my dude; you're doing the Soviet Montage Theory, right?"

"Ja, you?"

"Continuity errors in Hollywood films."

"Nice."

It must have been around 10pm when Phil and Zasha left for Filthy's. Zasha making sure to hug everyone in the room apart from River; since she had decided she was angry with him; and giving Reece an extra tight squeeze, cooing, "Ooh Reggie-Babies" before letting go.

Meanwhile, Phil gestured a 'one swoop' wave to the group before leading Zasha out the door.

"When should *we* leave?" Damian asked, head tilted and smile wide as he turned towards Reece.

"Up to you," she smiled back, slurping the last of the alcohol from her glass.

"I just meant because you're *still*..." Damian motioned down to the large blue work shirt and chequered pyjama bottoms she was wearing; he had been wondering for a while when she planned on changing and had soon accepted the fact that she might go out like that.

"Oh!" she laughed, standing up quickly from the couch and almost falling back into Damian's lap, "...yeah, give me a second, and we can go."

The second she was out of earshot, both River and Will came from their opposite corners to council.

"Buddy," River started, "do you really think it's a good idea to go out, just the two of you?" River's voice was just easing out of frustration at Zasha to a patronising nurture.

"Yeah, man, like it's pretty intense, don't you think?" Will said, reaching out to land his hand on the back of Damian's shoulders, making him all the more uncomfortable.

"Look, I appreciate the concern, but I'm fine! We always have a good time together, and besides, it's not like we didn't ask if you guys wanted to come."

Will and River exchanged a look of 'that's true' before silently agreeing to not acknowledge it.

"I just don't want you to get your hopes up."

"I won't, I'm over the whole thing anyway. I'm good!"

As he spoke, the lounge door opened, and Reece walked back into the room. Her hair was down; it was in a bun before; but now her hair lapped over her shoulders in gorgeous dark waves, the front layers sweeping away from her eyes. And her eyes, like deep pools of hazel honey. Damian looked at her lips, full and crimson, and her skin, dewy as ever.

Shit.

"That was quick. You look great though, Kid!" River praised.

"Not bad, Reggie!" Will also sang.

"Well, thank you, kind Sirs," she laughed, blushing a little. "Well, you ready?"

"Y-yes."

The dark streets were lit with dim blinking lights, the orange hue reflecting off the puddles of water in their way. Reece linked her arm with Damian, and at points, rested her head on his shoulder as they walked. He was short, but she was shorter, so it worked.

"I like this, by the way," she said, looking down at the fitted chequered shirt he wore, the deep bottle green and blue weave bringing out the cool tones in his skin. The beard also being a contributing factor to what Reece described as a "Hot lumberjack" look.

"Aw, thank you!" he grinned back. "Yeah, I really need to get a new shirt, though. I've worn this—what—4 times out already."

"It is your 'going out shirt' I've noticed."

"Well, when you look this great in it, what can you do!" he charmed, tensing his right bicep just a little.

"Ha, I love it!"

Damian was always more confident around Reece; something about her just put him at ease.

"Oh, shit," Damian winced, looking up at the sky and having a single raindrop land in his eye.

"What?"

"It's starting to rain."

"I hate this country," Reece laughed, unlinking her arm from Damian so she could grab his hand instead and pull him along as she started to run.

"What are you doing?" he shouted, jumping over puddles in his way.

"Do you know how long it takes for this much hair to dry!" she yelled back, but over the whistling wind and soon after heavy rainfall, it was hard to make out.

Weaving through dampened street crowds and darting into busy night traffic, the two managed to run the whole way to Lavery's, curving round the newly built Centra on the corner and up past the bus stop at Benedict's. Arguably, the two did look a little flushed when they finally arrived, ready in queue to have their ids checked, and Reece hardly resembled her driving license on a good day.

"Where were you born?" asked the bouncer at the door, a large, heavy man with a dark beard and tiny earpiece.

"Camden Town."

"Birthday?"

"3rd of the 4th, 99." (Just a day older than Damian, and she never let him forget it.)

"Go on in."

Lavery's was a building split into 3 floors, the first being a more relaxed bar and dining area, the second a weekday pool room and weekend club, and the third a beer garden and roof terrace. Lavery's had an old 'cowboy bar' feel; sunken brown lighting, wooden benches for bar booths, and old chunky photo frames hung distressed on their walls. The club was decorated with hundreds of stringed bulbs across the high ceiling and electric candles dotted on every second table.

Looking around, Damian began to feel anxious. The floor was barren, and open spaces made him feel uncomfortable.

"We should get a drink," he decided, making a beeline for the bar, Reece following.

"Can I get a uhh, pint of Guinness and uhh—" Damian turned to Reece as if to ask, "And you?" but he already knew "...and a Kraken and coke please." Looking around to catch Reece's surprised smile of affirmation before adding, "Oh! And could you top that with a Guinness head? Thank you so much."

"Well, damn," she gasped, eyebrows up and head tilted.

"I know my company." Damian continued grinning for the next while, flipping out his phone to pay with a well of confidence as if he held a bottomless credit card.

"Thanks, Damian." Reece beamed, taking her drink from the bar counter, agreeing, "Next ones on me."

With Damian nodding back, blushing a little.

It was late enough to expect a crowd, and yet the dance floor remained uninhabited for some time. "There's a table over there," Damian shouted, pointing to a small wooden bench running alongside the wall.

"You're not going to dance?" Reece shouted back, head tilted once again as she saw the whites of Damian's eyes expand, which only made her laugh.

"Maybe in a bit, when other people—" Before he could pull away, Reece had grabbed his hand and led him not just onto the dancefloor but right smack in the middle. "Reece! We're the only ones—"

"Shh!" she laughed. "Just dance with me!" With a drink in one hand, and Damian's hand in the other, Reece began to twirl herself under the fairy lights, her used white trainers making it easy to spin on the polished floor.

"We can't be the only ones—"

"Yes, we can!"

Damian stood frozen. He wanted to retreat, hideout in the corner until more people joined the floor, until he could be lost in a crowd. Moments passed, and he could feel gathered stares from the sides of the hall. His shoulders and neck became solid, and he felt sick.

Reece stopped dancing, still smiling but now just looking straight ahead at Damian, watching the nervous cogs in his head jitter and turn. "Dance with me," she said once more, this time softer.

Damian looked straight back at her, her stare unshaking and a mischievous smirk across her face. She was hard to say no to, and she knew that.

"Fuck it!" Damian shrugged, letting go of her hand and walking back to the bar.

Yet Reece's smile only grew as she watched Damian lift his glass to his lips; his gulps so loud she could hear them from across the room; down his pint and re-join her on the dance floor, reaching for her hand once more to jump and bop with her to a remix neither of them knew.

Jackson watched this from a dark corner, leaning on the window between the smoking area and the dance floor, pint in hand but hardly touched.

He had come there with his best friend Sonny and a couple of Sonny's 'photography friends' that he wasn't too keen on. They were all slightly older and far more accomplished and did little to humble the fact. Jackson had desperately wanted to fit in with all of Sonny's friends, but as they stood there, on the other side of the glass, cigarettes between fingers and lips, Jackson only became more frustrated. The smell of smoke made him sick, so not only were they rich, they were rich, and they smoked, which only made them cooler, according to Jackson.

After a while, Sonny came back inside, his posse following behind. Sonny was a short man, stocky yet firmly built with narrow dark eyes and a clean-shaven face. He had short, well-groomed hair that began black at the roots but froze off into peroxide tips. Sonny also had an expensive style, plastered in big unsubtle brand names. So much so that you might think he was sponsored. He wasn't.

"Fuck. Is that Reece and Damian?" Sonny gasped, firmly grabbing onto the lapel of his fitted black trench coat, feeling embarrassed by association, even from the other side of the room.

"Ha, yeah."

"Fuck. I couldn't be doing that, so I couldn't," he said, shaking his head, watching as Damian unapologetically 'dad-danced'; arms at 90-degree angles and side-stepping like Will Smith in the movie 'Hitch'.

"Ha, well, he needs it to be fair, the man's tightly wound," Jackson explained, lips pinched.

"Well, fair play to her then."

"Hmm."

Jackson watched with a smile on his face, even over the loud music; he could hear them laugh, even more so when Damian attempted to dip Reece under the lights, and her old shoes sent her sliding. And it wasn't long before other charmed viewers started shifting from the sides of the wall onto the dance floor, soaking up the child-like energy to perform 'big fish, little fish' in a large circle.

After a few more songs, Jackson continued to watch as Damian and Reece's atrocious dancing finally slowed, and they made their way to the bar. It was there when a tall, slender woman wearing fitted black jeans and a sequin vest approached them, fondly hugging Reece and smiling at Damian. Jackson had recognised her instantly, her name was Tara, and she was a waitress with Reece at Scalini.

She was easily one of Reece's more attractive friends, and he had known her to model outside of work. She had a flawless caramel complexion and dark sultry eyes, her face was long and thin, and her smile pouted. Jackson had told Reece he could put up with her large and slightly crooked nose because she was tall, and after spending so much time with a girl that barely reached his shoulder, that was everything.

They talked for some time, Tara using her hands a lot to gestate her stories and finally pointing to a space on the floor occupied by more Scalini folk. Reece's eyes lit up as she saw more of her friends dancing and ran over to hug a girl named Jamie.

Damian was also familiar with a few waitresses and was more than happy to reconnect with a small pretty girl called Molly.

Molly had been to a few house parties at the flat, and Damian had always thought she was "Delightful."

One of the restaurant managers was also there, his name was Rocco. Rocco was a tall, dark and handsome Italian man, a fair few year older than Reece.

Upon seeing her, he had wrapped both arms around her, greeting "Ah Bella!" before offering her a drink, to which she politely declined. Her second rum and coke were already hitting her in a way that she could tolerate an annoying waitress called Andy, and that was enough.

After a while of dancing, badly and out of sync with the group, Reece had seen Jackson, sitting alone in a corner booth. She caught his eye instantly and motioned for him to join her, but he shook his head, pointing to the smoking area. She sighed, tilting her head, and walked over, keeping her doe eyes pinned on his.

"Why do you come out with people who have no interest in being *out*?" she asked once she was stood in front of him, smirking a little.

Jackson just laughed, shaking his head, unable to answer.

"You look nice. I like the yellow," she said, pointing at the sweatshirt, but still no answer. "You sure you don't want to join us? It's more fun than—" As she spoke, Jackson grabbed her hand and pulled her into the booth next to him. "Oh, okay!" she laughed in shock as she fell into the soft seat.

"Do you think I'm...cool?" Jackson asked.

"What?"

"Yeah, like, do you think I'm cool? Like a cool person?"

"Ha, uhh, I think if you have to ask, you—"

"Yeah, I know, it's just so frustrating!"

"What is?"

"Shhh."

Time had passed, and with the help of Damian, Jackson was finally convinced to join the group, with the promise that Reece would 'introduce him to Tara.' Now, Reece would stand by the fact that she is an incredible wing-woman. She had seen many episodes of 'How I met Your Mother' and was confident in her abilities. Jackson, however, would later inform her that she is a train wreck and to 'never try to help him again.'

"*Have* you met Jackson?" Reece childishly grinned, nudging Jackson forward and nodding as if to say, "My work here is done," before walking back to the bar for water.

Tara stood shuffling for a moment, taking a deep breath in, her eyes darting around the room awkwardly. Jackson too was extremely uncomfortable, hands in jean pockets and stiffly rocking back and forth.

They stood like this for some time before Tara finally explained, "We actually have met before, I'm sure?"

"Yeah, at one of the flat parties."

"Yeah! Wild night, didn't someone pee on the floor?" Tara began laughing, encouraging Jackson to also smile and respond, "Some bird also shagged in the bathroom!"

"What? No way!"

They continued to talk, slowly edging to the back wall, until all stories from that house party had been shared, then once more, they returned to silence.

Jackson, however, could have sworn he was in love and wasn't going to let the conversation die that quickly. "Yeah, so sorry about the whole, uhh, Reece..." he sighed, rolling his eyes.

"What? Oh, don't worry about it, she'd spoken about you before, so I thought she might do something like this."

"Oh really?"

"All good stuff, don't worry!"

"Like what?" Jackson took a step closer to Tara, locking eyes with her.

"She'd said you were charming and funny and that we'd really get along."

"Oh yeah? And what do *you* think?" he teased, leaning his elbow on the wall to his right, Tara politely smiling back. She had only then noticed how far they had wandered back from the group.

"I think we should get back to the others."

"Really? So, you're not going to tell me?"

"Hmm, maybe some other time." The curt reply made it evident to Jackson she was not interested, and the walk back to the Scalini circle was a quiet and short one.

Embarrassed but able to shrug it off, Jackson turned to Damian, who was looking lost after Molly had left early. "Where's Reece at?" Jackson asked, looking around the room, acting unphased by his recent rejection.

"Uhh, she's over there with some guy." Damian gestured to the bar where Reece was standing with what looked like a glass of water, and a tall, burly-looking man stood with her.

"Who the fuck is *that*?" Jackson snapped.

"Oh, that's Adomas. He's the pasta chef." Jamie added, a smile punched into her cheeks, her voice strained.

"Right."

Jackson knew of Adomas; Reece had spoken often of him and never positively, and as he watched closely, he noticed Reece becoming extremely uncomfortable around him. Her shoulders were tensed. Her eyes were constantly darting back and forth between the bathroom and the bar.

Adomas was an intimidating-looking man with short blonde hair and a scrappy beard. He also had a couple friends around him, of which were even more so rugged and large. According to Jamie, the friends didn't work at the restaurant, and she had never seen them before.

Damian also watched as Reece took her glass and attempted to leave, but the men surrounded her at the bar, chanting something he could not make out over the distance. The four men closed in, towering over her so much so that Damian and Jackson could no longer see her.

"Should we go over there?" Damian asked nervously,

"It's okay, just keep an eye on her, will you?" Jackson sighed, rolling his eyes again and leaving for the smoking area. It was seconds after that Damian beelined for the bar once more, weaselling his way through the large men to Reece's side.

"Damian!" Reece exclaimed excitedly, panic leaving her eyes as she saw him.

"Hey, are you okay?" Damian cooed, wrapping an arm around her.

Reece nodded, with a smile Damian recognised to be fake.

"She is fine. We are all friends." Adomas smirked, the men behind joined in muffled laughter. He spoke with a heavy Lithuanian accent, his words stodgy in sentence.

"Right, okay, maybe we should take you outside for a second, yeah?" Damian insisted.

Reece nodded, taking Damian's hand and taking a glass from the bar top in the other. "Thanks again for the drink!" she exclaimed, lifting the glass up, the fizzing clear liquid spilling over the rim.

"It is better when you taste it," Adomas hissed, a smile laced across his face.

"Uh-huh."

The ground was cold and hard beneath her back, her shoulders numb. It was dark, the kind of dark she could not tell whether her eyes were open or shut. It was just darkness. Reece could feel the pavement gravel underneath her fingertips, and her legs were pressed flat into the ground. The tip of her nose felt warm, and her cheeks were flushed and burning up. She could hear the faint sound of footsteps and the sound of a spinning bike wheel clicking past her head. She tried to move, but it was like wading through water; her limbs remained slow and heavy.

Just minutes had passed before she heard the sound of a man's voice cry out, "Fuck, I think this chick's dead!" And she wondered if she was.

It was moments after this that she felt the jolt of her body being pulled from the ground onto her feet, lifted, and thrown onto something hard beneath her torso. Her head was ringing, and the motion of swaying made her feel nauseous once more. Finally opening her eyes, she watched as the street beneath her passed by in floods, focussing on the sound of heavy footfall. Her hands were resting against something soft. She soon realised the thick yellow material and instinctively grabbed onto the fabric underneath the jacket, a well of panic filling her body. "Jackson?" she hazily moaned, the swaying coming to an abrupt stop.

They had been walking for over 10 minutes when Jackson felt the tension pull on the back of his shirt and heard her faint sob. Taking a deep breath, Jackson leant forward, keeping his hand on the small of her back, and put her back on the ground in front of him. She looked small and scared, her eyes large and dark. Jackson's hand was still wrapped around her, and he could feel her swaying in his hold.

"Are you...okay?" he asked, concerned but not showing it through furrowed brows and a cold stare.

"Uh, I don't—" Her eyes were fluttering and darting around the floor. "What happened?"

"Oh, so you don't—" Jackson stopped, and in 0 to 60, his skin became hot with rage. "You don't—!" Jackson began pacing like an angered father, one hand in his hair, the other on his side. "Do you know what this means!" he shouted, drawing attention from passers-by, who had stopped either to watch the show or witness the domestic, but he didn't seem to care.

"Jackson, I—"

"No! Just. Stop!" he yelled, continuing to pace a few metres away from her.

By now, tears were streaming down Reece's face, and she too didn't seem to care about the audience that had formed outside of the closed takeaways.

They were near the flat, she could just run. But as she thought this, she became paralysed with fear as Jackson turned back, stepped towards her, and grabbed her with both hands around the arms, shouting, "Do you not get why I'm mad?"

She shook her head. "Did I screw up things with Tara?" she wept, desperately trying to think of what she could have said or done.

"*Tara*? Fuck. Is that really—?" He stopped again, his grip slowly releasing around her arms and realising how cold her skin was before taking off his jacket and wrapping it around her shoulders.

Reece stood still, the coat draped loosely over her, her tears frozen on her cheeks. Scared to move in case he started back up again. This was the first time she had seen Jackson so angry, and she hated that she was the cause of it and hated it more that she didn't know why.

After a while, Jackson finally sighed, noticing the viewers slowly fall out; and sat on the curb. His long legs outstretched in front of him into the street. Reece too joined him on the curb, her knees tucked into her body.

"I don't remember," she sobbed again, her hands holding her head as it thumped and bleated and burned. "I just feel so sick."

The smoking area, despite the smoke, was a beautiful outside area. The wooden booths were lined with floral hedges and delicately painted signs describing old facts about the bar and city. Old wooden boxes were used for seating, and the whole area looked to be designed like a marketplace.

Upon entering, a wave of relief washed over Damian as he turned back to Reece. "Are you sure you're okay?" he asked, taking in a breath of smoky air and coughing a little as it hit his lungs.

"Yeah, all swell. That was just Adomas from work. He actually came to apologise for being a dick in the past."

"Oh, well, that's big of him. And he got you a drink?" Damian smiled, pointing to the glass in Reece's hand. "What is it?"

"I actually don't know," she laughed, bringing the glass to her lips and sipping. Her eyes pinching, eyebrows raising as the familiar bitter taste hit the roof of her mouth. "Vodka and lemonade," she said, her teeth scraping against her tongue to remove the aroma. "You want it?"

"Nah, I'm still on the Guinness!" Damian's voice played out childishly, pronouncing Guinness like 'Geen-iss' and chuckling to himself after he had done so.

"Right, ha."

Pretty soon after, the two bumped into Jackson once more, this time with Sonny and the following mob.

"Well, well, well, what's the craic!" Sonny cheered, opening his arms to Reece and squeezing as she fell into them.

"Hey! Haven't seen you in forever," she beamed.

She had always liked Sonny; despite his diluted entitlement; and had known him for a while at this point, being introduced the same night Tara and Jackson had met. Impressed by his knowledge of film and photography, the two of them spent most of the night talking on the black leather sofa, exchanging sips of pink gin and fruit twist Fanta.

"How are you?" Reece smiled once she pulled back, noticing a few other familiar faces in the group.

Harry, another one of Sonny's photography friends, stood shyly at the back of the crowd. Shorter than most and very slender, Harry, like Sonny, was Cantonese and had dark, serious eyes. His hair, also like Sonny, was bleached blonde, and he had a wide child-like smile. Reece liked Harry and was more than comfortable giving him a tightly squeezed hug, unlike some others she had seen.

Eric, for instance, was there too. A tall, large looking 'lad-type' with a scruffy dark beard and neck tattoos. He was a photographer and personal trainer and was often described by Jackson as "The one who fucks his clients." He was often seen wearing tight capri pants that fitted well above his ankles and stretched over his enlarged calves, making everyone uncomfortable.

And then there was Jay. Jay was tall and dark and easily one of Jackson's better-looking friends. Jay had large smiling eyes, with thick dark lashes, and was aesthetically built. He dressed well and smoked like he was being filmed, his fingers caressing his lower lip as he pulled the cigarette down away from his face, as if in slow motion.

Reece had spotted him out instantly, thinking back to when Jackson told her, 'if he could be anyone, it would be him.' Making her laugh a little as she realised why.

"Y'know, I'm not doing too bad. And what about yourself, big man?" Sonny charmed, now turned towards Damian.

"Yeah, all good. Just saving *this* one from a big creepy bastard."

Reece's eyes grew in size, and her cheeks flushed with embarrassment.

"Yeah, we heard about that fucker. Are you alright?"

Reece shot Jackson a look, her eyes narrowing, but Jackson remained unphased. "I'm fine. He's fine. Can we not? I can take care of myself." Obviously flustered, the group of guys laughed and scoffed.

"Sure, you can, Pet." Sonny winked; Reece had told him once that she liked it when guys called her, "Pet," but now was not the time.

The group ended up going back in together, some of Sonny's friends less enthused to dance than others, deciding to stand in a perfectly still formation just metres away from the Scalini group. Jackson and Sonny, however, had finally drunk enough to sway and fist bump along to whatever was playing, making sure to keep their male bravado intact.

Reece had also re-joined her friends and was currently dancing with Rocco. Jackson found this extremely weird as Rocco was quite a bit older than her, making a snide comment to Damian, saying, "She's dancing like a stripper."

Damian was also uncomfortable with how close they were dancing, watching as she would lace her hands around his neck and move in time with him. "Yeah, I think I'm gonna go!" he shouted over the roaring music.

"You sure?" Jackson shouted back.

"Yeah, I got class in the morning." He lied, it wasn't his reason for leaving, and Jackson knew that. With a final nod and exchanged smile, Damian left quickly, avoiding Reece and her boss as he left out the back.

"Why didn't we leave with Damian?" Reece asked after Jackson had begun retelling the events of the night.

"He, uhh...had class...in the morning." Jackson saw as Reece's face bunched up in confusion. "What?"

"Damian doesn't have class on Wednesdays. That's why we have our Subway dates."

Now Jackson looked confused. "You don't call them that, do you?"

"What?"

"Dates! You don't call them dates when you get food together?"

"Uhh, yeah, but it's not like—"

"Fuck me, Reece!" Jackson yelled, throwing his hands up into his hair and pulling on the strands.

"What!" she shouted back, her eyes welling up once more. She really couldn't handle people shouting at her...I say, 'people', I mean Jackson.

"How can you not see *it*!"

"See *what*!"

"He likes you! Fucking hell! He left because you were dry humping your fucking boss!" As soon as the words left his lips, Jackson felt regret. In seconds he had spilled Damian's most kept secret and thrown it at her.

Reece gulped back a tear, slowly shaking her head, eyes pinned to her knees. "You're wrong."

"Am I?"

"It's not like that. He doesn't—"

"Doesn't what? Take your side on everything? Do anything you ask of him—"

"Jackson, stop."

"Tell you, you're his 'favourite'."

"Please, just stop!"

"Pay your fucking rent!"

"I paid him back! I only needed a week!"

Seeing the tears now streaming down her face, Jackson took a deep breath, looked away, and looked back at her. "Yes, but would you have asked anyone else?"

Letting the tears fall past her lips, Reece whispered, "He would have done that for any of you."

But Jackson only repeated, "Would you have asked anyone else?"

"No."

Jackson didn't need to respond; Reece knew what that meant, and she couldn't help but think this was the cruellest thing Jackson could have done.

The two sat in silence for some time, Reece replaying past moments between her and Damian, her head ringing with each bulb that blew in her mind, and she felt sick with guilt. "Why did you tell me?" she whispered; her throat hoarse.

"You needed to know." He paused, taking Reece's hands in his, making sure she was listening. "Reece, you have that boy wrapped around your finger. You—"

"How though! I don't—"

"Because you're *you*." He paused again; his voice softer now. "Reece, when you walk into a room, it lights up, and when you flutter your fucking eyes and speak in that fucked up accent, it's sexy. So, like, what's a guy—*Damian*—supposed to do?" Jackson waited for his nerves to end. He looked at her mouth, it was slightly parted, and he could see she was tensing her jaw. He looked at her eyes, at her large dark eyes, noticing her pupils expand into them. The wind had blown pieces of her hair over her face, but she didn't move them.

"You shouldn't have told me."

"Yeah, well, you know now. So, you can stop being a fucking tease." He smiled, waiting for the curve in her lip, but it never showed; and continued the story. "And then you disappeared."

It was nearing the early hours of the morning when Damian left, and pretty soon after, so did Reece. At first, Jackson wasn't too concerned, but after a while, he grew worried.

"Have you seen Reece?" Jackson asked Tara, who had spent most of the night with Rocco and Jamie.

"Uhh, I think she went to get some water. That was a while ago, though."

Rocco had also mentioned that she started feeling unwell, and Jamie suggested 'checking the bathrooms'. Gesturing Sonny to follow him, they both searched the floor, starting with the smoking area and rooftop bar.

"She's fine man, that girl said she's probably in the toilet." Sonny said after Jackson had circled the outside booths for a second time.

"I swear that girls a fucking liability," Jackson snapped back.

On the other side of the dance floor, tucked behind a raised seating area and corridor leading to the bathrooms, Reece stood with her back leaning against the wall. Her hands touching the sides of her head and her knees bent a little. She had been in the bathroom for some time with an overwhelming feeling of nausea but had been unable to purge. As she stood there, the bright lights from the room hazed and expanded into blurry spotlights, and the music started to murmur and sink as if it had been pushed underwater. She was alone, or so she thought and felt safe closing her eyes, waiting for the feeling to pass.

Jackson found her pretty quickly; the deep bottle green top she was wearing caught the corner of his eye as he curved around the DJ's table to check the bathrooms. From across the hall, Jackson could see a group of large men around her and recognised Adomas immediately as the "Scandinavian looking fuck" he described him as.

Adomas was standing close to Reece, one arm resting on the wall above her head and the other hand holding onto her waist. He was laughing loudly, and the other men shuffled in place, one taking the side of his fingers and caressing Reece's cheek, another tugging on the loose strands around her face.

Seeing this, Jackson felt explosive rage, striding up to Adomas, grabbing him by his shirt's collar, and shoving him into the wall behind him.

"What the fuck are you doing with her!" he shouted, loud enough to make a scene in the club.

Adomas was the same height as Jackson but a lot wider and stronger. Grappling onto Jacksons' arms and throwing them outwards, Adomas watched him stumbled backwards. The other men, like bulls, grazed in place, fixing their hooves into the floor.

"Listen. You do not want to cause fight."

"Fuck I don't. Sonny, grab her," he commanded. Sonny following, his eyes narrowed as he pulled Reece from the wall, lifting her arm and wrapping it around his shoulders, carrying the weight of her unconscious body.

"She wanted us here," Adomas teased, "she did not want to be alone."

With each word, his voice pissed Jackson off, but realising he was severely outnumbered, he cursed once more and left to follow Sonny, until—

"Your girlfriend needs a man like me—show her a good time." And that did it.

Hearing this, Jackson swung back around, his right fist thrown at Adomas's face and missing by inches.

Laughing, Adomas grabbed Jackson by the neck and pulled back his paw.

Luckily, Sonny's uniformed squad had been close by, running over in time to pull Jackson back and surround the men.

Spectators who had been watching were unsure whether a fight or dance battle was going down, and pretty quickly, those around froze in their cliques to find out.

"Fuck this cunt, mate. Let's go," Harry called out, pulling on Jackson's shoulder to turn and leave.

"Yes. Take your bitch home."

"And then, as if you couldn't make things worse. You passed out outside of the kebab place, and some smick almost called the police because he thinks you're dead...And now we're here. Glad you're all caught up. Thanks for coming to my ted talk." Jackson took a deep sigh. It had been a long night.

"Jackson, I am so sorry, I don't—" her head shook, and she squeezed her eyes shut. Filled with guilt and embarrassment, she truly believed that was the last time she would ever drink.

"It's okay." Jackson smiled, his eyes in the top right corner of the sky as he thought of something funny. "Y'know, Eric might ruin your life and ask you for nudes. Jay might get you pregnant, Sonny might stalk you with his camera, and Harry might help him with his drone. And I might nutmeg your dad, but we're sure as hell not going to let anyone else do it!"

There was a second of silence before the two of them burst out laughing, loud enough it created an echoed harmony down the now-empty street.

"Thanks, Jackson."

"Yeah, whatever, now can we get the fuck outta here? I'm freezing my balls off."

BITTER

The sound of gentle bubbling could be heard from the stove as River stood dropping crushed cloves into the pot. The sweet and spicy smell of mulled wine filling the Flat 6's living room. With a yellow blanket wrapped around his shoulders, he opened the oven slightly, checking on the cinnamon rolls he was baking, this time without Damian and Reece's assistance. They were browning nicely, and this made him smile.

The others were in the lounge too, Nora and Will cuddled close under a blanket on the one sofa, Jackson and Amy not so close on the other. Amy was still upset about the 'effort' comment and made it known she was displeased.

Reece was sitting on the arm of the couch next to Will, looking up at Damian opposite her. They really hadn't spoken since the awful night at Lavery's, and both felt hollow without the other's company.

Zasha was stood by River's side, "Aw-ing" and "ooh-ing," at the baked goods and simmering treats as a way to mend the bridges between their previous arguments. It was working.

A large purple candle Amy had brought in from home was burning on the windowsill, and many were disappointed at its scent-less-ness.

"Yeah, well fuck off, it's from Auschwitz, okay? What's it supposed to smell like?" she laughed, watching as the expensive candle started to run and drip down the base, wondering whether it will make a mess, then forgetting about it.

Amy's grandmother's fern tree was still in the same place as before, resting on the white shoe rack. However, it was now bent in the middle, the red and silver baubles scattered around the base from where they had fallen, which Will kindly pointed out. Knowing fully well the damage occurred during a game of 'inside rugby', Jackson kept quiet throughout the discussion.

Nora was also very quiet, looking back and forth between the plastic Spar bag on her lap to the pile of wrapped gifts in the middle. Like she expected, her gift for Will had not arrived in time, and in a sweep of panic, she had run to the corner shop to improvise.

Like an awkward British family, the group decided to open their Secret Santa gifts one at a time, each and every one of them feeling this was an increasingly bad idea but, nonetheless.

"Fuck it, I'll go first," Jackson exclaimed after the question was raised and the room went silent. Rummaging a little through the pile, Jackson found the two labelled with his name and raised them for the group to see.

Damian had started filming, and so Jackson made sure to address the camera, and he started unwrapping.

The first gift was long, thin and cylindrical, the weight of the present making it clear it was a poster—that—and the fact it wasn't wrapped at all, just covered with a plastic bag from both ends, the name 'Jackson' scrawled on with a black marker.

Examining the poster, Jackson saw it was an Artic Monkeys album cover and was instantly excited. "Aw, no way! I've never had a poster in my room before," he beamed with child-like enthusiasm.

Next, he opened a gift that was indeed wrapped with brown shipping paper that came in a small square box. Ripping the sheet of paper from the box, opening the flap, and pulling out a large glass jar. It was a vanilla and mulberry scented candle in a dewy caramel wax. "What!" Jackson screamed. Pulling the glass lid off and smelling inside. "Artic Monkeys and candles! Fuck! How'd you know?"

"I didn't," River called out bluntly from the kitchen, side glancing Reece, who was shyly smiling.

"Well, thanks, I guess." There was a split moment of tension; Jackson knew River wasn't his biggest fan and was feeling guilty that River had gotten him. But the moment passed when Will declared, "River! You're up, Chief."

"Make sure to look at the camera!" Damian also chimed, which sent River into disclaiming:

"I do not consent to being in this video," —a serious complex that had been ignored on multiple occasions. Leaving the mulled wine on the stove, River sat cross-legged on the floor, in-between both couches and opposite the tree.

His parcel was wrapped in a plaid patterned wrapper with an abundance of tape around the sides. This made River giggle as he tried at first to unwrap delicately but gave up and pulled the paper from the middle, exposing a bundled t-shirt inside.

Pulling it out and stretching the sleeves outwards, he saw that it was a dark blue shirt with an embroidered bumblebee in the middle. A cursive tagline reading 'Bee Happy' underneath. "Aw, dude!" he cooed, his smile settling into the sides of his cheeks. "This is adorable! Really wonderful. Who do I thank?" Looking around the room, River caught Amy mid-blush.

"Yeah, I was told you like bees, so yeah," she stated, smiling but, not really.

"No, I do! This is great, thanks Amy."

In pattern, Amy dug through the pile and pulled out a soft parcel. Her gift was wrapped with shiny iridescent paper, and a silver curled ribbon was tied around with a bow. "Wow, uhh okay." she gasped, feeling a little on the spot as Damian moved in closer with his phone. Taking care to unwrap the gift, Amy lifted the cellotape pieces with her long nails and opened the paper up. Once again, stretching the arms out, Amy lifted a baby blue sweatshirt and showed the camera. "Wait. What?" she gleamed, turning the jumper around. "Goose and Gander, no way! I literally only told—" Amy turned to Reece, who was sweetly smiling back at her.

Months ago, Amy had told Reece that Goose and Gander were one of her favourite brands and desperately wanted more clothing from there. Specifically entailing that baby blue was a colour she wanted to wear more of. "This is so so nice, Reece, thank you!"

The rest of the group took no surprise to Reece being Amy's Secret Santa as only 2 days after the names were given, Reece had let it spill when she thought out loud, "Should I just buy Amy a kitten?" and thankfully, everyone but Amy was present.

"You're welcome." For the first time in a long time, tension seemed to disappear between the two, and it was great.

"I feel bad, though," Amy explained. "This is over the price limit."

"Maybe, but your birthday is next week, and I won't be around so—"

"That's so thoughtful, Kid," River sang.

Amy, adding in, "Yeah, well. No one's ever around for my birthday."

"Aw, babies!" chimed Zasha, running over to sit in-between her and Jackson so she could lean over and hug her.

"Dude, we'll definitely do something before everyone leaves for Christmas," Will assured, met with a collaborated nod from the group. "Okay. Reece, you go now."

Reece was nervous. She already knew who had her, and she had a lot of fun figuring it out, but now it meant that she wouldn't have a genuine 'surprised' face. And with everything going on with Damian, she worried it would make matters worse.

Reece's gift was well wrapped in red and green paper. There were 2 gifts, cello-taped together, making it difficult to separate elegantly.

The first gift was in a weighted square box; as she opened it, she saw a rounded Christmas mug filled with marshmallows and hot chocolate. "Aw!" she beamed, taking the mug from the box and showing the camera. "Thank you, Damian!" she cheered without thinking and was instantly met with:

"How did you know?"

"Who told you!"

"Aw, what!"

River, who knew exactly how she knew, muttering, "You are the literal worst, Kid," under his wine-smelling breath.

"Yeah, *this* one got it out of me pretty quickly," Damian joked, gesturing to the second gift.

Inside the second parcel was a pair of fluffy grey slippers with little pompoms hanging from the outer edge. Before Reece could comment, Damian sang, "Took me forever to get these! I didn't realise I had to shop in the kid's section! Spent ages looking through the woman's isles before I figured it out!" The group joined in pitying laughter, and Reece blushed a deep red.

"Aw, Reece and her fucking baby feet!" Jackson screamed, which only encouraged more ridicule.

"Pfft, jokes on you, I—" Reece stopped, unable to think of something witty to say. "Never mind. Thank you, Damian. I love them!" she said, before putting the slippers straight on her feet, the rest of the group leaning in, waiting for the confirmation. "Yes, they fit!".

Command unnecessary, Damian passed his phone to Will and picked his gifts quickly from the remaining parcels. Also wrapped in brown parchment, Damian first unwrapped a small; no bigger than a post-it; present. Neatly unfolding the edges and pulling out a shiny gold ornament.

It was a Game of Thrones Hand of the King Tyrion Lannister pin, which instantly sparked the fan-boy side of Damian they were all familiar with.

"Oh my god, no way! Yes, yes, yes!" his voice squeaking in high-pitched excitement. "This is awesome!" he continued before ripping open the second parcel, lifting up another piece of Game of Thrones merchandise. "Ohhh! I am so happy right now!" he exclaimed, his voice transitioning into a lower octave.

"What is it? Turn it around," Jackson said.

Damian, flipping the t-shirt the right way, showing a black cotton shirt with a white outline of a wolf illustrated on the front, the tagline reading 'The LONE WOLF dies, the PACK survives.' "I love it so much! Thank you..." he looked around the room, eyes squinting at Jackson.

"Nah, man, not me like."

"The thing is, right?" Zasha explained bashfully. "I tried to find something from that Skyfall movie you like—"

"Skyrim...*game*," Reece corrected, laughing with her.

"...But the guys at Forbidden Planet didn't have anything. So, I got this instead."

"Skyrim *is* my favourite game, they have this series in the Elder Scrolls that—" Damian began, but after looking around at the wide eyed 'you're going to explain this *now*?' faces, he abruptly stopped, finishing with, "but Game of Thrones is my favourite TV show, so it's perfect, thank you Zaz-Zaz."

Zasha was next. Her gift was also wrapped in the same shiny paper as Amy's and finished with a silver bow, beautiful cursive writing reading 'Zasha' on the front. Zasha instantly turned to Reece laughing, "Ha! Thanks for wrapping this, Reggie!"

The group laughing and nodding as if to say, "Ah, that makes sense."

Opening her box, Zasha lifted up an extremely large mug, so large it could have been, and probably was, a soup bowl. The mug was white with the 'Central Perk' logo on the front and painted green on the inside. "Aw, babies!" Zasha whined. "It's a big mug! I love big mugs!" Genuinely thrilled, Zasha turned to Will but was redirected to Jackson. "Aw Jackson, how did you know?"

"Hey! I pay attention too!" Jackson shot Reece a charming smile and turned back to Zasha, who had already put her mug down and wrapped her arms tightly around his shoulders. "Oh, guess we're hugging," he sighed, hesitant to hug her back. "And I could have wrapped that!" he yelled but was unsurprisingly met with a unanimous, "No, you couldn't."

Leaving just Nora and Will, they both exchanged a look of affection. Will obviously being the one to make the joke, "Well, I *wonder* who has me!" before searching around the floor.

"Okay, so, your gift hasn't *actually* arrived yet, so this is just an 'in the meantime' present," Nora explained, a little embarrassed as she handed over the plastic packet she had kept in her lap.

"Oh, okay," Will said, disappointed but smiling anyway.

Inside the bag was a series of odd things, including a large loaf of pound cake, a dib dab sachet, and a plastic lighter. Speechless, Will took out the items and spread them on the floor, missing a packet of gum at the bottom of the bag; Nora insisting, "Don't forget the gum!"

It was an odd moment between the two, Will tried to make the best of it, thanking Nora for the...things and agreeing how annoying it is when things don't arrive on time.

And at first, this was fine, but things tightened once again when Nora confessed, "I know, right! Like I actually only ordered your present a couple days ago, but they said it would be here!"

This put everyone in the room on edge, but Will was determined to be upbeat, replying, "Well, just more suspense for me, I guess! A film maker's greatest weapon!"

Nora's gift for Will did actually arrive only a couple of days later, but Will ended up being more excited for the pound cake when he opened the parcel and found out Nora had ordered him a small cushion with her face on it. Awkward for everyone involved.

Moving swiftly on, Nora reached for the small square gift left on the floor. It was wrapped in shiny green paper and was lathered in tape.

"Look, we can't all be good at wrapping!" Will paused for a second, his eyes lighting up in Reece's direction. "Or *can* we?"

"I completely forgot!" Reece cheered, shifting in her seat, welling up with excitement. Others were more than confused. "No, no, wait, we'll do it after."

"Okay."

Ignoring 'whatever that was,' Nora opened her gift, once again showing it to the camera, which was now back in Damian's hand. Nora held up a small air humidifier that was shaped like a cactus. "Oh!" she sighed, turning it around, inspecting all sides as if it would suddenly become something else.

"So, it's a USB, so you just plug it in. I thought you could use this when you, y'know, *are*—" Will goes on to 'charade' someone smoking, making sure to suck in and blow out air; obviously noting to a *different* type of smoking.' Nora looked confused.

"Uhh, I think you're getting that mixed up with a 'diffuser,' Buckeroo," River added. "A humidifier makes the air, well, humid."

Will looked up back in shock, mouth ajar. "Yeah, that too."

Everyone bar Nora found this funny. "Well, thanks," she ended up saying after the silence became unbearable.

"Right! You ready?" Reece jumped up, reaching her hand to Will to pull him from the couch.

"Ready for what?" Amy asked.

"Uhh, for the best thing you will hear in 2019."

Below is the rap both Will and Reece wrote for the flat. I am not joking. They performed this willingly, singing each verse alternatively, starting with Reece:

Reece

> River!
> Pres-i-dent of the so-ci-ety,
> Gosh we never knew you studied writing cre-a-tively!
> Guess we'll use big words like os-ten-ta-tious-
> And kind of e-ffem-in-ate-
> And don't get me started if someone ab-bre-vi-ates!
> Although this may be funny, try not to laugh.
> We want to raise the roof with our jokes, not your shaft!

Will

> Zasha why, Zasha wine, Zasha why fucking not.
> Living life on Instagram is all you've bloody got.
> Now we'll try not to burn ya,
> Like the:
> Toast, the chips, and lasagne...
> If you stop-
> Pleading like an immigrant
> Telling us you're fucking skint
> Why you talking trash, gurl?
> Wipe it up your ass, gurl!

Reece

> All I've gotta say is "Man like Jackson!"
> Split 3 ways but won't accept his nation!
> As shallow as a kiddy pool
> Learn to read, go to school!
> And listen when I say:
> "Don't go packing rubbers"

Cause no matter how they look,

Age is *never* just a number!

I'm just kidding, you're not always a creeper...

Heads in the walls, bodies in the freezer.

Will (Pointing to Nora)

You're *real* name's Maria,

That says a lot.

Giving your number to every boy on the block.

My bad, let's keep it clean-ah?

Get it?

Cause' you're Latin-a?

Just keep me right with this biblical tale,

Was it Marco that becomes fish-food for the Whale?

Bigger sex drive than Moby Dick.

Because you're just a massive prick!

Reece

Now what can we say about Damian?

When he's not gyming and staying fit?

We never see him eat, still looking like a beast!

Both of them now

Posh boy living in a shack!

Posh boy doesn't know he's whack!

Posh boy, that's a fucking fact!

But you'll never catch him sleeping,

Coz' the boy will be back!

Back to Will

Amy-cat, Amy-cat

Sorry, no-one got you're joke.

We just can't keep up with:

Toothbrushes and problems with the bloke!

Is it you whose been to Auschwitz?

Sorry, was finishing your pasta bake and biscuits...

My bad! That's too much to handle,

Both, once more

Let's finish this rap by blowing out your candle!

Most of the audience was entertained. River, however, was truly appalled. Jackson was still confused, thinking to himself, *17 still isn't that young!* And Nora was more than pissed off, making a scene as she huffed out of the room—only family called her 'Maria'.

"Well, can't please them all!" Will laughed, falling back down into the couch and leaning his head on the windowsill. "Uhh, Amy...?" he whined after he had placed his hair directly into the melting candle wax that had pooled and spilled over the edge.

"Oh, for fuck's sake!"

Within the next few days, the flat dropped like flies. Nora was the first to fly home to Barcelona, and then Damian returned to his quiet home in Bristol.

River following back to Guilford with an extended invitation to Zasha to spend Christmas with him and his family. A few days later, Zasha would fly out and meet him there.

Even though she only lived a few miles away, Amy also went home around the 18th, saying that this would be the last Christmas she would be with her boyfriend Callum; referring to their pending breakup; and needed to make the most of it. Leaving just Will, Reece, and Jackson; for an extra day; in the unheated flat.

"You're so lucky!" Will exclaimed, turned to Reece as he tried to shove all his unwashed laundry into the red suitcase.

"Ha, why's that?"

"You don't have to fly anywhere; you can just get a train."

"Eh, I guess. It's only an hour for you though, right? You're only in Aberdeen."

"Yeah, but—" Will took a deep breath in as he squashed and squeezed the remainder of his clothes into the suitcase, pulling at the old zip around the edge until it closed. "You don't have to carry a bloody broken suitcase around the country!"

Both Reece and Jackson tilted their head and squinted their eyes. "*Broken*?"

"Yeah, the handle is broken, like it's stuck at the bottom of the case. I can't pull it up," Will explained.

Jackson, laughing at the image of Will walking around the airport holding a bulky case to his chest.

"Oh, when did it break?" Reece asked.

"It's actually been broken for years!"

The room went silent for a second.

"Why didn't you replace the fucking thing?" Jackson asked, laughing still but now thinking Will was an idiot.

"Because it's like...my good luck charm... I've been all over the world with this case, it's part of the family!"

"You're a muppet," Reece giggled, now picturing the odd scene.

"Give that here," Jackson ordered, grabbing onto the handle, pressing in the button, and yanking upwards. Nothing. Jackson tried again, and still no success. "Well fuck, I tried, I'm going to sleep. See you next year." With that, Jackson left the room and went upstairs. Honestly, one of the more endearing goodbyes from the Irishman.

Quietly laughing, Reece held out her hand, gesturing for Will to push the case over to her. Reece looked at the red box for some time before reaching for the handle, clicking in the dirty button, and pulling upwards, the rest of the handle coming up with her.

"What the fuck!" Will cried out, throwing his hands over his mouth and taking a step backwards. "Lad, you're a machine! That case has been broken for years!"

"You can no longer call yourself a Scotsman." Reece grinned, her smile wide and eyes bright.

"Aw, dude, come here." Will wrapped his arms around her, the large warm hoodie he was wearing swarming over her frame. Although she hadn't noticed, the hoodie he was wearing was one of his own creations.

In the few months they lived at the flat, Will had started a small t-shirt printing business. He had only sold a few here and there to other film students, as most of his work including printing quotes and scripts from eclectic films, but he was very proud of his Fight Club pullover, despite who refused to notice.

"Have a wonderful Christmas, Pumpkin," Reece beamed, her soft, muffled voice talking into his shoulder.

"You too, Reggie."

Will left for the airport later that night, and Reece had planned to go in the morning but was worried about Jackson.

Jackson had often described how unwelcoming his mother's home was. She was currently living with her boyfriend and their two children, Jackson's sisters, and the boyfriend had made it very clear that Jackson's presence in the home was stressful. Reece had accompanied Jackson many times to the house when the girls needed babysitting and had never understood the tension. But things were always different around guests.

"Jackson, you awake?" she whispered from the other side of the door. No answer. "Jackson?" she spoke softly again. With no reply, she opened the door. The lights were off, and Jackson was lying face down into the pillow, his fluffy grey duvet folded perfectly with him sleeping in between the crease like a sleeping bag. "Jackson!" she hissed for a final time before climbing onto the end of his bed and crawling to his side, tucking herself under the covers and staring at the ceiling. "Do you want to come home with me for Christmas?" she asked.

Hearing this, Jackson rolled onto his back, his head turned towards her. Smiling wide as he realised, she was completely nuzzled under the covers, completely comfortable next to him. "What?"

"Do you want to come home with me for Christmas? I know things aren't the best at your house, so I—"

While she rambled, Jackson turned onto his side, wrapping an arm around her waist and pulling her into him, tucking his other arm under her head. "Shhh," he whispered back; eyes closed but still smiling.

"But I just thought—"

"Shhh...Do the *thing*."

Reece smiled. Holding onto the bridge of his arm, she started tracing her nails along his skin. "...Wanna come to India with me?"

211

INSECURE

L ooking back, it's fair to say the flat had more than their fair share of drama, chaos, and malfunction for one year. And you're right. But all this takes place at University. Academic schedule.

The new year mist and frost had settled on the streets of Belfast, the last signs of Christmas dissipating off into the air as neighbours tore down their festive lights, and all signs of green and red were stripped from their houses.

The early January days were quiet; all students were still at their homes for the holidays, and Jackson couldn't have been happier. He slept-in without the fear of being woken by 'pathetic student problems' like Will misplacing an SD card, or Zasha getting fined for late equipment return, or Reece getting fired, again, and frantically applying for any and all jobs on Indeed. Life was bliss.

He even had the freedom to bring home his tinder conquests and parade them around the empty flat, which later the others found out included all bedrooms.

"That's disgusting," Nora scoffed, being one of the first to return to the flat and the first to hear about Jackson's 'time alone.'

"Look, if you didn't want me to fuck in your room, you should have locked the door!" he laughed; he was joking; Nora's room was way too small to have good sex, but he liked that it pissed her off.

"Heh, you're a fucking idiot. And you're cleaning my sheets," she instructed, pointing a long finger at him before walking up the stairs, making sure to move her hips the full pendulum as he watched from the bottom.

Amy also returned that evening and likewise was less than impressed by the tales of Jackson's hook-ups.

"Why are you telling me this?" she spat. It had been over a month and a half since Jackson had suggested Amy to 'put more effort into her appearance,' and like a film student's career, her resentment wasn't going anywhere.

"Okay, seriously, what can I do to make it up to you. It's been fucking ages!"

"You can take it back!" Amy yelled, dropping her large handbag to the floor and pacing across the living room.

"Okay, I take it back."

"You can't take it back! You already said it!"

Jackson let out a loud laugh, throwing his head back against the couch. But Amy continued to pace angrily.

"Why did you even come back if you're still pissed?" he asked, looking at the loose floral material around her legs that were pale enough to see her black underwear underneath, thinking, *now I like those...* but choosing to keep that to himself.

"Because me and Callum have been fighting and—"

"Uhh, Amy?"

"What?"

"We've talked about this, don't complain to me about Callum, okay? You—"

"Oh *wow*!" Amy mocked. "Could you be more arrogant? I don't like you, Jackson! Okay? Get over yourself." As Amy spoke, she caught Jackson's smirk, and she became filled with rage. "Fuck you! We're supposed to be friends, and all I get from you is fucking abuse. Go fuck yourself!" She let out a sort of scream-grunt, as you could call it, before slumping down on the opposite sofa.

Jackson let the tension deflate for a second before announcing, "I wrote you a poem."

"What?"

"Yeah, to say sorry...For what I said."

"Right."

Jackson looked at the multiple files of notes he had stored on his phone, surprised to feel the butterflies of nerves as he read.

Amy,

We've been friends for quite a while.

And it sucks I'm the reason you refuse to smile.

I said you needed more effort in your appearance,

But what I say shouldn't make a difference.

I think you're great and I love you a lot,

So, you can go on to hate me,

But like, can you not?

After he finished, Amy's face remained cold as she got up from the couch, picked her bag from the floor, and left the room. Leaving Jackson alone.

"That's the last time I fucking try," Jackson scorned in a whisper.

The next to arrive back at the flat was River, Zasha, and Damian. By coincidence, they had all caught the same flight back from Heathrow. Zasha and River travelling together after their 2 weeks stay at River's parent's house.

When they returned, Zasha described the Harrison Household as "Perpetually surreal," and, "amorously charming!" as they all expected River's home to be, with Jackson having to search up what 'amorously' meant before nodding his head; as if to say, "Sounds about right."

"His mum even bought me a little present, so I'd have something under the tree, it was so lovely! And they had food everywhere! All the time. Like they had a big Christmas Eve dinner, a Christmas dinner, a boxing day dinner, a dinner on our last day. And there was always wine!" As Zasha lavished about her stay, the ending fact of bottomless wine seemed to excite her the most.

"It was a dream, in all honesty," River agreed, in reference to all the food and drink, but secretly suggesting to the 14 days Zasha managed to go without causing a scene at his expense.

"Sounds glorious!" Damian cheered.

Damian too was sporting the spoils of his Christmas as he wore Gymshark labelled clothing for head to toe.

"What about you, Bud? How was your Christmas?"

The four of them had settled once more in the Flat 6's living room as Damian began to tell of his wonderful time. "I even reconnected with a girl I used to see!" This perking up the ears of all in the room.

"Who!" Jackson yelled uncontrollably.

"Uhh, well in first year I met this girl called Clodagh and—"

"Wait a minute..." River uttered, his mouth turning upside down and shades of green spoiling his face. "Clodagh, as *in*..."

"Yes— *that* Clodagh."

As the 'unknowing others' began to wonder 'who this Clodagh might be,' Reece had arrived at the flat.

"Oh, hey guys!" she beamed, standing in the doorway dressed in a uniform no one had seen before. She was yellow.

"Reggie!" Zasha shrieked, standing to throw her arms around her and pull her back down into the couch. "Aw babies, what the fuck are you wearing?"

"Ha! I got a new job. Yeah, I had my first shift at 'We are Vertigo' today, I literally trained in from Coleraine at 7 in the morning to make it there for 9. Mental. I hate my life. How are all of you?"

This shocked no one. This in fact, was a very 'Reece thing' to do, so little time was spent discussing her new job.

"Well..." River began. "Damian was just telling us he's talking to...Clodagh again..."

"Clodagh as *in*..."

"Yes."

"Oh, Damian," Reece sighed, taking a bottle of Echo Falls from her bag she had picked up on her way back and swigging some before passing it around, purposely missing out Jackson and handing him a separate bottle of beer.

"Okay. Who the fuck is this Clodagh bird?" Jackson asked, throwing his hands up. "Is she hot? Is she crazy? Is she crazy hot?"

"Well, *I* think—"

"No."

"Oh, come on, she's not *that* bad," Damian pleaded, but both Reece and River's head shake was enough to shut him up.

"Should you tell them?" Reece asked River.

"No, you do it."

"Right, okay. So, Clodagh is a friend of a girl both River and Damian lived with in first year. Ash, right?"

Both River and Damian nodded.

"Right, and Ash is crazy as it gets, but she described Clodagh as 'crazy'. So already we were all like, 'uhh okay, everyone lock your doors.' So, one night, me, Will, River and Damian were in their kitchen and Ash walks in with Clodagh, and they are plastered! Like, Michael McIntyre 'gazeebode'. And Clodagh's standing there, and she's wearing the *shortest* shorts I've ever seen and a hello kitty vest top that just... does not fit her."

"I love the sound of this," Jackson interrupted, feeling like a proud father.

"No. It's not—okay, so she comes in and instantly sets her eyes on Damian and is shouting stuff like 'I'm gonna fuck that boy' and 'he's mine' and acting like a loud horny predator. Making everyone uncomfortable—except for Damian, apparently, who just goes along with it.

And this girl just grabs him by the collar and pulls him down the corridor, throwing him on his own bed, and like—everyone hears the door slam closed and then just screaming!"

"Oh fuck!" Jackson says again.

"No, not *good* screaming—" Reece exchanged a quick glance with Damian before continuing, "and then like...2 minutes later, she comes back into the kitchen without Damian and acts as if nothing happened!"

Damian had stayed silent through this detailed play by play, and once it had all been said, he kept that way.

"So, like, what the fuck happened?" Zasha asked; with a level of confusion, you could see her brain envisioning the scene.

"Great question! What happened, Damian?"

"I, uhh... Don't know."

"Pfft, well, that's a lie!" River belittled.

"No, seriously, I never could remember. Like, I remember going back into the room with her, and I think I took off my shirt—"

"My *man!*"

"Ha, but other than that, nothing. I woke up the next morning with a tonne of hickeys, though!" The group fell silent once more.

"So, was she hot or not?" Jackson asked for a final time. Without saying a word, Damian scrolled through his phone and showed a picture. "Okay, so *not.*" Sending the group into a fit of giggles.

"You guys are unbearable!" Damian winced, which only made them laugh louder.

Finally, Will returned to the flat, and within 24 hours, the flat was back to its full occupancy. His hair had grown incredibly long in his time away and had been straightened over the curves of his head. And as he walked, the lack of movement made it obvious it had also been gelled down.

"Now, this is a look!" River expelled, eyes bright, thinking that Will resembled a young Dicaprio.

"Yeah, do you not have running water in Aberdeen? Did you have to trek to a well or something?" Reece quipped, hugging him tightly but not a fan of the hair at all.

"Nice to see you as always, Reggie. Nah, man, I just woke up one day and decided this is how my hair is going to be from now on. Think it's kinda cool, don't you?"

Damian nodded his head slowly, respecting the decision and wondering whether he too could get away with that much product.

"You look like the Director of Grease..." Reece continued, "...or just a greasy director, I'm not sure."

"Ha!" Jackson screamed.

Rolling his eyes, Will sighed and turned back to Reece. "Anymore?"

"No, I'm good."

"Good."

"Hey, Jackson?" Reece asked after a second of silence.

"Yes?"

"Remember not to include Will in on the water bill...He won't be using any."

"Right!" Will shouted, dropping his fixed case to the floor and storming upstairs. "I'm taking a shower! And I hate you all!"

"What the fuck?" Zasha whispered, a slight disbelieving laugh in her voice.

"Right! Like, how self-involved do you have to—" Amy paused, watching Zasha wriggle low into the mattress and pull the top of the duvet over their heads. "What are you doing?" she asked, following Zasha's lead and sinking down into the sheets, quickly engulfed by bedspread and darkness.

"Ah, this is better. Go on."

Although she could not see it, Amy was smiling, an unfamiliar warmth in her cheeks heating the small space of air between them. Holding up the covers just high enough to create a camp-like shelter, Amy continued, "And a *poem*? Like— how does that make it any better? How does it take away the fact that he basically called me ugly?"

"Because he's a cunt!" Zasha hissed, a little louder than she intended. "Amy. You are so fucking beautiful! And Jackson and everyone else knows it! I don't know why he thinks he can just go around saying shit like that. He's just a—"

"It just hurts worse, y'know? Coming from him."

"I know." It was already incredibly warm under the covers, yet Zasha still nudged closer to Amy, laying her head on her shoulder.

"Hey, Zaz?" Amy stressed, now feeling claustrophobic and somewhat anxious.

"Yeah?"

"Can you move? Like, it's getting a bit Lesbian under here."

"No."

"Okay."

Zasha knew how much Amy needed it; despite how much she didn't want it.

The two lay like this in silence. Hummed by the sound of each other's soft breath and the motion of the top sheet rising and falling with every exhale. The silence only lasted a minute or so before the agitation and frustration of Jackson's behaviour was revived, and the sound of muffled angst caught Reece's attention as she came up the stairs.

Reece stood in Zasha's doorway, looking at the two human-like shapes jostle under the covers. It was an odd sight, but Reece couldn't help but smile. She could hear their faint voices but could not so much make out what they were saying. Looking around her room, Reece saw that the large bohemian tapestry that hung on the wall above Zasha's bed had fallen from one corner, revealing a small dent in the plaster. Her desk, which was usually covered in assorted books, pictures, and ankle bracelets, was now empty; its contents spilled onto the fall around the feet. And the string of fairy lights which usually spindled around the window and across the wall had been pulled and was dangling from the first hook. If Reece didn't know Zasha any better, she would have assumed there had been a robbery, but she did, and was less than surprised.

"Zasha?" Reece laughed, watching as the two of them froze for a second, squirm back to the top of the bed, and uncover their faces.

"Reggie!" Zasha beamed, squiggling some more to the centre and gesturing for Reece to join them at the other end. "Come sit, come sit!" she sang again, catching Amy's stern look and clenched jaw but choosing to ignore it.

Smiling, Reece ran over, lifting the blanket from the end of the bed and tucking herself in, her back against the wooden desk so that she could see them both. "Oh my gosh! Your bed is so warm!"

"Isn't it. We were just having a little cuddle—"

"We weren't cuddling, fuck's sake," Amy scoffed, her head shaking, eyebrows raised.

"No, it's cute, definitely needed sometimes."

"See!" Zasha cheered, once again louder than she planned.

"Right, well, I'm too old for a sleepover, so I'm gonna go," Amy mocked.

But before she could leave, Reece exclaimed, "No, stay! I was just about to ask Zasha about the obvious...sex...that happened here."

Zasha shrieked in laughter, covering her mouth and sinking back down under the covers.

"Y'know, I was wondering that too!" Amy beamed, now remembering when she had first walked in and noticed the carnage. "Who have you been fucking?"

Zasha lifted her head back up, her cheeks flushed and her eyes focussing on anything but Amy and Reece.

"Well?" Amy asked again.

"Okay, fine!"

Both Reece and Amy held their breath, expecting to hear that River was somewhat involved, leaving them both seriously intrigued and insanely uncomfortable.

"So, you know how me, and River were seeing each other?"

They both nodded, a look of, "I knew it!" plastered on both their faces.

"Well, right before Christmas... Y'know the night when me and Phil went to Filthy's?"

Reece gulped, she hadn't thought about that night, since that night, and she instantly felt sick when it was mentioned.

"Uhh, I think so. I think I was working," Amy answered, her eyes pinned to the top left as she tried to recall.

"You were."

"Yeah, so, keep in mind, me and River were never exclusive or anything like that."

Both Reece and Amy's hearts sunk into their chest.

"And I bumped into Alexander Bailey, y'know, the President of Players, and we just kind of..."

"Fucked?" Amy laughed, her eyes emotionless.

"Yup."

Reece looked a little more concerned, her top lip pointed up in the corner, eyes wide.

Both Amy and Reece knew well of Alexander Bailey. He spent a lot of his time orchestrating events in the QFT, where they had most of their classes. He was a tall, broad man with dark brown hair and a dwarf-like beard. He had a large nose and high cheekbones resting on a long face. It was known that just last year, he broke his jaw when a friend had run into him holding a beer bottle and was recovering from jaw reconstruction, which raised more questions from them both, but they thought it best not to ask.

Reece took a second, and then— "Wait...Alexander Bailey? Like, there's *another* Alex!"

This caused a choir of laughter between the girls, Zasha cupping her hands over her face and shaking her whole body dramatically. "I know! Bad Zasha, bad Zasha!"

"How the hell are we ever gonna keep up? Do we just refer to him as 'Bailey'? Like we do with Warner and McManus?"

"No, no, he goes by 'Alexander' so we should be okay. But, seriously, though...He wrecked me!"

"Eurgh." Reece looked disgusted.

"Well fuck." Amy looked jealous.

"You see that dent?" Zasha gestured to the small hole in the wall. "That was from my head."

"Bloody hell!"

"And *these*." Zasha pulled down the soft blue t-shirt she was wearing to show her shoulders. Faded but still visible; there were small finger-like bruises over her body.

"Fuck!" Amy yelled.

"I'll tell you what, there must be a thing with *'Alexs'* because—"

"I really don't want to know," Reece jumped in. Zasha could see Reece looking mildly uncomfortable, she was holding onto the sleeves of a long black t-shirt, and her lip was still puzzled in the corner.

"Ha, what?" Zasha asked.

"I mean…does River know?"

The question caused silence to sweep over the room, and it was obvious that Zasha was caught off guard. And as if it was choreographed, both Reece and Amy motioned towards the door to close it. Reece had seen River cooking downstairs earlier, but the walls were thin, and Zasha was loud. Nestled back in bed, the two waited for Zasha to speak.

"So, here's the thing…" Zasha went on to explain that during her stay with River over Christmas, the two of them decided that it was best not to continue…whatever it was that they were doing. And they should just go back to being friends. *Poetry*. "So, I don't see the point in telling him."

"Fair enough." The explanation seemed justified to Amy, though Reece had more questions.

"But you guys live in the same house. How are you going to keep it from him?"

"Oh! Me and Alexander have had sex here a bunch of times." This made Zasha laugh loudly and uncontrollably. "He's been coming here most nights and leaving in the morning."

"What!"

"And no one saw or heard you?"

"Nope."

"That's like some CIA, FBI—"

"MI5."

"MI High shit." Reece loved that show.

"Yeah, makes the sex hotter too. Y'know when you have to keep it a secret."

"Yeah." There was a faint longing in Amy's voice as she spoke, the breathy exhale coaxing the three into another silent reflection.

"Well! I need to pee. Be back in a sec," Zasha chanted as she danced over the legs across the bed.

With the sound of the door closing behind her, tension fell over the room. The same feeling of a mouse trapped with a falcon dawned. Yet they both felt they were the mouse.

Amy looked across at Reece, anxiety trapped at the top of her throat.

Reece looked back at Amy, a swarm of sickening wasps in the pit of her stomach. She saw the face of a statue, poised, still, and unforgiving.

And Amy saw the face of a siren, assumingly innocent but a threat, nonetheless.

The silence could have lasted forever; time would stand still all the same. But like ques, films with talking animals and vegans, Reece couldn't stand it. "Amy, are we okay?" she asked, her voice breaking through the icy shards.

"What?"

"Are we *okay*? I don't know how to explain it, but I just get the feeling I've done something to upset you, and I—"

"No, you haven't." Amy looked down at her intertwined fingers on her lap. A red blush warming to the sides of her thin face.

"So, am I making this up?"

Amy took a second before answering, saying things like these out loud makes them real, and she wasn't sure whether the reality was worth it. "No. There has been some weirdness, I guess. On my end, not yours."

Reece took a deep breath. This stalemate had been going on for months, and she was more than ready to call a truce.

Amy also took a breath before continuing, "Look, I know it's stupid of me. Like I know, okay. But I guess since you and

Jackson have gotten so close, I've gotten a little...Jealous." She stopped, looking up to see Reece's reaction, looking for a smirk, a glint of pride, or any sort of malicious reveal so she could justify her behaviour, but there was none.

Reece only looked confused. "Jealous?" she repeated, her lips slightly parted, her eyes growing like a kitten.

"Yeah, like, you get the nice 'let's go get food' Jackson, and I get the 'you're ugly' Jackson. Just a little bit fucked up, really." Amy was sincere, a veil of relief washing over her, but she grew shocked when Reece began to laugh. "What?"

"No, I'm sorry!" Reece began, but couldn't stop giggling. "It's just so stupid!"

"I know! I told you I—"

"No, not that. It's stupid because these last couple months I've been so jealous of you and Zasha." Reece took a moment before explaining, "Like you guys are always together, going on drives and visiting each other at work, and you're even planning to move to London together after Uni. It's a lot."

This seemed to make Amy smile. Through everything, it was nice to know that she wasn't alone, and she wasn't the only one missing a friend. "Well, fair enough," Amy laughed. "Maybe we could share them a little bit more?"

"Yeah, definitely."

Ceasefire was called just in time for Zasha to walk back into the room and cosy up under the blankets. "What did I miss?" she asked, turning to Reece and seeing the toothy grin on her face.

"You can't see Amy anymore."

PRETENTIOUS

"So, you're serious about this?" Reece asked, in a deeper tone than usual, trying to cover up her excitement.

"Well yeah, I can't let you go alone! You know what you're like!" Jackson laughed, shaking his head slowly.

"Hmm..." Once more, Reece tried to conceal her hysteria but failed seconds later. "Okay! Thank you, thank you!" she shrieked, throwing herself onto Jackson's lap to wrap her arms around his neck, refusing to let go until she felt the hug reciprocated.

"Alright, alright, go call her!" Jackson could feel the energy through her skin like an electric shock, and he was pretty sure he could hear the static.

"Okay, I'm calling her now. This is so exciting!"

"What's her name again?"

"Latika."

Latika was Reece's oldest friend from when she lived in Oxford. They met when they were both just 10 years old when Reece's family had moved schools for the 6th time.

Latika was a small soft girl, with brilliant dark brown hair that bounced in plaited waves. Her skin was chocolate, though the lightest in her family, and her lips plump and full. When they met, Latika would wear black square glasses, though as she got older, she transitioned into wearing contacts revealing her round golden eyes. Next to her brothers, Latika stood out like basil in a spice drawer, as she was short and beautiful, where her brothers were large and plain.

Reece hadn't lived in England for over 4 years at this point, though they stayed in touch, visiting each other when they could over summers and calling when they could, to update on gossip, news, and general breakdowns, most of the contents including either: Reece's horrific track record with guys or yet another incident where Latika's strict parents had overreacted and/or fought about something irrelevant.

However, the last call was juicier than usual, with Latika explaining how one of her brothers had gotten engaged to a girl no one knew he had been dating for the past 2 years. *Scandalous stuff.* And so, upon discovering the news, both families had arranged for a wedding to take place in Kerala, India, the birthplace of the bride to be, leading to the reason for the current call.

"Latika!" Reece called out, pacing up and down her room, Jackson watching from her bed, holding a large soft toy in the shape of a highland cow.

"Hello, my love! How are you?"

The sound of Latika's voice echoing through the speaker, Jackson playing close attention to her accent, wondering when the New Delhi charm would kick in.

"All sweet. I was actually calling about something kinda weird."

"Go on..."

"Well, you know how you've always said that if I ever wanted to come with you when you go to India that I could—"

"Oh my god, Reece! Is this going where I think it's going?" The excitement in her voice was as clear as a white wine spritzer.

"Well...I was wondering... if I could come with you to your brother's wedding?"

"What! Yes! Yes! Yes!" Latika shrieked, her perfectly British accent making it clear to Jackson that he might actually have to go to India to hear what he's looking for.

"Really?"

"Of course, you idiot! What—like how—when did you decide this?"

"Uhh, a couple of days ago, actually. I was just thinking about how cool it would be to be there with you. I haven't seen you in so long, and this year has been mental. And then you told me about your brother, and look, I know it's his wedding, and it's completely fine if he doesn't—"

"What are you on about? Gurl, you know you're part of the family; he'd love to have you there! Don't be stupid... I just feel bad."

"Oh, why?"

"Well, because of Indian traditions and all that, the sister of the groom has to do all the planning and rituals and stuff. So, me and my family are actually travelling up a couple weeks early to prepare. So, I wouldn't be able to travel with you."

Reece took a deep breath, side glancing Jackson, who was sat up and listening intently. "Yeah, I thought so, which is actually why I was hoping I could bring someone with me, so I wouldn't have to travel alone, also—"

"So, you wouldn't be the only white person—"

"Yeah, that too."

"Ha! Thought so, who you thinking?"

"Jackson. He's actually here now if you wanna talk to him."

"Fuck yes!"

The two didn't talk for long at all, blaming it on the 'signal' and 'bad weather' as the two ping-ponged back and forth with, "Huh?" and, "Reece, what did he say?" It was a nightmare. Latika having an issue with the lack of syllables in Jackson's sentences and Jackson being too distracted that an Indian girl sounded like a roadman.

"This is pointless," Jackson sighed, saying goodbye to Latika as clearly as possible before handing the phone back to Reece, and picking up the toy once more to hold to his chest.

"Listen, we probably gotta start looking for flights, but we'll talk more later?"

"Yeah, okay, eek! This is so exciting, okay, talk later. Bye-eee!" Latika exclaimed, stressing the 'eee's in a joyful shriek before ending the call.

"*So?*" Reece sang, taking a step towards the bed.

"*So* what?"

"She's cool, right!"

"Ha, yeah. She's dead on. How'd you say her name again?"

"Latika"

"Lah-tee-kah!" Jackson repeated in his best British accent. Lowering his register an octave and swagging his shoulders with each sound.

"What is *that*!" Reece laughed, copying his attempt.

"That's how she speaks! Bit of a smick like, a British smick—which is so much worse!"

"She's not a smick! And we call them 'chavs' by the way."

"Nah, smick is right. My name's Lah-tee-kah!"

"Stop that."

"Lah-tee-kah!"

"No."

"Lah-tee-kah, Lah-tee-kah, Lah-tee-kah!"

"I give up."

The news travelled fast of the two's plans, and it's fair to say the reactions were a mixed bag.

Zasha - Thanks for the fucking invite.

River - You're going *where* with *him*?

Amy - Right.

Damian - Yo! Thats sounds incredible!

Nora - Ok. Will, have you seen my charger?

Will - You two are gonna get it *awn*! Nora, it's right *there*!

Phil - I've actually been to India before, so...

However different the responses were, all the holiday talk sent the flat into a flight-finding frenzy, with Amy spearheading the search.

"Right, Vienna for £132 return!"

It was one of those rare moments; usually reserved for public holidays; that all 8 members of the flat had convened to the living room in Flat 6. Christmas had passed after all, and the group had not received a government fine for anything, so this occasion was a gem indeed.

You also might have noticed that Flat 6 was always the preferable location in situations such as these. They had heating, fully functioning lights and their floor was completely clear of unexplainable pools of water, a luxury they took for granted.

"So, it's on this Thursday in the Brien Friel Theatre," Zasha explained, perched on the top of the one-seater sofa, her legs resting on the arm.

"I'm sorry, I blanked out. What is?" Reece blinked her eyes down hard to wake herself up. She had been sat next to River explaining his thesis on 'second-person pros' for the past half an hour and was struggling as it is.

"My play! *'Blossoms'*, remember?"

"Ah, yes. Yes, of course, I'll be there."

"Good. Everyone else?" Zasha scanned the room, taking in turns to make threatening eye contact with each and every member, taking a few extra seconds on River, who still had not stopped talking; despite no one listening. "River?" she asked, her eyebrows punched upwards on the beat.

"What? Yes, dude, I'm there, 100%."

Zasha nodded. *Next.* "Amy?"

"Hmm?" Amy was sat on the opposite sofa to Reece and River next to Nora. Nora had been showing Amy some digital art she had been working on, and Amy had been trying her best not to mention the similarities of 2004 clipart. "Oh right. What's the play about again?"

Zasha instantly became animated, her pupils dilating in excitement and passion. "Well, it's all based on a rape case from last year—" she began, her volume and subject pricking the ears of Will and Jackson, who had been standing in the kitchen corner discussing 'Galactic Football'. "Y'know, the girl that was raped by those rugby players?"

Zasha spoke of an unnerving trial that took place in the early months of 2018, where a Belfast woman had reported being sexually assaulted by 3 different Ulster Rugby Players at Mason Jackson's house after they had returned from a night out. 9 weeks and 4 cross-examinations later, the defence was found not guilty due to insufficient evidence for non-consensual activity, yet the case remains one of Ireland's most speculated trials.

"Well, the play is all about rape culture, and it targets victim shaming and toxic masculinity," she explained proudly, though she was disheartened by the male unease in the room.

Damian especially, blushing hot red flames at the word.

"You see how you're feeling right now, that's how we are going to make every man feel in that audience. It's brutal."

"Sounds epic, can't wait," River applauded, holding his gaze long enough with Zasha that he too, began to blush.

"Jackson?" Zasha asked next, with as much authority as she could muster.

"What?"

"You're coming."

"Why? It's a student play, I'm not a student."

"So? You could really benefit from hearing what we have to say. Men like *you*—"

"Men like *me*? What does that even mean?"

"I just think it would be in your best interest to—"

"No, thanks."

"What the fuck, Jackson!" This angered Zasha incredibly, and she turned to catch the reactions of the others, hoping that they would share her frustration, but no one cared enough to try. "Will, you'll come, right?"

"Are you going to tell me, I '*have* to'?" There was a cold sternness to his words and a thin icy glare in his eyes. He had been waiting for Zasha to address him since the conversation came up and was glad it unravelled in this manner, his abruptness taking Zasha by surprise.

"Uh, no?"

"Then no, I'm good."

"You're *good*? What the fuck is going on?" Zasha was laughing a little, once again looking around to see if anyone else shared her bitter confusion.

"I'm busy," Will cut back, cracking his neck.

"Busy doing what?"

"Do I need to tell you?"

This made Zasha laugh even more. "I'm sorry? What the fuck is wrong with you?" she mocked, throwing up her hands.

"Why does something have to be wrong?"

The two continued to play this game for quite some time, with Zasha becoming more and more agitated and Will continuing to deflect in nonchalant passphrases.

"What's all that about?" River leant over and whispered to Reece, but she just shook her head, and the group remained quiet until finally, Will snapped.

"I just don't see why you always have to throw your opinions in people's faces. I get enough of that here; you don't expect me to spend my free time listening to it, do you?"

"Ha! Wow, see *this* is why 'Blossoms' is needed, for little boys like you who don't like being told 'no'."

And with that, Will sighed and confessed, "I, don't even know how to respond to that." And he left, shaking his head on the way out. The room stayed still for a moment, Zasha's mocking snigger being the only sound until Nora broke the tension.

"It's also a good time because abortion is being made legal in Northern Ireland."

"About fucking time!" River exclaimed.

Others such as Amy and Damian chiming along too, with Zasha adding, "Exactly! It's a fucking joke it's taken until 2019!"

"Yeah, right?"

"It truly is a failure of a democratic society to have to have waited this long," River stated proudly. Others taking the opportunity to voice their appraise, asides from Reece, who had purposely kept quiet through all of this, though her silence was noted and addressed instantly. "You're being a bit quiet there, Kiddo," River pointed out; a long smirk drawn on his face. "Got something to say?"

With this, the room fell silent once more, the other girls especially turning their attention to Reece and wearing the same scorn. Reece could feel the judgement already, and still, she bit her tongue.

"Well? It's not like anyone could disagree." River was baiting her, and she knew it, and she would have remained passive if she didn't sense the cruel delight River took in cornering her.

So, she took a breath, looked him straight back in the eye, and said—with as little emotion as possible— "It's going to be a sad day when that law is abolished."

And all hell broke loose.

"What the fuck!" Zasha shrieked.

"So, you think women shouldn't have the right to their own body!" Nora scoffed.

"That's so fucked up," Amy judged, covering her face with her hand.

"Fucking hell, Kid!" River exclaimed, pretending to be shocked but still smirking from ear to ear, asking, "well, tell us, please! I'd like to know."

Once more, Reece took a breath. She could see the fumes airing from Zasha's nostrils and wondered whether the Landlord had fixed the fire alarms. "It's murder. What do you want me to say?"

"It's not fucking *murder!*" Zasha mocked.

"Ah yes, thank you. I was soo wrong—3 seconds ago. I'm glad you corrected me." Reece quipped back, only enraging the mob further.

"How is it murder? Tell me! I'm *dying* to know." River was on fire.

"Despite when you believe life starts—"

"Oh, and I'm guessing you're one of these nutters that think 'life starts at conception'?" he interrupted, knowing fully well she was indeed one of 'those nutters'.

"Hmm," Reece calmly sighed before repeating, "I said, *despite* when you believe life starts. If the law is abolished, abortions will be able to take place as late as 24 weeks."

"Your point?"

"River, babies have been born at 24 weeks, and they have a fully developed heart, limbs, and nervous systes—"

"Yes, but not every woman is going to have an abortion at 24 weeks. Most abortions take place within the first trimester... When they're just a bunch of cells."

"So, I must support a law that only kills children *some* of the time?"

"It's not fucking *murder!*" Zasha shouted once again, shaking her head. "And even so, what—you're going to tell me that even in rape cases, you wouldn't allow the girl to terminate the pregnancy?"

"Yeah, or what if the child is disabled?" Damian added.

"Or if the parents couldn't take care of the baby?" Amy piled on.

"Again. You're asking me to base my support on the minority of situations." For a split second, Reece had their attention and didn't intend on backing down. "In every pro-choice argument, the most unfortunate cases are brought up; and you're right, cases like rape and child disabilities are awful, but they do not justify abortion being legalised on the whole. And after all that, if you still can't understand why, I'm against abortion. You have the intelligence of a potted plant."

A single second of silence passed before—

"Yeah, I think I speak for all of us when I say we've had enough of your bullshit 'Christian propaganda,'" River spat. "Do you really think I'd be pro-abortion if it was the killing of children? No. It's a lethal injection into a group of cells. It's humane. They feel nothing. It's *not* a baby!" River was joined by the nodding of heads around the room.

And with a straight face, Reece stood up from the couch and walked to the door, sighing. "Think what you like. But River?"

"What?"

"Why would the injection have to be *humane*, if the baby wasn't alive to feel it?" With that, Reece turned and left, catching Jackson's worried gaze on the way out.

The remaining 5 took little time to reflect before rehashing it all again.

"I actually can't believe that!" Nora scoffed.

"Pfft. Will wants to talk about people shoving their opinions down your throat. He should have been here for *that!*" Zasha laughed.

"Fuck me dead, that was a lot!" River gasped, another high-pitched shrieked laughter escaping his lips, causing him to throw his hands over his mouth.

"It's funny what you learn about people when you live with them," Amy joked but was instantly silenced when Jackson scolded her.

"You're kidding, right?" The 5 of them now turned to Jackson and watched as he strolled through the middle of the room to the door.

"What?"

"Each to their own or whatever, like I'm pro-choice too. But man, you asked her, didn't you?" he said, now looking at River, but before he could answer, Jackson continued, "and no harm like, but if you're not *man* enough to listen and respect a different opinion, then that's on you." Jackson watched the smirk on River's face fade into a snarl, next looking down at Damian, who was sitting cross-legged between the two sofas. "And man, don't you have a disabled friend?"

"Wait, that's uncalled for!" River blurted, his eyes darting between Jackson and Damian.

"Yeah, that's why—"

"Just saying."

"No! I just meant if you could know and decide, you—" Before Damian could finish, Jackson was already out the door, and he slowly lost the confidence to continue.

There was a different atmosphere in the room after Jackson left, it was hard to come back after being told-off, and they all felt some-what embarrassed.

Back in Reece's room, Reece was sitting on her bed in the dark, her knees tucked into her chest and her black hood covering her eyes. She was wearing the same grey slippers

Damian had gotten her for Christmas and a pair of River's chequered pyjama bottoms; they were way too big and were being held up with his nightgown tie, both of which he hadn't noticed were missing.

Walking into the darkness, Jackson loudly sighed; the room was dimly lit by the orange street lights that escaped through the borders of her blinds, just enough that Jackson could tell Reece was crying. Moving slowly, as if not to startle her, Jackson sat in the middle of the bed, his back pressing against the wall behind him.

"You, okay?" he asked, tilting his head and watching the single tear fall down her cheek.

"Yes."

"You're not okay."

"I *am* okay."

"You're not—are we really going to do this?"

"...Yes."

Jackson laughed, "Why didn't you just tell them to fuck off? You have to start sticking up for yourself."

"I know, I just—"

"No, you're too nice. You have to start thinking like me."

Reece lifted her head from her knees, "Oh yeah? How's that?"

"Well, you gotta start thinking 'are they my friends, *because* they're my friends? Or are they my friends because it's *convenient*?" His words sparked terror in her eyes.

"Are you saying we're just—"

"Some of you are. Like River and Zasha, for instance, we live together, so it would be *inconvenient* not to be friends."

"And me?"

Jackson tilted his head, a boyish smile on his face. "What do you mean 'and me'?"

"Am I your friend for convenience?"

Sighing, rolling his eyes, and brushing the hair out of her face, Jackson leant in teasing, "I don't get into bar fights for just anyone."

Reece's smile punched into her cheeks, and a warmth flushed across her face.

"Right!" he announced. "I've done the friendly thing and checked on you. Now I gotta get ready for a date."

"A date? It's like 11pm. With who?"

"Amy."

"What!"

COLD

Like clockwork, the early January frost was followed by the late January snowfall, coating the streets in a thick white fluff. The snow so glossy you could mistake it for icing, and the snow so thick, the shorter pedestrians were cut off at the knees. The few cars that were permanently parked outside the flat resembled large snowballs, and Amy was less than impressed with the time it took to emerge from the mound.

"If I didn't look so good in these boots, I'd hate the snow," she moaned, sludging through the white mass on the way to her car and using her long forearm to clear the windshield.

Will watched from the pavement; arms folded as he shuffled in place to keep warm. He was wearing a large yellow quarter-zip jacket, made from rough, dry material; his hood pulled up and pulled taught around the chin so that only the centre of his face was visible. "Can't see why you would hate it. I'm having a great time!" he mocked, now jumping up and down, creating a crater in the snow around his feet.

"Hmm."

Opening the car door, Amy could hear the trapped ice in the crevice of the handle break, and small shards fell into her leather gloved hands. "Eurgh." Wiping them off on her black riding coat and stepping inside the car, she looked back at Will. He was laughing. "Why are you laughing?" she asked, frown already loading.

"Heh-heh, I just didn't know you were a horse-girl!" he teased, his lips turned down in the corners, his eyebrows raised.

Very few in the flat knew that Amy was indeed a 'horse-girl', but if you had asked, Amy would have told you she has been riding for many years, even entering competitions across the country. Though one had recently been cancelled due to the weather; and had even joined the QUB Equestrian society, but that was a sore subject as Amy had been waiting over a year for an embroidered jacket. She even had a horse of her own, a beautiful black mere named Bella, which she tried to ride at least once a month when there was an open slot at the stables, all of which adding to the mocking Jackson would give, calling her a "Privileged protestant."

"Fuck up!" Amy snapped, turning the key in the ignition and pulling off from the drive; the bundles of snow that had been delicately resting on the roof, flying off the edge and spreading into a powdered mist behind her.

Waiting until Amy's little red car was out of sight and laughing to himself as she once again misread the one-way sign, Will turned to head back into the flat, making sure to triple check the front lock. Walking up the stairwell, Will could hear Reece's distinctive laugh from the Flat 6's lounge.

"Would you just keep still!" Jackson yelled, trying to take a photo of Reece's profile against the blank wall.

"I'm sorry!" she giggled, her face contorting in odd ways to try to subdue the hysterics.

"It's really not that funny."

"I know! I don't know why—okay, I'm good. Go now," she said, her face finally relaxed and unmoving, that is, until the flash from Jackson's phone made her blink.

"Fuck's sake, Reece!"

"Urgh! I'm sorry! Take it again. I promise I'm ready!"

This carried on until Will came back into the room, and all laughing and smiling ceased. Instantly there was a weight in the room, one that can only be described as a heavy bitterness. "What are you guys doing?" Will asked, his face straight and the lack of song in his words.

Reece clenched her jaw, looking back at Jackson for some kind of cover.

"Uhh, we have to take some photos for the visa application," Jackson answered back plainly.

"Ah, for India?"

"Yeah."

"Exciting stuff." Will nodded, still standing in the doorway, unsure if he was welcome any further in.

The tension was no shock to anyone involved, as just days before this, an argument had broken out between the two flats when Nora had let it slip to Reece that all in Flat 6 had decided to live together again in the upcoming year. Which was all well and good, that is, until Will spoke out, saying that Reece's 'messiness' was the reason for her not being included in the grouping.

Zasha and River also didn't make the 'cut' as their constant fighting and melodrama had caused a strain on poor Will, and Damian had already stated he would not be living with Jackson due to some conflicting opinions on 'drugs in the flat'; meaning, he was excluded by default.

"Are we good?" Reece asked Jackson with a degree of urgency, motioning to the photos on his phone.

"Yeah. You're all set."

"Okay, uhh, we'll complete the application later?"

Jackson nodded back, smiling just enough to warrant one in return before she left, keeping her eyes pinned to the floor as she passed by Will and his bright yellow coat.

A moment of silence passed before Will let out a loud, exhausting sigh. The answer was obvious, yet still, he asked, "She doesn't like me very much right now, does she?"

Jackson sighed too, walking from the corner wall to the sofa, slumping down into the worn-out leather. "She's not your biggest fan, but she'll get over it."

Seeing the olive-branch, Will sat down next to Jackson, folding his long leg over the other in a perfect right angle. "I said my piece. It is what it is."

Upstairs, River was still in bed, he hadn't made it into class for weeks, so at this point, it was only natural to wake late into the afternoon. Stretching his long thin arms above his head and waiting for the routine crack in his neck, he let out a loud moan, vaguely resembling the sound of a kitchen appliance starting up.

"Shhh," Zasha moaned, headfirst into the pillow next to him, her hand flapping above her head to motion him 'quieting down'.

River looked at the top of her bare shoulders that were visible above the covers and smiled. Once again, his doe eyes scanned the floor and caught sight of the square pink wrapper that had been thrown to the ground late last night, wondering what this all meant. But before he could question it, Zasha yawned once more, turning onto her back and looking up at him, smiling.

"Morning," he whispered, knowing fully well it was nowhere near morning, but deciding, "afternoon" didn't sound as sweet.

"Hmm, hey," she cooed, her blue eyes blinking slowly as she sat up.

"Listen, Zaz, I think—"

"Shhh," she commanded once more, pressing her fingers to his lips, unintentionally but seductively, nonetheless. "This is good," she whispered, nodding her head ever so slightly.

"*This?*"

"*This.*" Zasha took a second, taking a short sharp breath and continuing on the inhale, "I think I love you, River." As the words were released, Zasha felt a swarm of butterflies in the pit of her empty stomach. She watched as River's face blushed a fierce deep red, and his jaw drop just enough to remain cute.

"I, uhh. I'm gonna make you some tea!" he squealed, just short of falling out of bed and scrambling for his robe. This made Zasha laugh, calling him a "Dork" as he jaggedly kissed her on the forehead and darted out the room. Zasha hearing the quick excited footsteps all the way down.

In the kitchen, River paced with jittering excitement and impending worry. Both Reece and Damian were in the lounge watching his nervous behaviour, both equally confused.

"Okay, what's happening here?" Reece asked, her five fingers stretched out and motioning in a circle in River's direction.

"Yeah, you don't look okay," Damian pointed out, side glancing at Reece, hoping for some telepathic answers.

"I uhh...Ha!" River squealed like a teapot on a stove. "Zasha, she—"

"Oh no," Reece sighed from the bottom of her voice, thinking, *he must have found out.*

"What has she done *now*?" Damian sighed in a breathy exhale, wondering how many hours he will have to spend this time, listening to the two go back in fourth in the same overplayed argument.

"Zasha said she loved me," River finally confessed, dropping from where he stood into a crossed knee on the floor, large teacup in hand.

"Oh!" This was worse than Reece could have imagined. "But I thought you two were just gonna stay friends?"

"We were! But then last night we were hanging out, and things just kinda escalated, and now today... It's all just wild!" River's eyes remained fixed on the lounge door, cutting in-between Reece and Damian on either couch.

"Well, maybe this is a good thing!" Damian cheered. "If she's saying all that, maybe she's ready for a relation—"

"Yuergh!" Reece blurted out, cutting Damian off.

"What?"

Reece panicked, knowing fully well, Zasha was not ready for a relationship but knowing it wasn't her place to say why.

"Kid?" River asked a strain of worry in his voice.

Taking a second to think, Reece took a breath, curling her knees under the green blanket on the couch and twiddling her thumbs beneath it. "I just think, before you jump into anything, you have to find out exactly what she means, like, exactly what page she's on, y'know?"

This seemed to confuse River more. "What do you mean? Surely if she's saying, 'I love you,' that means she—"

"River, please. Just make sure."

With that, River nodded, "Okay, I will," before getting up to finish the cup of tea and leaving to return to Zasha upstairs.

"It's *Wednesday*!" Damian exclaimed after River was out of sight.

"Ja!" Reece cheered back, paying little attention to why it was brought up.

"Want to go to Subway? I'll pay!"

And instantly, there was a weight on Reece's chest and a sickening feeling in her stomach. She remembered what Jackson said on the curb that night and felt an overwhelming sense of guilt. "I uhh, actually can't today. I have some work to catch up on," she said softly, her eyes pointed down at her lap.

Damian could tell something was wrong but couldn't remember the last time he saw Reece actually do any work, so the mentioned 'catchup' was deemed necessary. "Oh, okay, no worries, no worries. I'm gonna head up anyway and get myself some grub. Want me to pick you up anything?"

Damian was selfless, sincere, and had a heart of gold, bigger and more precious than many Reece knew. "Nah, I'm good, thanks though."

"Okay."

Within the minutes River had left, Zasha had dressed herself in one of his large blue t-shirts and was sitting in a pair of his shorts, phone in hand, texting.

Opening the door slowly so that the hinge's creak was bearable, River re-entered the room, cup of hot tea in hand. It was a Lapsang souchong type of tea that made Reece giggle whenever mentioned; but apart from green tea, it was Zasha's favourite; River being more on an 'Earl Grey' man himself; surprising to no one.

"Here you are," River beamed, handing the cup to Zasha, more collected than his last appearance.

"Aw, thank you, babies," she said, taking the cup and putting it straight on the windowsill to finish her text.

"Who you talking to?" River asked quizzically, releasing quickly that perhaps he would sound overbearing unless he added, "your mum?" afterwards.

Without a beat, Zasha answered, "Just a friend," before putting the phone face down into the sheets and reaching back for her tea.

Within the hour, Jackson had found Reece sitting alone on the empty stairwell, watching the falling snow from the corner window. Her hair was tied, which it rarely was, into a black wavy bun on the apex of her head. This took Jackson by surprise; her face looked so different without the large amount of hair covering the sides of her face, making him think, *she should wear her hair like this more often*. "Reece?" he called down the stairs, startling her.

"Oh, hey."

"Want to go on a walk?"

Without words, Reece's face brightened, and she nodded her head.

Despite the snow, ice, and typical Belfast climate, it wasn't cold. Reece felt perfectly happy skipping outside in the snow with nothing more than a chequered shirt and ripped jeans tucked into tan hiking boots.

Jackson however, no matter how warm and happy, would not be skipping, choosing to instead, broodingly wade through the snow, hands tucked tightly into the pockets of his beige corduroy jacket, the one with the white fur collar.

The streets themselves were already spoiled, the dirt and grime from turning car wheels leaving a trail of brown sludge down the road, the pavements looking worse for wears as crowds of students had traipsed through, leaving all kinds of footprints. The two walked until they reached the front of the Queens University building, the Lanyon Building. The outside lawn being one of the few untouched places in the area.

"I love the snow," Reece exhaled, her smile as bright and wide as the acre of unsullied snow, stopping just before the border to not ruin it.

"Yeah," Jackson agreed, taking out his phone and filming her as she danced and twirled in the blizzard.

"What are you doing?" she laughed, her arms stretched out and her mouth open to catch the snowflakes on her tongue.

"You're in 4K!" he yelled, feeling the wind at the back of his neck pick up. However, his excitement quickly faded when his phone notified him of 'no more space', and he was reminded why he didn't film in 4K more often. Putting his phone back into his pocket, he waited until Reece tired herself out, slowly turning back around to face him.

"What?" she asked, noticing the seriousness of his pose, his shoulders were pulled back and taught, exaggerating his wingspan, and his chin was lifted and flexed.

"What have you decided to do about next year?" he asked, his eyes blinking as drops of snow fell into them.

Reece hadn't given it much thought, perhaps too embarrassed to even think about it after her scolding from Will. "I uhh, don't really know. I'll probably see what the others are doing."

As she said this, she noticed Damian walking on the other side of the road, Subway bag in hand. He had noticed her and had kept eye contact until he walked out of sight. Even from afar, Reece could see the anger and confusion on his face as he watched her with Jackson. "Oh, crap," Reece sighed, biting her lower lip and feeling the same sickness as before.

"What?"

"Damian saw me."

"So?"

"*So*? I told him I couldn't go to Subway with him because I was busy, and now he's just seen me out here with you!"

"Why'd you say *that*?"

Reece shot Jackson a look of, "You know why," but Jackson remained cold.

"You know you can't live with him, right?"

"No, it won't—"

"You know you can't," he repeated. Reece scoffed at this, turning out of his eye line and kicking at the snow in front of her. "You know I'm right." He could see the side of Reece's lip point upwards as if she was about to snarl.

"This is all your fault," she mumbled.

"What?"

"This is all your fault!"

Jackson's laugh was caught short when he realised that Reece was actually angry. "You're kidding, right?" he mocked, standing taller than ever.

"No! This *is* your fault. If you hadn't of told me, everything would have been fine!"

"Fuck would it 'be fine'. If I hadn't told you, you'd still be stringing that boy along, you—"

"What!" Jackson's words made Reece furious. "I wasn't 'stringing him along' I never did anything to—"

"You have that boy wrapped around your finger, and you know it!" Jackson shouted, watching as Reece took her small claws and dug them into the snow, her fist curling over a ball, fingers squeezing it until it was hard like stone. "You serious?" Jackson mocked once more, his question answered when Reece threw the ball of snow towards him, the icy rock hitting him at the top of his chest. "Ah—ow!" he winced, becoming angry himself. "What the fuck was—"

"Stop saying *that*! All you did was ruin things and make things awkward between us! You had no need—"

"Ha!" Jackson laughed, brushing the snowy debris from his chest and taking a step towards her. "If it wasn't for me, you'd actually be planning to live with him right now, and you'd only prolong the awkwardness because he'd end up telling you, and you'd have to deal with all this to his face! I gave you a way out!"

"Eurgh!" Reece screamed, releasing another snowball and watching it hurdle towards Jackson, this time hitting into his left shoulder.

"Would you stop that!"

"You hypocrite!" she yelled, viciously kicking the snow at her feet towards him.

"Why am I—?"

"You're living with *Amy*!"

Jackson paused at this, taken back by her confrontation. "That's not the same," he mumbled back, eyes now gingerly pinned to his feet, shoulders slumped back to their normal position.

"*How* is it not? You know how she feels!"

Jackson shook his head, teeth chewing on his inside cheek. "I'm never telling you anything again."

"Ha!" Now Reece was laughing. "You didn't need to! Anyone with half a brain cell could have figured it out!"

"What? How?"

"Oh my gosh!" she exclaimed, her hands scrunching into her hair, making it wilder than ever. "You're only living with us because of her, to start!"

"Jee, thanks."

"Shhh, you know this is before I knew you," she assured gently before continuing, "she can't stand you talking about other girls! She didn't speak to you for a week when she found out about the other Amy" —a pretty blonde Irish teacher from Tinder— "and then there was that thing with you calling her 'ugly'—"

"I did *not* call her—"

"She hasn't been the same with *me* since we started hanging out—"

"That's because—"

"And I'm pretty sure if you had given her an inch, she would have broken up with Callum by now for you!" Reece yelled, watching Jackson's face twitch, his eyes lighting up. "What is—"

"Think I could give her more than an *inch*, like!" he screamed, having to turn away and hold his stomach as he laughed, his whole-body cramping.

"You're an idiot!" Reece screamed back, unamused and kicking more snow at him until there was an empty well at her feet.

Jackson was like this for some time, running in circles like a child, bopping his head as he did.

"You're such a hypocrite," Reece sighed once more, with a final attempt to throw a snowball at him, this time with it crashing into the side of his face.

Jackson stopped running, his whole body froze, and his eyes narrowed.

Well, crap, she thought, watching; as if in slow motion, Jackson turn towards her, his feet dug into the snow like a charging bull, and run towards her, lifting her off the ground and tackling her deep into the perfect snow on the lawn. A loud 'pfff' of white powder erupting from beneath them and dissipating into the air as they hit the ground.

Jackson caught his breath, the contrast between the cold snow around him and Reece's warmth below him sending pins and needles through his skin. He looked down; Reece was speechless, her lips parted, but no words formed. Her hair had fallen out of the grip in the attack and was sprawled out onto the snow, some strands covering her face. He looked into her eyes; he had never seen them like this before; he had always thought they were brown. But here, the daylight brightened the deep green pigment in them.

"Are your eyes green?" he asked quizzically before being pushed with a great force into the grass beside him with a grunted, "Urgh!"

The two lay there, like dead angels, both looking up at the blue sky, watching the tiny white flakes fall around them. Both catching their breath, feeling the snow beneath them melt into their hair and clothes, but for a moment, neither of them cared.

"I probably shouldn't go on this Malta trip with her then, right?" Jackson asked, turning his head to face hers.

"Wait, what Malta trip?"

"Amy booked a trip to Malta for me, her, and Zasha in February. She said she invited everyone... You didn't know?"

Reece shook her head, unsurprised at this point.

"She's also booked for us to go to Berlin in March, and she said something about just me and her going to Belgium to visit our friend Ethan in April."

"Wow. She made plans for a June wedding too? How are you affording all these trips anyway?" she questioned, knowing fully well there's no way his new job at the Spar would cover it.

"Oh, I'm not. Amy's paying."

Without words, Reece rolled over towards him, her small fist plummeting deep into Jackson's arm, causing him to cry out, "Ow! Reece! What the fuck?"

"Such a hypocrite!"

MARTYR

Less than a week had passed since Zasha's, "I love you," and River still hadn't found the right time to question her about it. "Things are just really good right now, y'know?" he said, looking up at Damian on the other side of the bed.

"Hmm?" Damian had been trying to finish up a piece of coursework for the last hour but found it hard to concentrate with River's incessant talking.

"Zasha," River reiterated. "I want to ask her about the whole 'I love you thing,' but I don't want to mess anything up."

"Oh! Right, yeah," Damian agreed, looking up over the top of his computer screen to meet River's gaze with an affirming head nod before returning to his paragraph.

"And there's no way I could misinterpret that, right? Like, you don't just go around saying that to people!"

"Uh-huh."

"I don't know...May-bee she meant it like a friend? But then you wouldn't say that to a *friend* straight after sex."

"Definitely not."

"This is buck-wild!" River screeched, laughing loud and high enough to startle an already anxious Damian. "I can't believe my biggest problem right now is a girl saying she loves me!"

With that, Damian gave up, closing the lid of his laptop and sliding it off his lap, his fingers intertwining in its place. "I think you should do what Reece said and just ask her about it," Damian suggested coldly. Reece, being a sore subject since he saw her and Jackson outside Queens.

"Yeah, but things could get awkward and—" River paused, noticing the defeat in Damian's eyes. "Oh, Bud," he sighed. "How are you doing with all *that* anyway?"

Damian took a moment, taking a deep breath, trying to keep his face as neutral as possible, but the boy wore his heart on his sleeve, and it wasn't long before he cracked. "I just don't get it!" he started. "I don't know what I did! One day we're friends, the next day, she's avoiding me and hanging out with fucking—Jackson—and it's all just messed up."

River bit his tongue. He had known for some time that Reece 'knew' after she confided in him about what Jackson had told her. And he hated Jackson for telling her. "Do you think she *knows*?" River baited, testing the waters like an ice pick on a frozen lake.

"No. No way," Damian said confidently.

There was a lull of silence between the two, River thinking that if he was ever going to tell him, it would be now...And deciding against it. "You know, you should really move your TV into the lounge."

"What?"

"It would be a great way to bring the flat together!" River exclaimed positively, confused as to why his suggestion was met with a very stern and unbudging, "No."

"Ha, alright there, Buckeroo, a bit selfish, but you do you, I guess."

"Please leave."

Like a rebuked child, River left the room, sulking downstairs into the lounge, looking at the space between the two walls thinking, *a TV would look great there,* before cheering himself up with a cup of tea and Weetabix minis. Just as he was pouring the milk, River heard a strange scraping sound coming from the other side of the front door. Putting the milk jug down, he stepped into the corridor to listen closer. River could see shadows moving from under the door and the low rumble of men's voices. River's first thought was to call Reece, but she was out with Jackson babysitting his sisters for the day, and everyone else he was currently on good terms with was in the next flat.

In a state of panic, River leaped up the stairs and barged once more into Damian's room. "Damian! There's men outside the door. I think they're trying to—"

Hearing this, Damian leapt out of bed and into action, his short quick legs jotting down the staircase to the front door, River making sure to keep a few steps behind.

Taking a deep breath and holding it at the top of the inhale as a last effort to grow in posture, Damian unlatched the lock and pulled the door open.

Behind the door stood three large foreign men dressed in dark clothing and one wearing a ski mask and holding a long metal rod. The two without a mask had dark wired beards and large flaring nostrils. The man in disguise seemed to be a lot fairer, with light brown eyebrows and lighter eyes.

Damian braced himself for a struggle, trying to think of any and every combo attack on Apex Predators, thinking, *why the hell don't I own a volt!*

But to his surprise, upon seeing the little gatekeeper, the three men turned and fled down the stairs, shouting something in a language neither Damian nor River understood.

Running down after them, Damian called out, "Yeah! You—get to fuck—you...fuckers!" Waiting until they were out of sight before closing both doors behind him.

River was still sitting perched on the middle stair, his long fingers cupped over his mouth in horror. "Who were they? Should we call the Police?"

"Some Romanian twats, I think...Pretty sure one of them was holding a crowbar!"

"Fucking hell!" River gasped. Until this point, River had been considering living alone for his final year of Uni, though after this, he decided that he—to some extent—liked life, and either needed a flatmate, or a gym membership. "Hey, Bud," River perked up, joining Damian at the bottom of the stairs. "Want to live together next year?"

"Yeah, alright."

Later that evening, Reece returned from babysitting with Jackson and had met up with River in his room, who was more than excited to tell of his life-threatening day.

"And I swear, he wanted to kill me!" River exclaimed, tucking himself into bed next to Reece and passing her the squishy yellow 'duck' for her to hold.

"He's got a point, though," she laughed, nuzzling into place.

"What do you mean?"

"It's *his* TV!"

"Hmm." River rolled his eyes, opening his laptop on his lap and thinking how small it looked compared to Damian's 30inch flat screen.

"So, what we watching?" Reece asked, leaning over to rest her head on the side of his chest. Smiling, River wrapped his left arm around her, squeezing her a little before suggesting, "... We could watch the 'Goofy-Movie'?"

"What?"

"Look. It's actually *insanely* good. There's a musical track in this film that is actually heart-breaking. And the relationship between the dad and the son is—"

"Hu-wiugh!" Reece pretended to throw up, making a disgusting retching sound that River, well, found disgusting.

"First of all. Hate that. You know I do. And second of all, you have the worst taste in films! And you're a film student!"

"I do *not*!"

"You hated 'Notting Hill'!"

"Uhh, yeah, because that film had the worst soundtrack, every character was annoying, wimpy, and soppy. And it—"

"*Worst. Film. Student. Ever*," River repeated, looking down at her little scrunched face. "Okay, no Goofy Movie, but you will watch that with me one day."

"Hmm, we'll see. Ooh, what about Treasure Planet!" Reece's eyes lit up, in a sort of child-pleading, "Can I have more ice-cream?" kind of way.

"Uhh, hell yeah!" River cheered back, "I haven't watched that film in years, and I'm pretty sure the main character is hot as fuck."

"James Pleiades Hawkins, and yes, he is!"

The two had barely made it through the opening scene when Zasha waltzed into the room, bundled in large bohemian flared trousers and a white wool pullover. There was a scowl on Zasha's face as she entered and saw Reece sitting where she had spent the last week sleeping.

"Hey, you!" River beamed. "You're looking cosy."

"Hmm," she replied coldly, perching on the end of the bed, her nose turned upwards away from the two. "River," she sneered. "Want to watch something with me?"

Both River and Reece side glanced at each other in a disbelieving manner. "Uhh, sorry Zaz, I'm already watching something with Reece, uhh. Maybe tomorrow?" There was a shake in his voice like he was scared that his refusal might set her off, and rightly so.

"Yeah, I noticed *that*..." she smirked. "Since when have you two been friends, anyway?"

Once more, her question encouraged confusion between the two.

"Uhh, for a while now, Zasha. What's up?" Reece asked, slowly lifting her head from River's side.

"Oh, no, no, nothing. Don't worry, I think it's cute." Zasha had developed a condescending tone to her words, and the pinched smile in her cheeks made it worse.

"Are you okay?" River asked, his subconscious mind scanning the room for heavy things she, could and would, throw at him, his eyes landing on the large copy of Pride & Prejudice on his desk and thinking, *nah, Zasha hates Jane Austin.*

"Yeah, I'm fine! Just fine. Was actually wanting to talk to Reggie about something."

"Oh, okay. Shoot."

"Hmm." Zasha took her time, her eyes moving slowly between the two as if scanning cracks in their firewall. "Well, it's actually about you and *Jackson*..."

Reece caught her breath.

"You see, I'm worried that you've lost all self-respect."

"Wait, what?"

"This whole...*India* thing has really got me thinking about things, and I just think you need to start choosing your friends more wisely."

Reece's mouth parted; her eyebrows pinched together. "Zasha, is this about not being invited? Because I told you I only had 1 plus-one and Jackson—"

"No, it's not that. I couldn't care fucking less if I'm honest. It's about *you*."

"I don't understand."

"It's about you being friends with some *like* Jackson."

Reece stayed silent, waiting for the explanation.

"If I'm being completely honest...he's a cunt—a misogynistic fucking—immature child, and you just seem to put up with all of it!"

"Jeesh, Zasha! I—"

"And it just says a lot about you, if I'm honest. Like, what kind of person stays friends with someone like that?"

"Did he *do* something or *say* something to you? Because I don't get where this is coming from."

"I told you. It's not about him. It's about you."

It was clear to Reece, Zasha; like a middle-aged woman in a supermarket, was just looking for a fight. "Look, I'm not going to do this with you right now. But if that's how you feel, maybe you shouldn't be going to Malta *and* Berlin with the guy."

The last dig threw Zasha off-course, knocking her into a second of silence so Reece could get up and leave, telling River she'd, "...Be back with snacks," and leaving the two alone; even though the look on River's face was pleading for literally anything other than that to happen.

"What's going on, Zaz?" he asked softly, stretching out both arms, inviting her in for an embrace.

"Nothing! I'm just, eurgh! She doesn't see *it*, and it pisses me off!" Zasha rose from the bed, every so often twitching in a fit of rage. River watched as her fingers traced his desk, and he held his breath when they brushed over the hard copy of Pride & Prejudice, finally releasing when they passed and pulled open the top drawer of his desk.

In a split second, River's eyes doubled in size, and his heart stopped beating.

"What the fuck are these?" Zasha snarled, lifting out the bundles of wrapped letters addressed to 'Emily.' "Who the fuck is Emily?"

"She's just a friend! She's the one I told you about, the one from camp!"

Zasha scoffed, flipping through the packs and counting at least 8 letters addressed to her.

"What? Are you, like, *obsessed* with her or something?" her snide remark opening a wound River had forgotten he had, but realising he didn't have the time to be reminiscent.

"No, Zaz. We just write to each other, like—"

"What do you write about? Have you told her about me?" Zasha was now looking directly at him, her glare like looking into the barrel of a gun.

"Everything, uhh, Uni, books, the Society—"

"*Me?*"

"Uhh, you've been mentioned, yes. But those ones haven't even been sent yet! Like you're holding all the ones that—"

"Oh! So, you *haven't* told her about me? Why's that?"

River choked like a deer in headlights and prayed she would just pull the trigger and end him then and there.

"Right," she scoffed, taking the envelope resting on the top of the pile and ripping it open, snatching the folded letter inside.

"Zasha! You can't just—"

"My Dearest Emily!" *Oh boy*. "Something amazing happened last night, and you're the first person I wanted to tell! Zasha said she—" Zasha stopped reading, her claws crunching in on the sides of the letter until the page was pulled so tight River was only waiting for the rip. "You told her, I *love* you!" Zasha screamed, scrunching the letter and throwing it across the room, storming out and slamming the door behind her.

Without thinking, River fell out of bed, scrambled to his feet, and followed her into her room.

"Zasha!" he exclaimed. "I don't see what's wrong! Just tell me!"

"Eurgh!" she screamed again, lifting a candle from her desk and smashing it against the wall, leaving another dent in the plaster.

"Fucking hell!" River shrieked, backing up against the closed door. "Is it because I told *Emily*? Or is it because I told *anyone*?"

"Oh my god, River! How thick do you have to be? It's because I didn't fucking say it!"

River choked again, he could feel his throat closing up and the air inside his lungs thinning.

"I don't—"

"Well, I said it. But not like *that*! How fucking self-involved do you have to be to think that I would love you like that!"

River couldn't breathe.

"I swear, every time I think you finally get it, you go do something like this! You go ahead and make up this bullshit fairy tale in your head that we're somehow a couple! River. *We. Are. Not. Together!*"

River seized, for a moment, his whole head became fogged, and his limbs went weak. He could hear the pounding of his heart slow like he was underwater, and he could see the light at the surface dim as he sunk.

"You want to know how *not* together we are?" Zasha screamed, ripping her phone from her pocket, clicking on the text chain between her and Alexander Bailey, and thrusting the screen in River's face. "See? While you've been thinking I'm your girlfriend, I've been fucking Alexander Bailey, in *this* fucking room!"

River could hear the words she was speaking, but they were drowned out by a dark voice in his head. Saying nothing, River turned and left, walking slowly down the stairs, not even registering Zasha's "Where the fuck are you going?" from behind him.

Downstairs in her room, Reece listened to the carnage upstairs, her heart in her mouth, and wondered if Damian was listening too. She listened to the sound of River's heavy steps down the stairs and the lounge door open and close. Bracing herself, she held off for a second, thinking whether she should talk to Zasha or River first, but her mind was made up for her when she heard the lounge door open and close one last time and the front door slam shut.

Thinking River had gone for a walk, Reece ran up the stairs into Zasha's room, but before she could speak, Zasha shouted, "Just get out! Get fucking out!" from the corner on her bed.

Leaving instantly, Reece thought if she ran, she could catch up with River. So, pulling her little black pumps on that were outside the door, and not caring that she was still in Christmas themed pyjamas, she yanked open the front door, throwing herself forward and almost knocking into River at the top of the stairs. "River!" she shouted. "I thought you had left, I was literally about to chase you down, and you know how much I hate running...River?"

River was sitting on the floor, his back leaning against the Flat 6's door, his left arm cradled in the other. His eyes were squeezed shut, and his breathing was short and punched.

"River?" she asked again, but looking closer, she saw that he was sitting near a pool of blood. The red hue slowly spreading outwards within the cracks of the floor.

"Reece?" River whimpered finally, opening his eyes and revealing his arm.

"Get up."

The two sat on cold hard plastic seats, dozens around them stacked and placed alongside like children in an assembly hall. The white lights overhead so bright they caused moving black spots in the corner of your eye. There was also a particular smell in the room, like rusted car parts and detergent, both equally unpleasant. River looked over at Reece, trying to make casual small talk as if nothing happened, but Reece was only cold towards him.

"Look, Kid. I didn't—"

"Don't '*Kid*' me right now, okay?" she scolded. *Reverse roles*. "You don't get to joke about this."

"Okay."

The two waited for what seemed like hours until River's name was called, and he was motioned into the Triage centre. Taking a seat on a long cushioned 'dentist' chair, River stretched his back and waited for the click. Smiling to himself when it was a 'good crack.'

The nurse to his side looked less amused as she stood holding a clipboard in front of her. She was quite a pretty woman, with mousey brown hair and a pointed nose. She had faded freckles across her face, and her lips were painted pink.

"So...River? Would you like to talk me through how this... *incident* occurred?" Her voice was soothing and calm, and it quickly became clear she was more of a psychiatrist than a standard nurse.

"Just having a bad day, really," River charmed, raising his eyebrows and smirking from one side.

"Okay, and can you tell me what happened to make it a 'bad day'?"

"Hmm, let's talk about you..." River looked at the embroidered name across the lapel on her white coat. "Doctor Catherwood," he smiled, acting like he was the 'angsty bad-boy' in an American sitcom trying to get out of detention.

"I don't think that's appropriate right now," Doctor Catherwood explained, making a small note on the page in front of her. "The bandage was a good idea," she said, gesturing to the bound material around his arm.

"Wouldn't be my first choice."

"Can you just be serious, for like, two seconds!" Reece growled, the harshness in her tone alarming the Doctor.

"Okay, I think it's best if you leave, you can wait outside," she instructed Reece, who was more than happy to leave River to whatever game he intended to play.

After about 20 minutes, River returned to the waiting area, his spirits revived as he slumped down in the seat next to Reece, a smile from ear to ear. "Welp. I have to see a counsellor," he sang as if words had no meaning at all.

"Uh-huh."

"They said we'll probably be here a couple of hours."

"Great."

"Should've brought snacks!" River laughed, looking down at Reece, in her baby blue snowman pyjamas, and the jagged rip in her top across the hem, which only made him laugh more. "You're a mess!" he teased, throwing his head back and reeling in attention from other patients who were sitting close by.

"*I'm* a mess? You're kidding, right?" Reece growled back.

River had never seen her like this. So heartless, cold, and unforgiving. "Look, I'm sorry, Kid—"

"*What* did I say about—"

"Reece! I'm sorry, Reece. It's just easier for me to crack jokes than to actually accept what I did."

Reece took a breath, her dark eyes fixed on his. "Why did you do it?"

"I don't know," he paused. "It used to help when I was a kid. When I was feeling anxious or hurt. Especially in school, I just had a really rough time, and it was a release, y'know?"

Reece said nothing.

"And I hadn't done anything like that in years! But tonight, I don't know. I guess Zasha just brought those same feelings back, and it's the only way I knew to make it stop."

River waited for Reece to say something, to say anything. But for a long time, she said nothing.

"Okay."

"*Okay*?"

"River, I'm going to say something to you, and you don't get to dislike it. Okay?"

"Uhh, okay."

"Okay. I'm telling you now. *I. will. Not. Sympathise* with you. I understand hurt and needing an emotional release. But I will never understand or show pity for what you've done."

Once more, River fell into silence, waiting for the rest.

"I'm here because I care about you, and no matter what stupid crap you pull, I'm here for you. But if you're looking for someone to hold your hand, that's not me. I'll make the bandage, but I won't pick you out Hello-Kitty plasters. Understood?"

"*Understood.*"

"Okay." Reece exhaled; a burden of tension released from her shoulders. "We should have brought snacks!" she laughed.

"Oh my god, the snacks!"

8 hours and 3 different counsellors later, Reece and River finally returned to the flat like soldiers from the front line. They couldn't have looked worse. With bags for life under their eyes and their hair frazzled and splitting off in different directions; from where they had tried to fall asleep in different positions on different chairs; they made their way back up to River's bedroom. Falling hopelessly under the covers together, trying to decide whether they had the energy to watch 'Treasure Planet' after all.

"Fucking hell, it's 6am!" River shrieked in a whisper, obviously getting his second wind.

"Uh-huh."

"Let's see what my quote of the day is!" he said excitedly, reaching for his phone and searching for his new favourite app. "Okay, here we go. 'Live each day as if it was...your last.'" River paused, looking over at Reece to share in the irony, but she had already fallen asleep, small yellow 'duck' in arms. "Ha. Sweet Dreams, Kiddo."

MINDLESS

Weeks had passed since the forementioned incident, and the early signs of spring were beginning to show. The black ice had finally melted from the roads leaving hot tar in its place, and tiny yellow flowers were erupting from the once cold earth and blooming in bright, happy petals. The tall trees that lined University Avenue had finally restored to their healthy green hue, and the soil beneath was dewy and rich. You could also smell the spring. Unlike the snow, spring smelled like fresh linen, the type that's washed with the expensive brands you only see when you go home for the holidays, and the smell of bark and pinewood hovers at head height. There're bugs, too. One of the more acute signs of spring are the flies that hang about in the kitchen, and not just because week-old food has been left on the counter.

Reece loved spring, but this year it was different, this year, she felt saddened by yellow and insects, and she hated that she did.

"I saw a bee," she sighed, dropping her bag to the floor and slumping on the couch next to Damian.

"Aw, Reece, I'll make coffee," Damian comforted, leaping from the leather to the old kettle tucked in the corner of the Flat 5's kitchen.

"Am I missing something?" Will asked, looking around the corner for Damian's guidance.

"River loves bees!" he shouted, opening all the cupboard doors in search. "Reece, where's the mug I got you for Christmas?"

Too depressed to panic, and knowing fully well the mug was sitting behind her blinds on the windowsill in her room; probably filled with old coffee; she sighed again stating, "Somewhere in my room, but it's dirty."

"Right. This blue one will have to do."

Reece looked over at the blue mug. It was Rivers. "Hmm," she whined, thinking, *if I drink the coffee fast enough, I won't notice the mug.*

"He's not *dead*!" Will exclaimed, laughing a little as Reece reacted by throwing herself backwards across the couch, the back of her hand on her forehead like a waiting lady in the 1800's.

"But I haven't seen him in weeks! I don't think he's ever coming back."

"He's living with Phil right now, isn't he?" Will asked, knowing exactly what the inside of Phil's flat looks like and wondering how he would cope.

"Yeah. Eurgh. Bloody—Phil, stealing our friends," she moaned, the smell of the coffee coming towards her and lifting her back upright. "Thanks." She smiled at Damian, who nodded, and resumed sitting next to her.

"Well, Zasha's gone away with the others to Berlin for the next 2 days. Why don't you bring him back?"

This was true, and surprising to everyone after the last review of their trip to Malta.

The details differ depending on who you ask, but the gist of the drama was that, within 2 seconds of arriving at the boat they were staying on, yes—boat. Zasha had realised she had left her phone in the backseat of the taxi they had taken from the airport, already causing a riff of stress in the group.

On the next day, Amy had wandered off, following a litter of stray cats across the island, and had gotten lost. Both Jackson and Zasha spent the whole day searching for her, only to find she had walked in the opposite loop.

And finally, in the airport on the way back to Belfast, Jackson had lost the girls while they shopped in the duty-free and they almost missed their flight; but it's okay because Zasha found a baseball cap with a bottle opener on it.

The three of them spent the following days in silence after they returned, stating "Never again." But when you've already booked flights, and the hostel is non-refundable, 'never again' really means 'until next time.'

"Yeah, I already asked him," Reece told Will. "He says 'he'll see'. I think this whole place just depresses him now—the selfish jackass."

Will laughed. I think a part of him was just happy that Reece was directing her angst at someone else, gave a nice change in pace. "Why are you guys sitting in here anyway?" he asked, looking around at the hollow lounge, the bare walls, and the puddle of water in the corner. "Eurgh. I hate your lounge. Why don't we watch a movie or something in our flat?" he suggested.

Both Reece and Damian side-glanced each other, a look of disgust scrawled across their face.

"Is Nora in?" Reece asked, her top lip pointing in the corner.

"Uhh, yeah, she's upstairs with Marco. Why?"

"Eurgh!" both Reece and Damian exclaimed. Shaking their heads as if they had eaten something inedible.

"Ha! What?"

Once again, the two looked at each other, eyes pleading on who should explain. Damian looked sadder.

"You ever watched 'The Room'?" Reece asked, thinking, *he's a film buff; of course, he's watched the worst film ever made.*

"Are you talking about the remake with Dave Franco or the original?"

"The original."

"Yeah."

"Have you ever watched 'The Room' while your flatmate is having loud, aggressive sex in the room above you?"

"What! No, why would you...Oh...Oh!" Will's face enveloped a look of horror as he realised.

The Room was already a heavily sexual film, with intense, albeit poorly filmed, but intense sex scenes in every other cut. But the thought of watching that while listening to Nora and her boyfriend 'go at it' upstairs was another horror altogether.

"I can't unthink that!" Will squirmed.

"We know. And, like...It's a long film!" Damian explained.

"And we had surround sound... if you get me," Reece continued.

All three of them now shifting uncomfortably.

"Okay, so, I'm moving in with you!" Will decided. "Guessing River's room's free?"

"Hmm!" Reece whined again, thinking how she'll have to start paying for her own Netflix account.

"I'll call him!"

Threatened with arson and burning all "...His precious books," River did end up taking Reece's offer to come back to the flat for the few days Zasha was away. Trudging his green suitcase into the living room and being less than surprised when a pancake came flying past the side of his face, hitting the wall behind him.

"Yeah, okay, so *that's* happening," he said to himself, fully prepared to embrace the chaos he had missed from 82 Rugby.

"We're making pancakes!" Damian shouted from the nook in the kitchen.

"They're making pancakes," Will repeated, seated on the leather couch, plate at the ready.

"If that's what you call it," River laughed, leaning the case against the wall and waiting for the—

"River!" Reece shouted, dropping the frying pan back on the stove and running over to him, throwing her arms around his waist and squeezing. There was something familiar about this hug, and River, all of a sudden, felt like he should have brought wine.

"Missed ya, Kid," he beamed, resting the side of his face on the top of her head.

Damian also came over to give River a hug, more reserved than their usual embrace but friendly, nonetheless.

"So, what going on with the—" River pointed to the pastry on the wall that was slowly falling to the floor.

"We're making pancakes." Reece smiled, as if it wasn't obvious.

"So, I've been told. But what's with the—"

"It was a bad pancake."

"I see... You'll clean that up, right?"

Both Damian and Reece laughed as if to say, "Obviously!" but 5 months later, when Reece would come back to clean the flat and hand in the keys, she would find that very same pancake, tucked away under the TV-less TV stand, and look fondly back on this moment thinking, *it was so much less gross 5 months ago.*

The next batch was a lot better, and River was happy to partake in the pancake flipping contest with the rules, "If it folds, it goes cold." A terrible game to play, especially when they were all awful at flipping pancakes. There was a lot of waste.

"You know what this reminds me of?" Damian began, but the spark in Reece's eyes let him know she was thinking the exact same thing.

"The eggs!" They both screamed. "Guys, do you remember?" they turned to Will and River. "What? In Elms?" Will reminisced.

"Yeah!"

"That was hilarious! I will never forget the look on your face Reece, as you tried to clean up the broken egg from the floor! You were retching! I ended up just scooping it up with my hands!" Damian wheezed.

Even the event's memory turned Reece's stomach, and she could feel the pancakes working their way back up. "That was so gross," she said, having to take a seat and wait for the nausea to pass.

"Wait, what was this?" River asked, vaguely remembering.

Damian delighted in retelling the story. "Do you remember, it was that night in our kitchen in Elms? I think it was me, you,

Will, Reece, and I think Ash was there too. And we were all standing about, and then Reece, me, and Will started throwing eggs around the room and catching them.

And then I threw one to Reece, and I don't know how but it hit the ceiling above Reece's head, cracked, and landed on the floor near her feet, and she was beside herself! Every time I touched the raw egg, Reece would gag!"

"Sounds about right," River agreed. It really didn't take much for Reece to feel sick, raw eggs, the word 'neck' and don't get me started on her fear of holes.

"Aw, I miss Elms," Reece sighed, joined in a peaceful remembrance by the others.

"Yeah. I wonder if we'll all miss this flat when we move into our new places." Will's words struck a chord. The three of them hadn't really thought about it. They had plans for the upcoming year, but no one had actually considered that they might miss their current flat.

River, for sure, knew he wouldn't.

"Oh, what are you doing next year, Will?" Reece asked, her head tilted.

"Uhh, so I've actually got a place sorted with Nora, McManus, and Warner."

"Oh!" This coming as a shock, not only because she thought Will, Nora, Amy, and Jackson were a solid group, but because he was now living with both her and Zasha's ex, a bitter realisation as she was the one to introduce Will to McManus in the first place. "But I thought you all—"

"Yeah, I know. I think Jackson's a bit pissed off with me right now. But him and Amy were just taking too long to finish their applications, so like—it is what it is. And Warner knows the Landlord of the new place, so we got it for a bit cheaper."

"Oh, cool, cool. Where is the flat?" Damian asked, hoping it wouldn't be too far out.

"Wolseley Street."

"Aw, awesome!" he cheered. "Yeah, our place is on Cromwell Avenue, so we're right around the corner from you guys!"

"*Our* place?" Will questioned, looking between Reece and River.

"Yeah, we signed the lease last week."

You see, a lot had happened since the last talks of living situations. Since the whole 'River and Zasha incident', Zasha and Reece had decided it was best not to share a flat in the new year, and Zasha would instead live with her friends Ginny and Anna.

Reece had also concluded that she likes very few people, and a summer apart would surely ease any awkwardness between her and Damian. Although Jackson still heavily disagreed, saying, "You'll regret it!" but Reece had also come to the conclusion that Jackson was wrong about almost everything.

"It's actually such a nice place!" Reece beamed. "And it's right on Botanic, away from the Holy Lands."

"It's a dream, really!" River added, remembering when he guilt-tripped Damian into giving him the biggest room with the headline: 'Box Room—Mould—Zasha,' describing his unfortunate year; bringing up the pressed suit in his cupboard, which had still not repaired after many trips to the dry cleaners.

"I'm happy for you guys!" Will smiled. "So, what are we doing tonight then?"

"Ooh, there's free entry at Limelight before 10 tonight?" Damian suggested, turning to River.

"Ahh, I think I'm just gonna stay in tonight, Bud. Maybe we could drink here?"

The four of them agreed, and they ended up having a pretty lovely night, choosing to stay in and reminisce about more moments from 'first year.'

Will telling of the time he and Reece had rented a Belfast bike and cycled alongside the river. Reece, standing precariously on the back wheel, arms out and screaming as Will swerved her in and out of pedestrian traffic.

"I remember that!" Reece beamed. "...We also went down that long hill next to Scalini's, and my boss shouted at me through the window!"

"That's right! Aw, man. What a ride!"

River then mentioned all the midnight showings at the Movie House on Dublin Road, he, Damian, and Will attended. The Star Wars trilogy being his fondest memory.

"That was wild. I remember not having slept in days because of all the coursework I had, but I had such FOMO" — fear of missing out— "I had to watch 9 hours of Star Wars!" River chuckled.

"It was an incredible night, to be fair. I remember we all came back at what—7 in the morning?" Damian asked.

"Must have been."

Damian too, went onto describe a beloved memory. "Do you remember Will's birthday?" he asked the group, a sweeping look of excitement on all their faces. "Aw, that was such a funny night. I remember it was all of our flat, Zasha, both Alex's were there, and I think Matteo?"

Matteo was a classmate of Will and Reece's. A tall, handsome Italian man with a strong jaw and thick accent. He was currently living with Phil.

"Yeah, he was! Ha! That man does *not* like me!" Reece laughed, thinking back to all their cold exchanges.

Matteo was also a very stern man who never took lightly to Reece's childish humour and dwarf-like stature.

"He's a hard man to please, that Matteo," Will chanted, the others nodding.

"And I remember, me and Reece were dancing in the kitchen, and we were drinking...what was it—"

"Rootbeer and vodka!" Reece sang.

"Yes-ss! And we got so drunk, I started dancing with the Christmas Tree!"

"Urgh. I hate that we still had that up in February," River scoffed.

"That was the night before you left, Will." Reece carried on, "Yeah, you were flying back home the next day, and I remember walking back from Limelight with you, and I wanted to stay up with you until your flight."

"Aw, that's so sweet," River purred.

"I mean. It *could* have been! But you passed out before we got to the stairs, and I had to carry you up 6 flights!" Will protested, smiling from ear to ear.

"Oh yeah..."

Phil also joined the group later that night. Strolling in with swaying shoulders and bopping his head like a crow.

"Hey, guys, what's the craic!" he cheered, happy to listen to the shared stories and happier to tell tales of his new relationship with his polyamorous girlfriend. "I mean. I won't judge," he said, shrugging his shoulders.

"I *mean*...You can judge a little!" River giggled.

"Nawh, like. She *says* that's what she's into, but with me, she's different, y'know?"

"No poppet, you're getting mixed up. Polyamorous means she's into *different* guys."

"Ha! Shut-up, Reece."

Jokes on her, Phil and Cara, have been together 3 years now, happily married, with an adorable baby boy.

Kidding.

Their relationship was doomed from the start.

The days of Zasha's absence passed quickly, and as the expected arrival time grew closer, River went through the stages of grief.

River - I'm fine! I'm over it.

River, 5 minutes later - This is all her fault! She did this to me! I was fine until I met her!

River, immediately after that – No, maybe this is my fault. I just get too attached, you know?

River, 20 minutes after that - I think I'm depressed. How do you know if you're depressed?

River, as the front door opened - Welp. I'm dead.

Though, to everyone's surprise, as the front latch clicked open, only one set of footsteps was heard.

"Yo!" Jackson called up from the stairs, Reece instantly running over to meet him outside the flat doors, throwing herself into his arms.

"Hey!" she cooed, nuzzling her head into his chest.

Feeling the warmth of her body against his, Jackson dropped his bag to the floor and cuddled her back, only for a second, though, because Jackson doesn't cuddle.

Pulling away, Reece looked up at his face, and she was certain she could see more frown lines than usual. "Well, how was it? Where are the others?"

Jackson sighed, reaching for his bag once more. "Uhh, it was good, yeah! A lot better than Malta, actually...Amy went home to see Callum."

"And Zasha?"

"Yeah, uhh, I should probably tell the others too," he said, walking into the living room and exchanging passive greetings with the others.

"Well, Chief! Good to have you back!" Will exclaimed, with his usual charm, though he could tell Jackson wasn't in a charming mood.

"Tell us about Berlin!" Damian yelled.

"Look, guys. I'm so fucking tired now—so I'll give you the highlights, but then I'm going to bed."

Agreeing this was a fair arrangement, the four listened intently as Jackson described the trip.

"Right so, we actually stayed in a hostel that was right next to the hostel I stayed in a couple years ago when I went interrailing, which was pretty cool." Jackson paused his story to show pictures of the outdoor sign and street markings before continuing, "But when we got to the hostel, they tell us we've only paid for two beds because I had thought Amy had booked and sorted everything, but it turns out she had only booked for her and Zasha—" Jackson had a look of "I know!" written across his face, his hands gesturing outwards to motion, "why do I even bother?"

"So, I'm broke as fuck, so Amy ends up paying for my bed. So now I owe her a fuck tonne for Malta, and—"

"Wait, I thought she offered to pay for Malta?" Reece said, distinctively remembering a whole, "Hypocrite" argument.

"Yeah! Me too! Apparently not, though, so I owe her like 400 quid—"

"Oof!" River yelled. Thinking about the last time he had that much money and remembering it was last month. It paid for rent.

"I know! But it's fine. I have a job now, so I'll get it back to her. Whatever. So, we're at this hostel right, and the girl working at the desk is on tinder so—"

"You *didn't?*" Will sang.

"I did. She's old, right, but dead-on, and still fucking hot. And we also visited the old amusement park and did a bunch of other shit. So yeah."

The storytelling lasted longer than they were expecting; in all honesty, Jackson looked like death, and you could tell he hadn't slept in days as his mouth remained open even when he wasn't speaking.

"So, where's Zasha?" Reece asked again.

"Oh, fuck! Yeah. So, in the airport on the way back, Zasha loses her passport and—"

"Wait, didn't she do that in Malta as well?"

"No, that was her phone. Fuck's sake. I get frustrated even thinking about it. Eurgh! So! She loses her passport at the airport, and they wouldn't accept any other forms of I.D—obviously. So... Long story short...We left her in Germany."

"What!" The chorus of the 4 screamed.

"Yeah, like, not much else we could do, is there?"

"Uhh, I don't know, stay with her? You can't just leave her there!" Reece gasped.

"That's fucked up!" Will cried out. Damian nodding profusely.

"Ha-ha!" River just laughed, a girly, high-pitched squeal. The other 4 hearing this and slowly turning towards him. "Sorry! It's just—never mind. Carry on."

"Look, we didn't want to leave her, but like, I'm broke, I couldn't afford to miss my flight. And Amy, well, didn't want to stay either, and let's be honest. If anyone is going to be okay in a foreign country, it's Zasha."

The rest of the group seemed to agree with this, slowly nodding their heads.

"And apparently, she's already found a Russian family she's agreed to work for, for a place to crash until she gets a replacement travel visa."

"What *kind* of work?" River asked, now a little worried for her safety.

"Oh, like babysitting or some shit like that. Apparently, they're pretty sound, like." After a second of silence, Jackson took it as his sign to leave, stretching up from the couch and yawning a loud yawn, just in case they didn't believe his whole 'tired' excuse. "Well. Night," he said, swiftly leaving Flat 5 to go to his own.

The rest remained silent for some time, thinking about Zasha and praying she'd be okay. The sweet silence was interrupted, however, when River broke out into another relentless giggle. "I'm sorry! But this is karma!"

Zasha was stranded for over 8 days in Berlin. Sustained by friends and family sending her money and Jackson's 'hostel hostess' connection giving her a place to stay when her Russian family had moved back home.

UNSOUND

From as early as 6 in the morning, the gridded streets of the Holy Lands were buzzing. The low rumble of students lining the paved walls and chanting from their rooftops and balconies. The sky stayed grey for the duration, coated in thick clouds of smoke and soot, and through the fog, a rally of Police cars and S.W.A.T vehicles got into position, guarding the corners of Jerusalem, Rugby, and Damascus.

Our favourite flat was also up from the early hours of the morn, hosting the same energy as outside their walls.

"I'm already on it, like!" Damian said, holding a bottle of Heineken up in the air before sloshing it into his cereal.

"That's disgusting," Will winced. "But I love it! Good on ye man!" Taking a bottle from the pack and searching for a bottle opener. "Uhh, dude, where is it?" he asked Damian, who was already regretting his decision of beer and All-Bran.

"Uhh, it was just here—"

Standing in the kitchen corner of Flat 6, Reece looked over her shoulder. "Why don't you just...?" she began, holding out her hand for Will to pass her the bottle. The glass was cold against her fingers and made her shiver a little. "Look," she said, taking the bottle and positioning the cap at 90 degrees on the counter's edge, the base of her palm slamming down hard on the top. The sound of the cap popping and springing off the mouth of the bottle making a satisfying 'clink'.

"Well, thank you, Reggie. Guess you need to stick around!"

"Ha," she mocked, turning back to the chopping board and lifting a large white knife from the surface. "Wish I could."

"What you making there, anyway?" Damian chimed in, his stomach-turning.

"It's called a Penne Torinesi," she explained, taking a large red pepper and holding it down into the wooden board.

"A what-a-what?" Will laughed, walking over to her side.

"Penne Torinesi,"—a pasta dish typically made with chicken, courgette, blushed peppers, and pine nuts— "Fancy chicken pasta," she explained. "One of the only benefits of working at Scalini's, really."

Will thought for a moment, his eyes lighting up before quipping back, "You mean, other than your bosses' tongue down your throat!"

Damian choked.

"What!" Reece gasped, her hand slipping from the board. "Who told you that!"

"Heh-heh!" Will chuckled, his tongue pressing against the inside of his bottom lip.

"Seriously, Will? Damian?" Reece turned back to look at Damian, her eyebrows pinched together.

"Definitely wasn't me," he said, coughing up a bran flake.

"I'm gonna kill Jackson," she growled, flipping Will off and returning back to her peppers.

"Uhh, Reggie?" Will winced, his mouth now turning upside down like a fish.

"Oh!" she gasped once more, lifting her left thumb from the counter, watching a fountain of blood pulse from the top.

"Did you just? —"

"Uhh, must of...Hmm..." She examined her thumb, squeezing the flesh with her other hand to find the cut. "Ew! Look at this!" she laughed, holding the top of the finger and pulling it back and forth, showing the wound open and close. "It's like Pac-man!" she laughed some more, holding the cut near Will's face and watching him gag.

"I'm gonna be sick! What's *wrong* with you! How are you laughing?"

Damian jumped up from the broken wooden table to examine the injury. "Right, we're going to need some antiseptic wipes, a bandage, and depending on how deep the cut is, you might have to go to A&E," Damian instructed, his Biology degree finally coming into play.

"I have some plasters upstairs!" Will shouted, running out of the room, eager to be out of the blood's way.

"Guys!" Reece sighed. "It's fine! Look, I just need to—" she turned the tap and ran her thumb under the cold water, the stream fleshing into a pinkie-colour as it drained. Waiting until the water runs clear, she dried her thumb on the side of her jeans, lifting it back up to Damian, "Look, see!" like a child showing a finger-painting to a teacher.

Though Damian's face was less than impressed as the wound opened once more and thick blood erupted from the crevice. "It's deep. You need to get that checked out."

"Pfft."

"I got them!" Will yelled as he ran back down the stairs and into the kitchen, muttering, "ya freaking psycho," under his breath as he tore the slip and wrapped the cotton plaster around her thumb. "Right! That's that, then. Gotta tell you, Reggie, sometimes you scare the fuck outa me!"

"Hmm." She smiled, squeezing her eyes shut and lifting her chin like an anime high schooler. "Right, okay, I actually gotta go!" she said after realising the time, kicking on her small black pumps and throwing the large yellow hoodie over her head.

"Dude! You have a severed thumb! I think this qualifies as a sick day!" Will laughed, watching as she put the hoodie on backwards and awkwardly danced her way inside to swivel it.

"Nope. Everyone will be calling in sick as it is. Can't leave them with no one!"

"You're too good for them, Boss!"

"I know." With that, she ran out of the room, swiping her little black backpack from the floor as she did.

"Wait! What about your pasta?" Will called after her, realising she had left an assortment of chopped bloody veg on the counter.

"Go to the damn hospital!" Damian also shouted, but the sound of the front door slamming from the ground floor made it clear she was out and away.

She actually ran past Amy on her way out, giving her a rushed wave goodbye as Amy pulled into the side of the pavement, her wheel jaggedly hitting the curb and lurching her backwards.

"Shit!" she cursed, looking out the window at the poorly angled park and thinking, *fuck it*, before getting out and going inside.

"Ame-Ame!" Damian revelled as she walked into the lounge. A nickname he had been experimenting with after; 'Ree-Ree' (for Reece) and 'Zaz-Zaz' (for Zasha) was a massive hit!

"Uhh, hey," she replied through gritted teeth, hating the nickname with every fibre of her being. Amy was dressed in fitted black jeans and an Ireland Rugby shirt; she had also painted a little clover on the apple of her cheek in green glitter.

"You look great!" Damian praised, looking down at his chequered green 'going-out' shirt, and thinking, *I really need some new clothes.*

"Ha, thanks, you guys on it already?" she asked, pointing to the empty Heineken bottle on the table and then fixing her eyes on the bottle in Will's hand.

"Hell yeah! You want one?"

"Yes!" she sang. "This is actually the first St. Paddy's day I've gotten off from work in years, I'm fuckin' buzzin'!"

"Amazing. Yeah, we were just telling Reece she should have called in sick!"

Amy paused, the excitement in her face slipping away for a moment. "Yeah, but like. It's not like she's exactly *from* here." As she said this, Amy realised she was talking to two more people who weren't exactly 'from here' and she laughed. "Ha! Fuck, sorry."

This making the others laugh out loud with her.

By noon, the flat's remainders were already 'gone' with Will eager to get everyone drunk as soon as possible and even breaking into the bathroom to hand Jackson a beer while he showered. And Zasha, no matter how patriotic she wanted to be, couldn't bring herself to drink beer that early, so she got plastered on wine instead.

The 5 of them, disclosing Nora; who had flown out to Barcelona for the week to visit Marco; and River, who had moved back in with Phil, also decided it would be a great idea to make a documentary film about the flat. But as mentioned, they were all pretty drunk, and the video ended up being a montage of Jackson exiting from different cupboards around the house shouting, "Wagwan!" and the video ended with Amy attempting to jump over Will's head on the stairs and almost falling on her face.

The Flat. Coming soon. Summer 2019.

Later that night, and many stops on their 'Pub Crawl' later. The 5 of them decided they would host a house party at the flat, inviting anyone they could find, clearly forgetting what happened the last time they did exactly that.

"What the—" River gasped as he walked towards the front door. Loud pounding music blaring from inside, light shining so bright from the windows you could see it from 5 streets over. River had been at Phil's for the day, and assuming the others (Zasha) would still be out, he thought he's sneak back to the flat to pick up some books and maybe bump into Reece. *How foolish.*

He didn't even need his key. Shocked, scared, and confused, when two complete strangers leaning on the wall outside the flat looked him up and down, muttered something between themselves, and opened the door for him, gesturing upstairs. "Yeah, I got it, thanks," he said, thinking to himself, *what the fuck is going on?* As he entered the flat, he was instantly greeted by his friendly and very drunk flatmate.

"River! Rivvy! Riv-Riv!" Damian yelled, lurching towards him, trusty Heineken in hand. "Where have you been?"

"Woah there, Buckeroo. Maybe you should sit," River suggested, holding Damian around the shoulders and motioning him to the bottom step on the stairs.

"Maybe *you* should drink!" he chanted back, the red loading in his eyes.

"I don't think so—"

"It's St. Paddy's!"

"I know, it's just Zasha's here and—"

"Zasha's not here!" Damian chuckled as if to say, "Durr!"

"Wait, she's not?"

"No-ooh! She's with a Mr Alexander Bailey!"

"Oh."

"The one with the fucked-up mouth!"

"That's him."

"I wonder how they—"

"Right!" River shrieked, stopping Damian in his tracks. "Give me that!" he asserted, gesturing for the bottle and downing the rest of it in one luke-warm-swoop. "Yeurgh! You need better alcohol, my dude."

"We shall get some!" Damian stood, like the captain of a search party, and marched through into the flat's lounge, returning just moments later with a large bottle of Bacardi he had pinched from the table when their good friend Mason wasn't looking.

"Geez! Where did you…You got mixer?"

"Nope."

"Fuck it."

In the opposite flat, Amy was having less of a charming time as she sat weeping on the black couch. Her cute clover smudged and running from the streaming tears. "I just try so hard; you know!" she told Jackson, who was trying to comfort her and eyeing up two girls dressed like Irish Dancers in the corner.

"Yeah, yeah, I know you do," he didn't.

"And it's like, I want it to work so badly!"

"Yeah, work's a dick!"

"What?" she whined, realising Jackson's attention was preoccupied, this making her sob more. "Jackson!"

"Hmm? Oh right, yes. Continue. Callum."

"Yeah, like. We're trying to make it work, and it's not working!"

"And this upsets you, *because*?" Jackson scoffed, thinking, *Callum's a twat* and *Irish Dancers are hot.*

"Because we've been together, 4 years!"

"Oh."

"Do you know how many guys I could have slept with in 4 years!"

"Oh!" Jackson perked up, completely unaware that's where *that* was going.

"I've missed out on so much!"

Taking less than a second to think about it, Jackson looked at Amy, placed a hand on her knee, and teased, "Well, maybe you don't have to..." slowly leaning in, stopping just inches from her face.

Amy held her breath, looking down at his lips and slowly parting hers, holding for just a second longer before closing her eyes and waiting for the feeling of his lips on hers.

But was more than shocked when Jackson screamed a loud "Ha!" Mocking, "That'd be fucking crazy!" before jumping to his feet, grabbing a strange boy's shoulder, commanding, "talk to her!" over the music, and running out of the room, the Irish flag he had tied around his shoulders trailing after him.

Amy sat frozen on the couch. Her jaw dropped, and her eyes unable to cry due to the shock. And she probably would have broken down right then and there if the boy Jackson had assaulted wasn't James.

James was a mutual friend of Zasha's and Phil and likewise studied drama. He was a lot shorter than Amy, with curly brown hair and large eyes, and had a lanky build. He was sweet and charming, and within minutes, Amy had developed an 'Amy Fancy' on him.

"I just feel so lost!" she blubbered.

"Oh, I know, like there's an overwhelming darkness inside that you can't escape!"

Pfft. Drama Students.

Unlike River, Reece fully expected to return home to chaos.

She had called Damian on the walk home from work and put two and two together when he answered the phone screaming, "St. Paddy's!" So was more than prepared to be greeted by strange doormen and chauffeured up into her own room. She was, however, surprised to see both Damian and River sitting on the floor of her room, swigging Bacardi from the bottle and trading Smeagol impressions.

"My *precious*!"

"No, it's, *my* precious!"

"*My precious!*"

River was also holding a sketchbook of Reece's and was pressing a deep red lipstick into the paper; defacing a sketch of Zasha she had drawn a few months back.

"Yeah, we're going to be arguing about this tomorrow..." Reece sighed, gesturing to the book in his hands.

"Huh?" River said looking up at her, unaware, before continuing, "no! It's my precious!"

"Urgh, I need a drink," she said, refusing the Bacardi and leaving to find something palatable, passing McManus and his new girlfriend on the way to the kitchen.

"Oh, hi!" Reece exclaimed, caught off guard and panicking a little bit.

"Hey Reece, what's the craic?" McManus charmed back, throwing an arm over Reece's shoulder for a brotherly hug.

"Ahh, uhh," she stumbled, pulling slowly back, waiting for anyone to say anything. But after the silence became unbearable, Reece squeaked, "So, this must be Lily!"

"Yeah."

"She's pretty." Reece paused for a second, her mouth contorting. "I'm sorry! I don't know why I'm talking about you when you're standing right *there*! Uhh. *You're* pretty!" Reece stuttered, wanting to die.

"Ha, it's okay, thank you," Lily spoke back softly.

Lily was, infact, a very pretty girl, petite and sweet with short straight hair and brown eyes. She had large white teeth that could only be described as 'adorable', and the smallest nose Reece had ever seen. Alex and Lily had been dating for a month or so at this point, so Reece had already mentally prepared for this moment.

Well, in theory.

"I'm gonna—yeah," Reece sighed, doing a 180, and returning back to her room. Pleading, "Gimme," with a degree of self-pity, holding out her hand for the long clear bottle to be passed into.

A couple hours passed, and at this point, the house party had taken its normal course of action. Some from the party leaving in small groups to either find a 'better' party, or just one that was going on later. Other's deciding to head to different clubs in the city centre before the doors close, and the remaining few either finding dark corners of the flat to throw up in. Or finding spare rooms to lock themselves in with a partner they had either come with or acquired throughout the night. The 'sex room' being the most popular, as a queue of both strange and familiar faces crowded around the closed door in hopes it would become vacant.

"I'm telling you now!" River whined, his voice waving in and out of pitch. "If anyone has sex on my pillow this time, I'm taking a match, and I'm setting this place a light!" he joked, but there was a certain level of seriousness in his voice that made Will and Damian wonder.

"I think you've had enough there, Laddy!" Will stated, pulling the coffee flask from River's grip, which was definitely not filled with coffee.

"No! I—" he began but stopped when he felt the rise of vomit in his throat, ballooning his cheeks. "Mmhm!" he murmured, eyes wide and shoulders tense as he ran from the bottom of the stairs into the small bathroom.

As if it was planned, both Will and Damian exchanged a look of excitement, both thrusting their pointer finger to the tip of their nose shouting, "Not *it*!" as a way of deciding who would be responsible for the man-child upstairs.

"Shit," Damian growled, having been just milliseconds slower than Will.

"Heh-heh! Have fun!" he teased, watching Damian sulk his way upstairs, now sober enough to hold resentment towards River the next morning.

In retrospect, it's probably a good thing River had barricaded himself in the bathroom, as just around this time, Zasha too had returned to the flat in search of Reece.

"Have you seen her?" she asked Will, who was still at the bottom of the steps.

"Yeah, uhh, she's with Jackson next door."

Zasha scoffed at this, pacing into the neighbouring flat and seeing Reece standing with Jackson at the broken table playing beer pong... or vodka pong. They ran out of beer hours ago.

"Ha! And drink!" Reece sang, doing a victory dance on the other end.

"I can't—I'm not—how the fuck are you so good at this? You're the least coordinated person I know!"

She had no clue.

"No, clue. But you gotsta drink!"

"Hmm," Jackson sneered, taking the plastic cup and downing its contents. "That's vile," he spat, rolling the Ping-Pong ball back to her.

"Uhh, Reece?" Zasha said, tapping her on the shoulder.

Now, if Reece had been any less drunk, she would have been very fearful in this moment. Nothing good ever seemed to follow when Zasha referred to her as anything other than 'Reggie.'

"Zasha, Zasha, Zasha!" Reece rejoiced, passing the ball back to Jackson so she could throw her arms over the top of Zasha's thin shoulders. "You're back—"

"We gotta go."

"Oh right."

With little more said, Reece, followed Zasha out the flat and down the stairs, making sure to grab the small bottle of vodka she had been keeping under the table for this very moment.

You see, Zasha and Reece had decided to work together to complete an assignment for their documentary film class. Back when they were on...friendlier terms. And had chosen to film a documentary about 'Living in the Holy Lands,' showcasing what life was like daily, and what better night to film than on St. Patricks Day in South Belfast! The only issue however, was Zasha and Reece weren't on the best of terms as of present, ergo, the vodka.

"Can we just get this over with?" Zasha snapped, flipping the GH4 Camera strap over her neck and passing Reece the Zoom.

"Aw, come on, Zasha. You can go back to hating me tomorrow, can't we just forget about all this crap for one night?"

Zasha thought about it. Recently she had been feeling like an outcast in the flat. Ever since that night with River, she had been treated like a villain. Rooms silencing when she entered, River moving flats just to get away from her, and she had even felt Amy pulling away. So, the idea of a temporary truce was more than welcome.

"Okay," she sighed, a familiar smile returning to her face.

"*Okay*." Reece smiled back, handing the small bottle over and laughing as Zasha twitched and freaked after the first straight sip.

"Yuck! Bad Russian, bad Russian!" Zasha cried, shaking her head from side to side, her fair, thin hair rising like static.

"Okay! Let's go!"

They ended up filming quite a lot, even getting a few shots of a Policeman arresting a young man for being drunk and disorderly; a street length of viewers chanting something in Irish, and even an ice-cream van passing through the streets at 1am, which didn't have anything to do with St Patricks Day, but was interesting none the less and they chose to include it. Walking back towards the flat, equipment slung over shoulders, the two drunkenly pounded on the outside door, having both forgotten their keys.

"Open up!" Zasha shouted, her head resting on the glass windows.

"Guys! It's cold!" Reece whined, picking at the stones in the wall and then feeling sick as it reminded her of her tropophobia. "Should we call them?"

"I don't have my phone, do you?"

"No. I don't have my phone...Do you?"

"No."

The two stood there for quite some time, Reece resting her head up against the painted blue door, trying to read the illegible yellow graffiti scrawled across the wall, thinking, *I bet Will did that,* before giving up and pulling back from the door, eyes pinned to the ground.

"Have you ever noticed that?" Reece asked in a hushed breathy tone, pointing to the spikey brown doormat reading 'Welcome.'

"No," Zasha confessed, laughing to herself, "ha. 'Welcome' that's funny."

"Ha, yeah. Well-come," Reece mocked, head pounding and eyes fading.

"Yeah. You know what's weirder, though?"

"What?"

"I'm pretty sure this isn't our flat."

Reece's eyes opened in alarm, now realising that the blue door, graffiti, doormat, and glass window were things definitely not associated with 82 Rugby. The realisation sobering them up, the two could hear the ongoing pounding music from down the street, the familiar corner wall and bright windows only a few doors away.

"Wait, that means—" The two began to laugh, realising they had just spent over half an hour crying outside a stranger's house.

"Why are we like this?" Reece wheezed, trying to catch her breath as she stumbled forward.

"Aw, Reggie, I've missed this," Zasha cried, wrapping her arm around Reece.

"Me too."

Dear Reader,

This is a story about 8 friends, and yes, from a very, very far distance, you can call them that. This is also a story about romance, danger, and heartbreak. A story about love and lust, and a story about truth and lies. You've seen them laugh, and you've seen them cry. You've seen them shout and scream and beg. And you've seen them get so close and be pulled so far back.

And so, dear reader, as we approach the end of our tale, I urge you to take caution. I fear you may have grown fond of the 8, some of you even becoming attached or sympathetic.

And I can't let that happen.

I need to remind you, despite my pretty words, that these are, infact, stories about

truly terrible people.

SELF-DESTRUCTIVE

It was cold in Will's room; he had always avoided turning on the heating in case the mould leeching from his bedroom window grew. It was cold, but he didn't seem to care as he lay on top of his bed in the early hour of the morning, legs outstretched, and eyes pinned to the blank ceiling wondering why he didn't ever put posters up there. He took a deep breath.

"Just a couple more days," he said to himself, pushing his head back far into the pillow and closing his eyes. For the past couple of months, Will had been feeling overwhelming pressure. He knew that if he was ever going to make it in the film industry, he had to start his portfolio now. And up until this point, he had only had a few gigs here and there, making short adverts or graphics for local coffee shops. And it wasn't enough. He needed more.

He had even discussed starting a production company with Warner and Matteo, another film student and Phil's flatmate. But they were going home for the summer, Will wasn't. Will was going to stay in Belfast and create something, make something. He had even written a couple of scripts, his favourite being about a man's ability to lucid dream, but after

Reece had told him it reminded her of a 'Nothing but Thieves' music video, he was put off.

"Just a couple more days," he kept saying to himself. A couple more days and the flat would be empty, and he could think.

Down the hall, Jackson too sat in his room alone, perched at the end of his bed sifting through the odd items in his top drawer. Smiling to himself, Jackson pulled out a little Chinese teapot. It was green with hand-painted yellow dragons across the ceramic, a gift Reece had given him for Christmas before she left for home.

She told him it reminded her of their very first day in the flat, when it was just them. He had told her that one of his favourite things about Chinese restaurants, was the little pot of tea in the middle of the table; how it was always there.

Though to Jackson, the little pot inspired a different memory. It reminded him of when he had taken her to the Ternary, a Chinese restaurant on the Donegal Square, with Sonny and Harry, and how when she was in the bathroom, they had poured salt into her cup. The memory of her squinted face making him laugh out loud.

Reece had also gotten him some Jasmine tea leaves, and months later, Jackson still didn't have the heart to tell her he was allergic.

In River's room, River sat in the corner of his bed, his arm outstretched in Zasha's hand. Delicately and gently, Zasha was painting green healing gel over his scars, a Russian medicine Zasha had spoken fondly of. "Does that hurt?" she asked, her voice the softest it's ever been.

"No."

River took a breath, even now, after everything, the touch of her hand on his was enough to make his heart skip a beat.

Just one more day, he thought to himself, one more day and he was going home. It had been a long year, and he wanted nothing more than to go back to his small cottage in Guildford, sit in front of the fireplace with his parents and read the books he had never been able to concentrate long enough to read.

Zasha, too, was looking forward to going home, if she could call it that. In just a couple days, she would be flying back to London to live with her mother and brother, in their small apartment outside Wembley. She would sleep on the couch since her mother wanted to keep the spare bedroom spare, and she would eat leftovers and walk her ugly dog. Her little Yorkshire terrier that she remembered River describing as a "Useless scrawny rat," and this made her laugh when she did.

Reece stood in the doorway of Damian's room, right shoulder resting on the frame, hands in pockets. She had been there for some time, watching Damian fold different sportswear items into a perfectly packed suitcase. The gallery of photos from the wall had finally come down, leaving hundreds of blu-tac marks and the shadows of the pictures from where the sun had bleached the border around them. The Game of Thrones calendar on the back of the door half lying out of the black bin bag in the corner, the large protein powder bottle discarded.

"You're not taking that with you?" she asked, pointing to the cylinder. "Even in a smaller container?"

Damian looked up at her, sighing as he did. "Nah, found out River was scooping it out with his hands and eating it raw, so thought best to chuck it."

"Ahh, thought River was looking a bit buff," she teased, crossing his room and sitting down on the bed next to him, placing her head on his shoulder and reaching for the Mimikyu plushie to hold in her lap.

Damian took a second, thinking about how in just a couple days, Reece would be halfway around the world with Jackson, thinking this might be his last chance to know for sure. "Can I ask you a question?" Damian asked softly, his words causing Reece's heart to stop. She didn't answer, yet he continued, "Do you think you and Jackson will ever—" he stopped. He didn't need to finish; his question was clear.

Taking a quiet breath, eyes straight ahead, Reece said, "Maybe once I did" —she paused, that was the first time she had ever said that out loud—"but I think after enough time has passed, the moments gone. You're too good of friends."

"Yeah," he whispered back. Resting his head on top of hers, both looking into the dark empty corridor.

For a moment, the flat stood still, like time had ceased. Even the air felt warmer like there was no room for cold in the void, and everything was quiet.

But you know the drill by now, quiet never lasts long.

The sound of the front door on the ground floor swinging open and slamming into the brick wall echoed throughout the building, and the loud scream and chatter of what sounded like 50 came rattling up the stairwell.

Ears from all corners of the flat pricked up, Damian being the first to stand to attention, grabbing a baseball bat from under his bed he had acquired since the last attempted break-in. Meeting in the corridor, River, Zasha, Damian, and Reece all froze once more as the sound of Flat 6's door flew open, the metal handle crashing into the wall.

"They have a key?" Zasha asked dubiously, leaning over the bannister in hopes of catching a glimpse, forgetting she can't see through walls.

"Must be Amy," River deduced. "I haven't seen her all day."

"Okay, but who are all the others? Should we go check?" Reece asked, turning to Damian.

"Yeah, I'll—"

"I'll go," Zasha insisted, "I don't think your racquet is going to help."

"It's a bat!" Damian hissed, leaning it against the rail and running down after her. Reece and River following closely.

Inside Flat 6's lounge, Amy had stumbled and collapsed on the black leather sofa. Her head, fallen face-first into the seat. Her legs had spread across the leather, and her skirt had ridden up to her waist, clearly showing her underwear through her tights.

As the others came into the flat, Reece and Zasha instantly ran to her side, lifting her upright and readjusting her dress, both exchanging a look of fear as they covered her with a blanket.

There must have been at least 15 others in the room, spread over the opposite couch, the dining room table, and seated on the kitchen counter, all of whom unfamiliar.

As the four of them came in, one particular girl, quite large and a lot older than the others, screamed, "Who the fuck are you?" as she stood from the sofa arm, flipping her tatted black hair from her shoulder and biting her pierced lip.

"We live here," Damian answered. "Who the fuck are you?"

The girl had quite a deep voice and spoke with a strand of West Belfast that Damian had trouble understanding.

"We're her friends, yeah. I think you should go."

Once more, Damian asserted, "We *live* here," giving River a clear side glance of 'go get the others' to which River nodded and ran upstairs.

"Look, we just wanted to check and see if she's okay," Reece told the beast, looking at the grease in her hair and ladders in her tights, unknowingly scowling at her.

"What the fuck are you looking at?" *Oops.*

"Hey, calm down," Zasha said, thinking, *her eyeliner is hideous.*

Damian scanned the room. There were a couple more girls there; all of whom seemed more human than the talkative ogre; and a lot more guys. All seeming to resemble stereotypical stoners, with thin, gaunt faces, sagging red eyes, and rollies between their fingers. 'Who the fuck are these people?' he thought to himself.

"Look, Amy's obviously out of it. We just want to take care of her—" Damian began but was interrupted when Jackson came barging through into the middle of the room, targeting the Gruffalo as he spoke.

"Get the fuck out, all of you!"

"Who the fuck do you think you are!" a tall, scrawny boy that had been hiding in-between the couches shouted and stood up. His blonde hair greased back in an ugly quiff. As he stood, a few other guys stood too, positioning themself behind him like an angry boyband. "Is this because I'm *gay*!"

"Wait, what?"

"Yeah! You wouldn't be kicking me out if I wasn't gay!" he squealed. Encouraging genuine laughter from River, who had been hiding in the doorway.

"We're actually kicking you all out, so unless you're *all* gay—" Zasha backhanded Reece across the arm.

"Shut up!" Zasha hissed, looking up at the intruders and bracing herself for their reaction.

"Just," Jackson took a breath, lacking the care about the boy's apparent insecurities. "Get the fuck out!"

"Or fucking what?" The boy took a step to Jackson, squaring up below his chin.

"Are you serious right now?" Jackson mocked, taking his hand and pushing back hard on the boy's chest so that he stumbled backwards.

"You fucking cunt!" the boy screamed, running back at Jackson and shoving him rearward.

It's moments like this I truly believe happen in slow motion.

Startled, Jackson was thrown backwards, his back slamming hard into the T.V. in the corner, and all three crashing into the floor.

Like the cry of war, one of the larger men at the back of the room charged for Damian, taking a swing for his face and clipping the side of Damian's jaw, slamming into the back wall as he did and pulling at the wires by his feet as he scrambled up back up.

And suddenly, the lights were out.

Muffled screams in the darkness came from all directions as 'the others' swung for and attacked the flat.

Zasha making a run for the door and knocking into River. "Call the Police!" she shouted, taking her hand and running into the bottom stairwell away from the riot.

Reece, who had seen Zasha leave, froze in place, standing in front of Amy in hopes to shield her, but was knocked off her feet when Jackson was hit once more; this time in his shoulder; and fell back into her, his elbow crashing into her lip as they tumbled like dominoes.

'Fiona' also played her part, her fist swinging aimlessly in the dark in hopes of hitting something, but only crashed into the wall as her weight was tossed about.

Both Will and Nora, who could hear all from their rooms, remained inside. The simple click and bolt of their locks in unison being the only sound they wished to acknowledge.

"Jackson, get up!" Reece screamed, squirming from the floor from where Jackson had fallen on her legs.

"Urgh!" grunting, he rose once more. More pissed than ever; thinking back to when he and Sonny used to get in fights on the streets as kids; *where's his fucking mob when you need them!* Even in the dark, Jackson could see one of the boys pull back his fist and swing, but Jackson had had enough, sidestepping the right hook and thrusting the boy into the back wall. The sound of his back cracking against the plaster, loud and ringing.

Still curled on the floor, Reece tried to shout, "Damian! Get—" but screamed instead when a hand reached in from the darkness and yanked her by the arm to her feet.

"*Go!*" Jackson yelled, pushing her towards the door.

"But—!"

"I said, *go!*"

Thankfully, Zasha had managed to get a hold of the Police, and they arrived quickly. 6 Uniformed S.W.A.T. Officers carrying tasers and firearms in their holsters marched up the stairs and into the flat, each shining a bright torch into the lounge and viewing the carnage.

At the sight of the Police, many from the flat ran, pushing past the men and sprinting down the stairs and out the door. Reece, Zasha, and River stood and watched as the few remaining were man-handled out, some officers' rougher than others as they threw the blonde boy towards the stairs, saying nothing as he screamed, "It was because I'm *gay*!"

Another officer approached the three and asked a few questions. "B&E?" The large Officer asked River, standing tall over him, with broad shoulders and deep-set eyes. He had a clean-shaven face and a small scar down his chin.

"Ah, no. We think our flatmate let them in, but she's too out of it to tell," River squeaked.

"Alright, and you spoke of drugs on the premise?"

"Yes!" Zasha answered. "They were smoking weed. They could have been doing other stuff, but we couldn't see."

"Alright."

At this point, Nora had also decided to grace the flat with her presence, waltzing down the staircase in nothing but a pink robe and glasses. Zasha scoffing as she saw this.

"Oh no! What happened?" Nora gasped, cutting in front of Zasha to speak to the Officer.

Another Official was talking to Jackson and Damian inside the lounge, detailing the fight that broke out., while another escorted the last remaining intruder.

"I told them! We're her friends! We *know* Amy!" The silverback gorilla screamed, but once more, the Officer wasn't listening.

"And the lights?"

"Yeah, uh, I think some wires were ripped out from the wall," Reece told them, pointing into the darkness where Damian was attacked.

Sighing, a blonde officer walked to the bottom of the stairs in Flat 6, his fingers tracing the wiring to a box in the top corner, opening the latch, and flicking the switch.

Instantly, the lights came back on, revealing the havoc. The T.V. that used to sit pretty in the corner of the room was now lying on its back on the floor, a large hole in the screen from where Jackson had fallen into it. The white shoe rack that was taken from the streets outside Magdala all those months ago had a broken leg and was leaning on its side. There was also a couple of broken glasses on the table, some shards having spilled onto the floor by the legs, and pools of spilled drinking circling the feet of the couch.

Taking some final notes and giving some final advice to, "Lock the front door," the officers left.

And the 6 remained silent for some time.

Sitting on the end of the couch by Amy's feet, Damian held his jaw in his hand, slight blue bruising already forming on the side of his face.

Jackson, too, held the shoulder damaged in his fall and was lightly touching the skin under his eye, which was pink and swollen.

"You guys look shit!" Zasha exclaimed, laughing and gesturing to the boys.

"Not just *us*!" Damian added, pointing to Reece.

"What?"

"Aw, Kid," River babied, cusping her chin in his hand and pulling at her bleeding lower lip with his thumb, revealing a cut across the flesh. It was swelling fast and turning a deep purple.

"How'd you'd get that?" Jackson mocked. "You did fuck all!"

"That was *you*!" she laughed back, the others joining in before transitioning into another quiet. Her thumb had been bleeding too, the slice having reopened during the scuffle, but that was old news.

"That was buck-wild!" River shrieked.

"Yeah! Like how did they even—" Damian started, but the sound of Will's footsteps down the stairs hushed him.

"Well, well, well!" Will sang. "What do we have here?"

At first, Jackson scowled at Will; he had knocked on Will's door before everything had kicked off, asking for help, but Will had refused saying, "Not my problem." But Jackson was too tired to care anymore, so instead he just sighed and explained everything that had happened, Will turning on the kettle as he spoke.

"And so yeah, fuck this place," Jackson finished, seeing the collection of slow nods.

"This has been such a crazy year!" Reece added, bringing up the very first house-party at Halloween. "I almost killed Lewis!"

"Yeah, and I chased down a taxi!" Damian laughed.

"I got my wallet stolen," Will shouted from the kitchen corner.

"I've had multiple mental breakdowns!" River jokingly sung, dancing on the spot, and grinning sarcastically.

"Uhh, I was just in a fight—" Jackson scoffed.

"I got stuck in fucking Berlin!" Zasha screamed, with enough "Oh yeahs" and "Oh fucks" to assume she won that round of 'who had the shittiest time,' but somehow one more seemed to beat it when Amy; who had been conscious for the last couple minutes; rose from her slouch saying, "I broke up with Callum."

And a chorus of, "Finally!" was chanted.

"Fucking hell, Amy. Nice of you to join us. Where the fuck were you tonight?" Jackson snapped.

Amy laughed, "Ha, I was just out in Thompsons y'know. Living my best single life. Then came back here...Did my friends leave?"

A moment of silence passed. Reece looked at Jackson, Jackson turned to Damian, Damian looked across at River, and River back at Zasha, before the 5 of them erupted into a loud, uncontrollable laugh.

"What-haat?" Amy whined, but the laughter continued.

"You know what?" Reece giggled through crying eyes, looking at River.

"What?"

"Someone should write about all this, about *us*!" River thought for a moment, head tilted, and lips parted.

"Yeah. They should."

And Will's eyes lit up.

END OF STORY